THE ORDER OF
THE RED LION

BY TIM BYERS

This is a work of fiction. All characters, organizations, and events portrayed in this novel are either products of the author's imagination or are used fictitiously.

The Order of the Red Lion

By Tim Byers

Copyright @ Tim Byers 2023

2nd Printing

ALL RIGHTS RESERVED

www.runnerdlibrary.com/runnerdpress

Published by runnerd press, a subsidiary of Runnerd LLC

Don Hahn, Publisher

Elizabeth Hahn, Publisher

Patti Naretta, Editor

Patrick Kelly, Reviewer

Regina Rexrode, Point n' Click Publishing, Layout

Gary Robinson, Logoglo, Cover Design

Manufactured in the United States of America.

PAPERBACK ISBN 979-8-9879371-3-6

To Megan,
Who loves stories.

PREFACE

Even if you've heard of it, you may not realize that Luxembourg is a real country. You're forgiven if you're not sure on that point, because its capital city is also called Luxembourg, or, for clarity, Luxembourg City. Officially, the country is The Grand Duchy of Luxembourg, which means it has a Grand Duke or Duchess, depending on the era. The country also stays under the radar a bit because it's relatively small compared to its neighbors, Belgium to the west, France to the south, and Germany to the east, occupying a little more territory than the counties that make up metropolitan Indianapolis, where I live. Though often caught in historical tugs of war between larger nations since the first recorded mention of the fortress city in the year 963, Luxembourg has been an independent country since 1839 and sought to remain neutral prior to both World Wars.

When I arrived in Luxembourg as a student in 1982, my experience was barely adequate to find it on a map. In my favor, however, was a love of history, particularly the World War II era, which had been fueled by countless hours building battle dioramas featuring 1/35th scale tanks, jeeps, and soldiers. Luxembourg, I learned, was at the heart of the Battle of the Bulge and would be the perfect starting point for great adventures exploring Europe.

Once my roommate and I had settled in with our host mom in the village of Strassen, the common routine for all of us at the Miami University (Ohio) European Center was to lug our backpacks to school on Friday, race to the train station after class, and get to Paris, Amsterdam, Cologne, or elsewhere for a weekend of sightseeing. Little did I realize though how my home base, this magical land with its capital city built on fortified medieval cliffs, would capture my imagination.

One day, our group of about one hundred students embarked on a local field trip. Across town, we arrived at a modest but impressive home, unique for the American flag that waved proudly in front. Waiting at the door were Ambassador John Dolibois and his lovely wife, Winnie. Mr. Dolibois, we learned, had not only attended Miami, but was the founder of our European Center.

A few years later I read his excellent memoir, *A Pattern of Circles - An Ambassador's Story*, and learned Mr. Dolibois' inspiring story. He was born in the shadow of the fortress city and, although thoroughly Luxembourgish, was known as "Hansi" because of his German ancestry. After the death of his mother when he still a boy, his father moved the family to Akron, Ohio, to be near his uncle's family. Hansi, now John, grew up quickly in his adopted country, enjoying the Boy Scouts and earning a scholarship to Miami University. Shortly after graduation, when Germany launched their blitzkrieg west through his native Luxembourg, John answered the call of his country. Because of his skill in multiple languages, he played a crucial role as an interpreter for military intelligence, eventually being sent to Europe to be a part of the team that interrogated top-level Nazi war criminals for the Nuremberg Trials. After the war, back in Ohio, John's vision for peace led to creating the Miami University European

Center in his boyhood home city of Luxembourg in 1968. A little more than a decade later, his career of service was recognized by President Ronald Reagan, who appointed John the United States Ambassador to Luxembourg.

So how did all of this lead to a fictional story about a boy named Hansi in pre-war Luxembourg? I suppose the answer spans both the years before and after my semester there. As a boy, I enjoyed stories but had difficulty finding the kind I enjoyed. So, I wrote some myself, including a kind of proto-*Red Dawn* thriller featuring seventh grade me saving myself and some friends from the commie invasion of our town. At this time, I also discovered thrillers from Alistair MacLean, famous for *The Guns of Navarone* and *Where Eagles Dare*. But it wasn't until I had a family of my own that I returned to the adventures of my imagination to create bedtime stories based on the same places and characters I envisioned for *The Order of the Red Lion*.

In case you're wondering, this story is just that, a story. What's real are some of the places, some of the words, and a few of the names you might hear on a walk along the Grand Rue— and hopefully the spirit of a proud and resilient people. One of them was John Dolibois, an ordinary boy from Bonnevoie, who accomplished amazing things because of his faithfulness, courage, and a sense of gratitude. I hope my story in its small way honors him, his people, and the land that gave me so much.

Mir wëlle bleiwe wat mir sinn

We want to remain what we are.

(Luxembourg national motto)

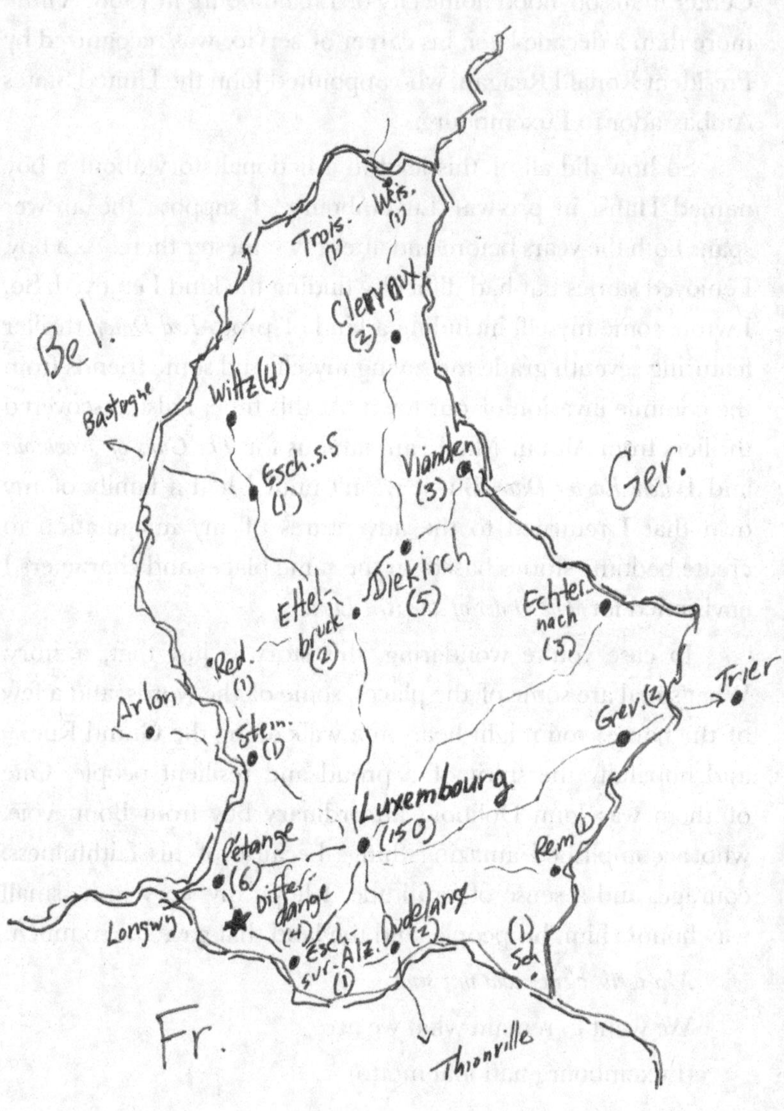

Bel.
Ger.
Fr.
Bastogne
Trois-V.
Urs. (1)
Clervaux (2)
Wiltz (4)
Esch.s.S (1)
Vianden (3)
Diekirch (5)
Ettel-bruck (2)
Echter-nach (3)
Red. (1)
Arlon
Stein- (1)
Grev. (2)
Trier
Luxembourg (150)
Rem (1)
Pétange (6)
Differ-dange (4)
Longwy
Esch-sur-Alz. (1)
Dudelange (2)
(1) Sch.
Thionville

CHAPTER ONE

Luxembourg City – August 1939

Papa's words gnawed at Hansi all day long.

"Meet me at the platform at five o'clock," he had said, hurriedly pulling his jacket on in the cramped hallway of their flat. "There's something I must tell you. *Alone.*"

Fourteen-year-old Hansi had seen that look only once before. The gray eyes, intense below a deeply creased forehead— it was the same expression Papa wore the morning Grandmother Maisy died.

He was off to work before Hansi could rub the sleep from his eyes. The words, like the collar of his best Sunday shirt, tugged at his throat all day long.

The bells of the Cathédrale d'Notre Dame rang four o'clock. Hansi, sitting on a bench along the wall of the ancient fortress known as the Casemates, stared out from the high cliffs across the valley and the sharp rooftops of his village, the Grund, below. His pencil, like a kestrel floating in the void, drifted back and forth above the blank page of the sketchbook in his lap. *What was Papa going to say? Why couldn't Maman know?*

Hansi often met his father at the train station at the end of the day. He enjoyed the time together, just the two of them. Papa would describe his work in the giant blast furnaces at the steel mill in Differdange. Hansi envisioned the place as a kind of zoo for dragons. His father, the brave knight appointed by Grand Duchess Charlotte herself, wrangled the mighty beasts to forge ore into a kind of steel unique in the world. Glowing orange ingots, like molten lava, would be pressed and rolled and stretched into mighty beams. Shipped across the whole of Europe, they would become a canopy over a train station in Paris, the skeleton of a stadium in Brussels, the beams of a bridge over the Rhine. Papa explained that, just like the forged blades of legend, the francs they brought to Luxembourg protected the tiny country from foreign invaders. Hansi swelled with pride that his father was at the center of it all.

Lately, though, talk of steel and dragons had been choked out by politics and rumors of war. Hansi's love of history, not shared by his classmates, came from his father and the time they spent together. Papa was a fierce patriot, not bashful to criticize both sides in the growing crisis. In the German Führer, Adolf Hitler, he saw a bully stomping into the Rhineland, Austria, and Czechoslovakia. In the French, British, and Belgians, he saw cowards, unwilling to stand up to the threat.

"Hitler just needs a sharp punch on the nose," he would say, reflecting the way you dealt with bullies in the working-class streets of the Grund. "But the French are afraid. And they'll regret it."

Meeting at the train station meant they could talk on their way home without arousing Maman's suspicion.

What could he want to keep from her?

The question both frightened and excited him.

He wants to talk man-to-man, but why?

Hansi tried to block the thoughts and focus on his drawing. The charcoal pencil hadn't moved. The sketchbook was full of fantastic scenes from his vivid imagination—steam-driven armored dirigibles floating over the spire of St. John's Church down in the valley. Rows of cannon, protruding from the cliff, rained fire onto the rooftops of the Grund while ranks of shimmering knights on horseback clashed below. Today was different. The blank page stared back at him.

In frustration he slashed a horizontal line across the page, then with equal carelessness a jagged line from the foreground to the imaginary horizon—the Alzette River. Using the side of the charcoal he shaded a black storm cloud rising in the east. It looked like something a four-year-old would draw. He ripped the paper from the book and let the breeze carry it away. Then, regretting his carelessness, jumped up to catch it before it was swept over the edge.

He was too late. A gray front moving in from the West drove strong gusts, pushing the page out over the cliff, unreachable above the hundred-meter drop.

He watched it go. It sped aimlessly east, following the ribbon of the Alzette, which thirty kilometers on would be swallowed by the Moselle and then the Rhine.

Hansi wondered, would Germany swallow tiny Luxembourg again, like it had when Papa fled to France to fight in the Great War?

The preparations all around the city were impossible to ignore. Sandbag walls had popped up everywhere. Air-raid sirens were installed on telephone poles and tested monthly. Even the Statue of Our Lady of Peace in front of the cathedral had been crated and hidden away in a bunker, probably in one of the tunnels somewhere below him in the Casemates.

Were the rumors true?

News reports focused on Poland made talk of war seem like a joke. Until this morning. Papa stayed up on things. He had lots of opinions. He didn't trust what others said about France's strong defenses along the Maginot Line. Hansi couldn't explain how he knew, but he was sure Papa wanted to talk about the looming war. It couldn't be anything else. But what could he possibly want to tell him?

Hansi closed his eyes and let the breeze wash over him, hoping it would carry his anxiety away with the lost page. It was no use. All he could see was Father's face, framed by the doorway of their flat, deadly serious.

There's something I must tell you.

Hansi opened his eyes and turned back from the cliff. To his surprise, he was no longer alone. Standing a few meters down the walk at the edge of the wall stood a girl in a navy-blue woolen skirt and a white blouse; her blond ponytail trailed in the breeze behind her.

Without warning she turned, and their eyes met. Hers were sky-blue, set in a round face. When she saw him the corner of her mouth turned up, not quite the beginning of a smile. She was pretty. His glance stretched dangerously close to a stare. Embarrassed, he looked away and then clawed clumsily to open his sketchbook. Hopefully, she couldn't see the rush of heat to his face.

He scribbled another jagged line and pretended to study the landscape. Who was she? A girl so pretty would certainly have no lack of friends. Why was she alone? A few moments later he chanced a look back. She had walked on.

He scolded himself for acting so nervously. What did he expect? A smile? A conversation? Two strangers suddenly becoming friends? More shame. Hansi wasn't around girls his own age very often. When he was, he would be possessed by an unfamiliar spirit, something both exciting and frozen at the same time. More shame.

It was time to leave for the Gare Centrale anyway. How could seeing the girl have distracted him so quickly? He had no idea. He didn't know why he was subject to such sudden strong feelings. He got up from the bench and stashed his sketchbook in his book bag. The walk would give him time to think. One last glance back. The girl was gone.

No sooner had he taken a step than a siren started up. The low whine grew higher and louder as its horn turned slowly on its mount.

The instructions for air-raid drills were clear. If you were in a public area, you had to seek the nearest shelter and wait for a second signal, the all-clear. Anyone caught ignoring it could be fined. But new shelters were being built all the time now, and he had no idea where to find the nearest one.

His intended path led away from the cliffs to an open space at the edge of the larger Casemates Park. The city lay beyond it. Surely there were shelters between here and the Gare, but it could be ten minutes or more before he found one. Plenty of time to draw the ire of a hawk-eyed gendarme. The path behind led into the Casemates, a more logical choice. The cliffs, riddled with caves, tunnels, and chambers—old fortifications long since left to tourists and explorers—were the perfect place for a shelter. Not to mention the same way the girl had gone.

He set off at a brisk pace while the siren blared overhead. The path sloped down through a cut in the stone and curved into the cliff before continuing along the heights. At this bend his intuition was rewarded—a sign fastened hastily into the stone read: Bomb Shelter.

Hansi stepped through a metal doorway at the mouth of a tunnel cut into the stone cliffs, where he continued down a narrow passage lit by yellow bulbs covered in wire cages. After several meters, the passage turned right and opened into a space wide enough for two wooden benches. The chamber was empty. He sat down, taking in the musty air and listening to the muffled siren moan on.

A moment later, a figure appeared in the doorway: the girl from the walkway. He tensed despite trying not to. She slid past Hansi and sat down on the opposite bench. They exchanged glances again, and this time Hansi nodded an acknowledgment. He waited quietly, trying to find anywhere to look but at her. He both hoped and didn't hope that someone else would join them. The silence grew awkward.

Hansi began to study the chamber as a solution to the problem of staring at her. The ceiling was jagged as if it had been cut out of the rock by hand, and along with the walls everything had been covered in whitewash. Curious, he touched the wall behind him. Sure enough, it was fresh.

His nervousness turned to impatience. This wasn't the first air-raid drill, and he already knew what to do. Gendarme officers had visited every school the previous spring, giving instructions about seeking shelter when the sirens went off. Drills began in May and continued all summer. Yet no one knew if or when war would come. In the meantime, though, they were a nuisance.

"*Moyen.*" The words came with a jolt. The girl was greeting him in Luxembourgish, Hansi recognized, but it sounded too slow, too deliberate, and too accented to come from a Luxembourger.

He nodded politely.

"I know, my accent's horrible," she said, continuing in Luxembourgish. "I'm a little out of practice."

He knew she wanted him to ask why, though he preferred to remain quiet and wait for the all-clear.

"Wondering how I know Luxembourgish?" she continued. "My mother taught me. She's from north of here, Vianden. My father is from across the Sure River. He speaks only German, and it drives him crazy when we speak in Luxembourgish. I grew up here until I was five, when we moved to Cologne. On my tenth birthday, we moved to Berlin. Two weeks ago, we moved here."

Still Hansi said nothing, but glanced at the tunnel, hoping for the second siren.

"What were you doing along the wall? Before the air raid?" she asked.

"Nothing."

"You had something you were working on. Are you an artist?"

Hansi held back a grin at the thought of being called an artist.

"Not really," he said.

"But you are drawing pictures, yes?" she persisted.

"Just scribbles really."

"May I see them?"

"No," he said, pulling his bag closer. "They're nothing, really." He looked up the corridor again. It was still quiet.

She slid toward him on her bench.

"I'm Karin," she said.

He looked up. She was close enough for him to notice wisps of blond hair around her temples and a slight hint of freckles on the bridge of her nose.

"I'm Hansi," he said and looked away again.

"I've always wanted to be an artist," she said with a laugh, "but I'm terrible at drawing. My mother promised me she'd take me on the train to Paris, to visit the Louvre. It would be such fun, don't you think?"

"I don't know," Hansi replied, shame rising. Five minutes earlier along the cliffs, he would have loved to have a conversation with her. Now he was ruining it.

"Well, now there's talk of war. So, I don't suppose I'll be going to France anytime soon. At least not for pleasure."

"What's that supposed to mean?" Hansi bristled at her assumption Germany could conquer France on its own terms.

"Nothing, really. I was just thinking—my father's work might take him anywhere if the war comes… back to Germany, to France, who knows? We may even stay here."

"Is your father a spy?" The question was laced with sarcasm.

"Of course not!" she snapped. Her blue eyes were fierce. She turned away.

Hansi let out a grin, proud of himself for the clever retort. The siren was still quiet and so was she. He returned his gaze to the jagged ceiling. A moment later his feelings changed again. *Why be such a brute? Wouldn't you like to be friends? What's wrong with you?*

"Actually, he's a diplomat," Karin said after a brief pause. "He calls it a 'trade mission.' All I know is that he's constantly on the telephone arranging meetings and shipments. Whoever it is he works with seems rather thick-headed."

"Thick-headed? How do you know that?" Hansi asked.

"Because he's always raising his voice with them," Karin said.

"Not very diplomatic for a diplomat," Hansi said.

"Are all city boys as rude as you?"

"I wouldn't know," he said. "I'm from the valley. I live in the Grund."

Just then the siren started up again. All Clear. Hansi stood up and took a step toward the exit, glad to leave. He glanced back at Karin and their eyes met again. Even with the look she was giving him now, he had to admit to himself she was pretty. Those eyes. Her mouth bunched in a tight frown. He was shocked by the sudden thought that he might like to kiss her. The thought set his face aflame. He turned away quickly to avoid the embarrassment, but needn't have worried, for in the next instant the lights went out and they were plunged into darkness.

CHAPTER TWO

When the lights went out, Karin gasped. Only the sound of the siren, eerie in the distance, penetrated the darkness.

"We should try to leave," Karin said in an anxious breath. Hansi heard the bench scrape along the floor.

"Wait!" he warned, but it was too late. More scraping, a yelp, and she fell against him.

Unprepared and unable to see, Hansi fell sideways over the bench and twisted, sinking down onto it with a thump that broke most of the force of the fall. Still, his back hit the wall. Then together they sunk down onto the cold, damp floor.

Pressed by Karin's body and disoriented, Hansi reached into the blackness. His hand passed through a lock of her hair and snagged it.

"Ow!" she cried.

In a panic, he jerked it away.

"Owwww!" The strands of hair were like a spider's web in Hansi's fingers. Near to panic, her body still pressing him against the wall, he could not push off the floor. But he had to get up, get free.

In the scrum, a hand came to rest on her back. The other found her shoulder. In the next instant, they both fell still. He felt her breath on his cheek. Their faces could only have been millimeters apart.

The moment transformed him. Her closeness, fragrance, and very presence changed the darkness from panic to something he'd never experienced before. The moment lasted but an instant, flooded by embarrassment. He was glad the darkness hid his face.

He moved her to one side, found his bearings between the bench and the wall, and then found her hand. He helped her to the bench and found a place beside her. She slid over. Their knees touched.

"I'm sorry," she said, a slight tremor in her voice. "You're right. Maybe we should wait for the power to come back on."

Hansi, frozen by her presence, was unable to answer. They sat in silence as the siren continued, a small connection to the world of light. Some minutes later, when it finally fell silent, the power of the darkness returned.

"Let's go," he finally said.

"I really think we should wait for the lights to come back on. I might break something on my way out of here."

"Give me your hand," he said. "I'll lead you."

He stood up and reached out into the darkness again. He touched her arm and felt the cotton sleeve. Then he found her hand. Other than his mother, he had never held a girl's hand before. Holding Karin's hand now sent a sensation through him he could feel in his feet. He hoped the feeling didn't reverberate through his hand to hers. His embarrassment was as deep and dark as the tunnel.

"Take small steps," he said, clearing his throat, and took a step forward. Karin held tightly and followed.

Hansi took a few more steps and was near the end of his bench at the doorway of the chamber when behind them they heard a heavy KLUNK!

They froze, and Hansi felt her grip on his arm. The sound came from the rear of the chamber, where the passage deeper into the Casemates was blocked by a metal door.

"What was that?" Karin whispered.

Then there was a second KLUNK! Before Hansi could answer, they heard a muffled voice, speaking in German. They froze in place.

"Why did you bring me here?" the first voice said.

"Shhh! Keep your voice down," said a second one. "I need someone with your, shall we say, particular skills."

"But it's been a good many years since I've…"

"No matter. I've been told it's like riding a bike, once you learn, you never forget."

"I've not ridden a bike in many a year either," the first one said with a laugh.

"I need someone comfortable with the dark," the second one said.

"That I am," the first one said. "But what if I still refuse? What you're asking me to do doesn't sound exactly right to me. I gave this sort of thing up a long time ago, and don't need to be running afoul of the law now. I think you should find somebody else."

Together their bodies were tensed to their limit to listen. It didn't take long to begin to feel the strain. Hansi sensed a rising cramp in his calf. When he could bear it no longer, he sought to relieve it by shifting his feet. His foot struck the bench with a sharp rap.

"What was that?" the second one asked.

Hansi held his breath.

"Probably just a rat," the first man said. "This place is crawling with them," he added with a snicker.

At that, Karin let out an audible sound, almost a yelp, and drew closer to Hansi.

"There's someone here!" the second one said. "On the other side of this door!"

There was a metallic bang on the door that reverberated through the entire chamber.

"Not as secret as you thought down here, huh?" the first man said.

"Shut up, you imbecile, and help me with this door!" the second one snapped back. The door latch clattered to life and then more clanging on the door.

Hansi pulled Karin toward the entrance. No longer caring about the noise, they frantically bumped and kicked their way along the benches until they were through the doorway of the chamber and into the tunnel. More pounding and clanging echoed from behind as Hansi led Karin through the darkness of the tunnel, dragging his hand through the fresh paint along the wet and sticky wall.

Halfway back up the passageway, the lights came back on in an explosion of light that hurt Hansi's eyes. Still, he was grateful to be returned to the world of sight. The sticky white paint covering his hand and sleeve caught his attention and he paused.

But then a sound echoed from the chamber that made his blood run cold—the awful scraping sound of a metal door against the gritty floor. The pair in the tunnel had solved their problem.

"Run!" Hansi said, pulling Karin ahead. Together they flew out of the tunnel into the natural light of the passageway in the cut of the cliff.

There was no time to think, only react by instinct. Hansi knew the Parc du Casemates like his own flat and turned right just outside the tunnel. "This way," he said, tugging at her as he bolted back toward the spot where he'd been sketching. As the path opened ahead of them, Karin accelerated and moved out ahead. Impressed by her speed, Hansi let go of her hand and chanced a glance back. The doorway was empty.

The pathway along the wall rose up to the top of the cliff and the space opened on their right to a grassy plain that covered the inside of the fortress. About fifty meters ahead was a gate at the western edge of the fortress. Just as doubt flashed in Hansi's mind that they could outrun their pursuers, Karin stopped dead.

"What are you doing?!" Hansi asked, in shock.

"Nothing," she said. "We haven't seen them, and they haven't seen us. Just walk naturally."

The idea fought every one of Hansi's instincts, but there was no time to argue. He turned to look back, but Karin yanked on his arm.

"You mustn't look back, no matter what! Remember, you don't know they're there."

Hansi heard the rapid rhythm of hard-soled shoes on the pavement behind them, approaching fast. His body tensed and his heart was still racing. Karin looked so calm by comparison. *How can she do this?* he wondered, fighting himself each step forward, wishing he could break into a run. His gaze locked on the gate ahead. Then, as the foot beats grew louder behind him, he took a deep breath and closed his eyes.

The clip-clop crescendoed past him and he opened his eyes. A lone man flew past, tall and wearing a wide-brimmed hat and a black trench coat. As he ran, the tails of his coat billowed wide behind him like a cape, making it look like he was gliding just off the ground. A few steps beyond them, the man stopped. Hansi had to force himself not to turn and run.

Karin sucked in another hard breath.

"Keep going," she whispered, taking his arm.

The man turned slowly around to face them, not five meters ahead. Hansi and Karin kept moving and took a step sideways to pass him on the walk, trying to act like everyday visitors to the park, hoping beyond hope he didn't recognize them. Hansi kept his head down as they passed but noticed smudges of white along the edges of the man's coat. Paint. Impulsively Hansi glanced at his own hands and then up at the man's face. Their eyes met. Hansi saw, beneath the shadow of the wide brim of the man's hat, below the narrow black curl that split his forehead, cold black eyes that seared Hansi's heart.

"It was you!" the man said, in German, and lunged for Hansi.

"Run!" Hansi shouted, jerking Karin forward. The man's outstretched arms just missed him, and he stumbled. Hansi let go of Karin's hand, and together they raced toward the gate, now just a short sprint away. Hansi hoped that if they could reach the street, they could lose their pursuer amid the busy commuter traffic.

The German quickly recovered, however, and soon gained ground behind them.

Hansi glanced sideways. Karin was faster than any girl he knew, and strong too, looking less winded than he as they ran. His own heart was pounding wildly. He couldn't get enough air. Still ten meters to the gate and the German was nearly upon them.

They beat him to it but by how much Hansi dare not calculate. Along the Avenue de la Gare, the city's main street, pedestrians had begun to emerge from the nearby shelters. The rapid steps of the German behind him would surely be upon him any instant now.

Without thinking, Hansi grabbed Karin's hand and darted out on the street, a wide brick boulevard busy with cars, trucks, taxis, and trams. There was a terrible shriek of brakes, successive horn blasts, and a heavy crash of metal, but in a moment, Hansi and Karin were in the center of the street, separated from the German by a wall of cars buckled at the bumpers. Turning left, they chased a tram rumbling toward the Pont Adolphe, the arched stone bridge over the deep valley, and jumped onto the running board on its far side. The tram lumbered across the bridge, leaving the string of cars in its wake, honking in protest. When Hansi and Karin looked back, the German was in the middle of the street, face red with rage, shaking his fist in the air.

CHAPTER THREE

Beyond the bridge, the tram stopped at the postal and telegraph office, giving Hansi and Karin a chance to move inside. Exhausted and in shock, they rode in silence past the shops, restaurants, and hotels before the tram stopped at the end of its line in front of the Gare Centrale, the city's main train station.

The stop, in the middle of the wide plaza in front of the brick and stucco terminal building, was the busiest spot in the entire city. Hansi and Karin filed out with all the other riders and pressed through the swarm of people waiting to board.

"Are you alright?" Hansi finally asked.

"I think so," Karin replied. "But he could be on the next tram behind us. We need to find a policeman."

They walked in a short circle through the sea of people in the plaza before returning to the street. There was not a policeman in sight, but after a few moments search they heard the rumble of another tram coming down the Avenue de la Gare.

"Come on," Hansi said, setting off toward the terminal. "We'll find my father." He glanced up at the spire high above the building where the clock read nine before five. If they couldn't find a gendarme, Hansi reasoned, meeting his father at the platform would be the next best thing, but that meant they would have to blend into the crowd for the nine minutes until his train arrived.

With each step forward it seemed blending in would not be the difficult task, but rather staying together in the dense throng.

"Is it always so crowded?" Karin asked, raising her voice.

"Not usually," Hansi said, understating the truth that he'd never seen so many people at the Gare before.

The moment they jumped off the tram, something seemed strange about the scene to Hansi. It wasn't until they finally managed to cram through the front doors and join the massive crowd inside that he realized something was missing. The trains. They were silent.

Hansi and Karin clawed their way through the mass of people to the far side of the building where the passageway was marked "To The Trains." When Hansi met his father after work, he would follow this down a flight of stairs, under several tracks, and up to the platform where his father's train arrived. But this afternoon, two gendarmes in dark blue uniforms blocked the way. Hansi saw a hint of relief on Karin's face. They approached the men.

"We need help," Hansi said to the first one.

"What's the trouble?" the officer asked from behind a finely waxed moustache and eyebrows that looked like shrubbery.

"Someone's following us," Karin said.

The moustache flattened out wide. "Who's following you?"

"A man," Hansi said. "He tried to… well, he tried to grab us."

The eyebrows shot up. "Kidnap you?"

"He's a criminal," Karin said. "We overheard him plotting something,"

"Plotting what?" The moustache twitched sideways.

"We don't know," Karin said, "But when he discovered we were listening he tried to catch us."

"He chased us all the way here," Hansi added.

"Please help us," Karin pleaded. "He could be right behind us."

The officer looked behind them at the huge mass of people jammed into the terminal and twitched his moustache the other direction. "That's not likely," he said. "A kidnapper would have an awfully tough time sneaking you two out through this mob."

"Are you going to help us?" Hansi asked.

The eyebrows dropped and he shook his head. "I'm afraid I can't at the moment," he said. "Jean-Paul and I are under strict orders at the moment not to move from this spot."

"But what about the man chasing us?" Karin asked, her look growing frantic.

"You should be quite safe here. Most of the city's gendarmes are within the sound of my whistle. Your pursuer is a fool to try something in here. Why don't you just wait over there? When this settles down, we'll see about the kidnapper."

"What's going on?" Hansi asked.

"You haven't heard what all this commotion's about?"

"No."

"The trains have been stopped."

"Stopped? Why? What's happened to the five o'clock from Differdange?"

"Look, boy, I know nothing about the schedule, but I hear they're going to make an announcement soon. Why don't you two go find a seat somewhere and wait."

"But what about my father's train?"

"There's nothing I can do about it. You're going to have to move along. I'm under strict orders to keep this area clear."

The look of worry on Karin's face was severe, and she stood firm on the spot. The gendarme leaned forward.

"Tell me, m'selle, what did your kidnapper look like? Jean-Paul and I will keep a lookout for him. Just find a place over there, my dear, and I'm sure you've nothing to worry about."

Karin described the man as best as she could and then she and Hansi moved back into the crowd. They came to a bench where an old woman stood. She was struggling to lift two cloth handbags that were filled with groceries onto the bench. Hansi approached her and tried to help her. When he lifted a bag, it startled her.

"It's all right, Madame. I'm just trying to help you," he said. "Please, sit down."

She fell more than sat onto the bench and glared at him. Her eyes were sharp through the curl of silver hair that fell from the scarf that wrapped tightly around her head.

"How do I know you're not pickpockets?" she said, nearly spitting. Karin, standing behind Hansi, gasped.

"If we were pickpockets, you wouldn't know it, would you?" Hansi replied with a grin. "Besides, I don't think we'd get far in this crowd. You see, I'm just here to meet my father, and, ah… my friend here is waiting with me."

Karin curtseyed. "Madame, do you know why the trains have been stopped?"

"Only that it must be something serious. In my seventy-two years, the trains were stopped only once, and that was Armistice Day in 1918, when General Pershing led the Yanks through the city on parade," the old woman said.

Nearby, a middle-aged man overheard her.

"You can bet the next army marching through here won't be so friendly."

"But at least the trains will run on time," added another man. A few bystanders chuckled at the joke.

The old woman's face turned red. She struggled to her feet, spilling apples from one of the bags.

"Fools!" she erupted, shaking her finger in the air. "You should be ashamed to joke about such things."

"Take it easy old woman," said one of them.

"I will not!" she protested. "Laugh now, but if they come, you'll see! Just ask the veterans of the last war. You won't find it so funny when you're rotting in a stinking trench somewhere, or a prison cell, or, heaven forbid, your grave! Mark my words—you'll regret your jokes. You think you're so clever? You should be ashamed of yourselves!"

Exhausted, the old woman fell back down on the bench. The men turned away.

Hansi and Karin collected the apples and put them back in her bags. She pulled a well-used handkerchief from her sleeve and wiped her forehead and eyes.

"Thank you, dear ones. Would you like an apple?"

She took Hansi's hand and squeezed it. Her hands were warm, but there was too much skin for the bones and ligaments. He was afraid to squeeze back too hard. She reminded him of his grandmother who had died two years ago.

"Pay no attention to them," he said, rubbing the apple on his sleeve. "They don't know what they're talking about. My father says Germany won't invade. He says the British and French won't let them."

"I hope he's right, but I fear he's not," she said.

Just then something happened along the back wall of the terminal, by the ticket counters, diverting the attention of the crowd.

"What's happening?" the old woman asked.

"I can't see," Hansi replied, stretching on his toes.

The old woman slid a few inches on the bench. "Climb up here," she said.

Hansi wedged himself in the space and managed to get a view above the sea of heads. Karin helped steady him.

"Someone's coming out of the office. He's going to speak."

A short, round man wearing a black wool uniform and matching hat climbed up a stepladder that had been set up outside the ticket office. Climbing the ladder was a great effort for him, and when he had reached a perch above the crowd, he had to stop to catch his breath. Then he removed his hat, revealing a head that glistened like his upper lip. He kneaded the hat with a nervous hand and cleared his throat to speak.

"Ladies and gentlemen, may I have your attention, please?" he began. "I regret to inform you," he said, "that all trains have been stopped until further notice."

The statement swept through the crowd like a shock wave, which reverberated back toward him with shouts and a surge that nearly upset him from his perch.

"Please! Please!" he called, one arm outstretched, the other clutching the ladder in desperation.

"When's my Dieter coming?" the old woman asked.

"I don't know," Hansi said. "What train is he on?"

"The five o'clock from Differdange," she said.

"That's your father's train, isn't it?" Karin asked.

Hansi nodded.

The official continued.

"A national emergency has been declared in order to investigate a possible threat to the trains," he continued, and another wave rolled over the crowd.

"A national emergency? What about my poor Dieter?" the woman cried.

"Does he work at the mill?" Hansi had to shout over the noise of the crowd.

"Yes, but what if he's in danger? My heavens!"

Hansi jumped down and put a reassuring hand on the woman's shoulder. "Don't worry, Madame. My father is on that train. It will be all right."

There was another surge of reaction from the crowd. Karin climbed up on the bench to see, only to jump back down an instant later.

"That's it!" she said. "He's gone."

"What about the trains? What about my Dieter?"

Murmurs spread through the crowd. Hansi spoke to someone nearby and learned that service would resume no earlier than nine o'clock.

"That's almost four hours!" the old woman reacted when she learned the rumor. "What will my poor Dieter do? What will I do?"

Hansi and Karin stood next to the old woman while the crowd boiled all around them. Luxembourgers were hardworking sorts who depended on timely trains. The announcement came as an overwhelming shock.

A new sound joined the chorus—a rain shower began to pound the glass ceiling.

The old woman touched Hansi's arm. "Will you wait with me?"

The question caught him. "My friend really needs to go home," he said, looking at Karin.

The wrinkles in the old woman's face deepened with worry. Karin looked anxious too, and so she pulled Hansi away. "What about the man?" she said. "He could be here, still looking for us."

"I know, but what can he do to us in this crowd?" Hansi thought for a moment and then said, "Listen, I've got an idea. Look at the crowd. See them heading for the door? I'd guess many of them are heading to cafés to wait this out. If we can blend in with them, I know the owner of the place across the street. We'll be safe there."

Karin looked doubtfully at the crowd pouring out of the terminal, then up at the windows high above them where the storm drummed on.

Without waiting for her reply, Hansi turned back to the old woman and told her his idea. "Manolo is a friend of my father. You can wait there with a warm coffee while I make sure my friend gets home. Then I'll come back and wait for you until the trains arrive."

"Manolo's? An Italian? Is it safe?" Though Italians had lived and worked in Luxembourg's cafés and coalmines many years, many older Luxembourgers were suspicious of them.

"He's a good friend. He'll take good care of us."

"But I don't even know your name," she protested.

"I'm Hansi and this is Karin."

"Karin?" the old woman said. "Is that German?"

Karin shot a nervous glance at Hansi. "Yes, Madame, my family is from Germany."

"It's a lovely name, dear. My grandmother's name was Karin. She was from Frankfurt and had crystal blue eyes just like you." The old woman smiled and then tried to pull herself forward.

"I don't know if I can make it off this bench, much less across the street in this storm," she said.

Hansi and Karin came to her aid, Hansi taking her bags and one arm, Karin the other. Once upright, they started to work their way through the crowd.

"Excuse me, Madame, what's your name?" Karin asked.

"Oh, dear, forgive my manners. I'm Marie Dumont. I live in Strassen."

"It's nice to meet you," Karin said with a smile. Hansi was pleased to see Karin's smile—the first one since their eyes met along the wall above the cliffs.

They were halfway to the exit when a whistle blasted, not the trumpet of a train whistle, but a high-pitched shriek from the passage to the tracks. Then several more, coming closer. When they turned to look, the mass was pushing back toward them.

Hansi maneuvered for a better look.

"It's the gendarmes!" he said. "They've got someone!"

"Who?" the old woman said.

"I can't see," Hansi answered.

The whistle blasts came closer, and the crowd parted just enough to make a narrow path.

Hansi saw four gendarmes, dark-uniformed, whistles protruding like cigars from puffed cheeks. They had a younger man in handcuffs. But the greater shock was seeing two men dressed in plain black trench coats and wide-brimmed hats following behind. The gendarmes jostled the younger man between them, dragging him, and at times nearly carrying him, straight toward Hansi, Karin, and Madame Dumont.

Hansi tried to protect the old woman from the oncoming surge, but when he turned back, someone bumped him, and he stumbled to one knee. For a moment he felt a flash of panic, afraid that he might be crushed beneath the crowd. But, with a fling of his arms, he caught hold of a stranger's sleeve and managed to stand again.

Now facing Madame Dumont, he took hold of her hands and pressed against the crowd with his back, trying to keep open space between them. Karin stood behind her, keeping her upright. The crowd pressed in hard. Hansi feared they'd be trampled together.

"There's too many—I can't breathe!" Madame Dumont cried.

"This way!" Karin called as she tried to pull Madame Dumont through a gap that closed as quickly as it had opened.

Someone hit Hansi from behind. He fell against Madame Dumont, just missing her head with his own.

"I'm sorry Madame!" he groaned as the crowd pressed in harder.

Like a wave, the pressure peaked and subsided and then, without warning, the path opened up to his back. He stepped back from Madame Dumont to restore the space between them. Then, together with Karin, they pulled the old woman forward to the edge of the opening.

Madame Dumont staggered forward and stopped beside Hansi just as the first gendarme officers passed by. She looked up just as the arrested man passed by, and then her legs gave out. Hansi tried to catch her, but it was too late. She fell forward into the path, twisting slowly down, and hit the dirty floor with a dull crack. Hansi let the bags fall, sending apples spilling out into the path. A policeman stumbled on one, smashing the clean flesh into the gritty tile.

The man in handcuffs saw Madame Dumont.

"Mama!" he cried.

CHAPTER FOUR

Karin lifted Madame Dumont's head from the cold floor. She blinked and fought to sit up but had no strength. "Dieter," she moaned. "My Dieter!"

The prisoner, whom Hansi now understood to be her son, leapt forward like a dog at the end of its leash, jerking to a stop just short of her reach. The officers dragged him on.

"Wait!" Hansi said. "It's his mother!"

The lead officer halted, looked with surprise at Hansi, and then at Madame Dumont still sprawled on the hard tiles. For a moment his eyes softened, but then, as if a silent voice had given him orders, hardened again. "We can't stop. We've got to get this man to the station for questioning."

"But she needs help!" Hansi said.

The officer hesitated again until one of the men in black trench coats stepped forward. "Why did you stop?" he asked in angry German.

"This is the man's mother," the officer said. "She fainted when she saw him."

"This is no concern of yours. Keep moving!"

"But she needs help!" Hansi said without thinking.

The German was a hulk of a man, standing almost a head taller than the gendarme lieutenant. He spun around to confront Hansi, who felt a shudder rush down the back of his legs.

"Who are you?" the German demanded, incensed.

Hansi answered in Luxembourgish. "I don't speak German," he said.

The German flashed a terrible grin. "Don't think you can fool me with that mongrel tongue," he said. "I know that every Luxembourg schoolboy speaks German from the first grade on," he said. "What is your name?"

"I'm… I'm just trying to help her," Hansi answered.

"Do you know this man?" the German asked, pointing to Dieter Dumont.

"No."

"Then I suggest you get out of the way unless you'd like to join him." He swung back around to the lieutenant. "Get moving!" the German barked.

"But she's his mother!" Hansi said to one of the other gendarmes.

The German snatched Hansi by the collar.

"You'll wish you'd never said that, boy," he said with the same terrible grin. "You're coming with us."

Karin sprung forward and took hold of the German's arm.

"You have no right," she said in perfectly accented German. "He's with me."

The German was vexed. "And who are you?"

"Karin Blik."

The German lifted an eyebrow.

Dieter took advantage of this distraction and broke free. "I did nothing, Mama, I swear!" He ran but a few steps before plowing into the dense crowd, and, because of the handcuffs, dove face-first onto the tile floor. The gendarmes had him in no time, but the chaos gave Hansi an opportunity.

Without warning, Hansi kicked the German's shin with all his might. The man winced and let go.

Hansi learned from Dieter's mistake. He aimed for a space between two travelers and wedged through it, then pulled himself, person by person, deep into the massive throng.

He heard the German swear behind him. Hansi knew the man's choice between Dieter and Hansi was no choice at all.

Hansi's movement through the crowd looked as much like swimming as it did running. He bumped and bobbed through the people, driven by a panic that suppressed all feelings of guilt over abandoning Madame Dumont and Karin.

He followed the flow through the large doors of the Gare into the plaza, convinced that mere coincidence could not explain running into two Germans in black trench coats in the space of a single afternoon. Why, Hansi wondered, was a German barking orders to uniformed officers of the Luxembourg gendarmerie? And why would they obey him? Something strange was going on, something strange and very wrong.

Wind drove raindrops like tiny arrows into Hansi's face as he ran across the wide plaza. This was not a typical August shower, the kind that flashed and boomed and blew through. It was the determined rain of an autumn anxious to arrive, driven by a change in the atmosphere, whose cold drops would not cease until it had swept summer's dust away.

The plaza was a boiling pot stirred by people leaving the terminal and arriving from the city. Hansi joined the crowd with the image fixed in his mind of Madame Dumont and Karin, dazed, terrified, and alone on the dirty floor inside. Who would help Madame Dumont? How would Karin get home? As he splashed across the pavement, he was determined to help them, somehow. But he would have to stay clear of the Germans.

Hansi fought his way to the far side of the plaza to the Avenue de la Gare. Traffic was jammed in both directions, horns honking and people milling among the stopped vehicles to escape from the Gare. Hansi crossed and looked up to a sputtering neon sign: Ristorante di Manolo. The door was jammed with people seeking relief from the storm. Hansi wormed his way past irritated patrons into the steamy eatery. The aromas of fresh bread, pasta, and coffee brought a surge of relief.

"Bonjourno, Hansi! You grow bigger every time I see you!" Manolo was a short man, broad, but not fat. His arms were like other men's thighs, with lines defining his muscles beneath the white cotton sleeves stretched tight around them. His smile was so broad that Manolo joked that it caused the pronounced gap between his front teeth. He snatched Hansi and clamped him between his huge arms.

Hansi liked Manolo. Unlike quiet and reserved Luxembourgers, Manolo was big and powerful like the storm outside. Hansi's father had become friends with him after years of stopping for a cappuccino or sausage after work. Hansi hoped to wait out the men in black coats here and then return to the terminal to help Madame Dumont and Karin. But he didn't say anything about this to Manolo.

"Papa's train is late," he said. "Can I wait in here?"

Manolo frowned. "I'm sorry, my boy, but I have no table just now. Many people wait for tables, you see," he said, pointing to the line.

"I don't need a table, Manolo," Hansi said. "I just need somewhere to wait out the storm and keep watch for Papa."

"Perhaps the terminal, no?" Manolo asked.

Just then a man wearing a black trench coat appeared in the window, cupping his hands to see through the frosty glass. Hansi caught sight of him and jumped behind Manolo.

"You in some kind of trouble, my boy?"

The man vanished as quickly as he had appeared. Perhaps he was just looking for a table.

"No," Hansi said.

Manolo studied him for a moment. "I tell you what. Come with me." He led Hansi to the front of the café where an artificial tree was positioned at the side of the large window. "Stand here. You wait for Papa."

The position was perfect—hidden behind the tree and yet with a view to the street.

"Thank you, Manolo," he said. "I mean, grazie."

Manolo smiled, patted Hansi on the head, and returned to serving.

A few moments later, a waiter brought Hansi a steaming cup of espresso, intensely bitter but warm.

As the minutes stretched, the rain lingered on. Streetlamps came on earlier than usual. The window was covered in condensation, requiring Hansi to wipe a porthole frequently for a view to the plaza.

Two-thirds of the way into the espresso, Hansi heard the seesaw wail of sirens and the flicker of lights moving along the avenue. A pair of plain, black Citroën sedans pulled up in front of the terminal, escorted in the front and rear by the black and white cars of the gendarmerie. The patrons hardly noticed.

Hansi rubbed a larger circle on the frosty window and saw officers pushing a path through the crowd like an upriver barge on the Rhine. Dieter's head hung in submission now as they dragged him to the first car and shoved him into the back. Hansi hoped Madame Dumont was all right and that Karin was still beside her.

The cars sped off north toward the old city, and before the sirens faded Hansi yelled a final grazie to Manolo and was out the door. He splashed across the street and plaza and then scaled the steps to the terminal two at a time.

Inside, the crowd had thinned a little. Hansi returned to the area where Madame Dumont had fainted, but she and Karin were not there. He searched the area nearby, but they were gone.

"Did you see an old woman here?" he asked a man passing by. "She fainted and was on the floor. A girl was with her."

The man didn't even slow down.

Hansi tried a few others, but everyone was on the move now and no one had seen them. He circled a larger area and returned to the bench where he had originally met her. Still no sign of them. Then it occurred to him—Karin probably sought help. There was a medical station in the terminal office where they could call a doctor. Before he could turn, he felt a hand at his neck, suddenly snatching him by the collar. At the same time, something sharp jabbed him in the back, below the rib.

"Don't make a sound, boy, or I'll have this knife sticking out your navel." The voice was as sharp as the stab; Hansi recognized it as the one he dreaded since the tunnel.

The German moved beside Hansi, clutching him by the neck with one hand and the knife with the other. Together they were like a son nestled under his father's arm.

"Keep moving," the German said and led Hansi to the men's washroom at the far end of the terminal.

Hansi complied in silence, feeling the jab of the blade every few steps. He looked into the eyes of the passing travelers, desperate to catch somebody's attention to communicate his distress. One woman looked at him and smiled, and Hansi tried to conjure an expression that would plead with her for help. Her glance lingered, and then her smile fell away.

In that instant, the German pulled Hansi closer. "It's a delight to see you, dear nephew!" he announced with a smile. It worked. The woman's smile returned, and they kept on. Then he yanked so hard Hansi could feel the German's breath in his ear. "Don't try that again, dear nephew, or you'll bleed to death right here." He jabbed the blade again. "Keep your eyes straight ahead."

Hansi obeyed, though what showed on his face was most un-nephew-like.

The washroom was the kind of place people tried to avoid. Whatever original decor existed lay beneath years of stains. The floors were wet from dripping, leaking, and overflowing fixtures; the light was low; and the atmosphere was nearly unbearable. The German shoved Hansi into a stall whose door was missing. The bowl had been clogged for a long time. When the German pushed him, Hansi nearly fell into it. The German took up a position blocking the doorway, legs apart and blade aimed right at Hansi's throat.

"We're going to finish our conversation now," he said. "Tell me what you were doing in that tunnel."

"What tunnel?" Hansi tried.

"Don't be a fool!" the German said as he thrust the knife forward.

Hansi jumped back and stumbled over the toilet bowl, cramming himself between it and the ceramic supply tank above him on the wall. "I don't know what you mean!" he said.

"How did you enter the tunnel? The entrances are closed to the public. Where did you break in? How did you do it?" The German thrust the knife toward Hansi with each question.

"It's a bomb shelter," Hansi answered. "There was an air-raid test. Didn't you hear the sirens?"

The German gave no answer. It looked to Hansi as if he were working something out in his mind. Then the knife jabbed forward again. Hansi was straddling the bowl and struggling to breathe. He felt the cold pipe on his back and the wet chain against his neck. His entire body quaked with tension.

"What did you hear in there? And who is the girl? What did she hear?" The German's voice was low and threatening.

"Nothing, I promise you," Hansi said.

The German put the knife up to Hansi's neck. The end touched his throat. Hansi thought the smallest movement, even a swallow, would draw blood. "You heard something—I know it! Tell me! I won't ask you again!"

Hansi was pressed into the stall as far as it was possible to go, and because of the smell, the sight, and the sharp blade, began to feel faint.

He measured out each word. "You must believe me. When the lights went out and we heard a noise, we got scared. Then we heard some talking but nothing we could understand. We wanted to leave as soon as we could, but it was dark. Truly, we know nothing!"

Hansi's terror was made worse because he couldn't remember the actual words he heard in the tunnel. He was not good at remembering details. He remembered the dark, the thumps, the voices, and Karin, but not the words. The German was convinced he knew more. Against hope, Hansi looked for a sign that he believed him. Instead, there was a look in the man's eyes even more terrible than before, and Hansi felt his legs giving out. In that instant, Hansi realized the German was going to kill him.

CHAPTER FIVE

The weakness in Hansi's legs caused his foot to slip, but the sudden thought that he might fall into the disgusting bowl was like smelling salts to a boxer. As he fell, he flung his arms out to catch himself. One hand tangled in the chain that hung from the water tank above, and he couldn't help but pull it. The action unleashed a torrent of water down the pipe and into the already overflowing bowl. He jumped back and straddled the bowl.

The German leapt back to avoid the surge, but it hit him at the knees in a gush that engulfed his lower half on its way to the floor. He slipped, never letting go of the knife in one hand, but missing the top of the stall with the other. He smacked his chin hard on the front lip of the bowl, causing another explosion of filth.

Hansi absorbed this second splash and felt a sharp pain in his thigh. Still, it was his chance to escape. Grabbing the sides of the stalls, he swung his legs in the air and dropped down to the only place available, the small of the German's back. Steadying himself by the tops of the stalls, he jumped off the writhing back, swung forward and out and was clear.

The floor outside the stall was a swamp. Hansi hit the surface and saw his own feet fly out from under him. He smacked hard on the slimy tile and slid away from the stall. The German was swimming in place on the floor. Hansi scrambled to his feet, covered in sewage, and skated for the door.

The terminal was not as crowded as before. There was air to breathe and room to run. And Hansi needed to run fast. Faster than the stench on his clothes. Faster than the pain in his leg. Faster than the German.

A few paces outside the restroom, Hansi risked a glance back but in the next instant wished he hadn't. He hit something so hard it felt like someone pulled the plug on the electricity in his body. Inside, everything went dark and quiet.

When he awoke—whether a fraction of a second or an hour later, he didn't know—it was with the feeling something invisible but heavy was pressing down on his chest, forcing all the air from his lungs. He tried to breathe but couldn't. Then the light began to return, and he saw a figure emerge before him, speaking to him, though he could not hear him or distinguish the features on his face.

"Hansi, Hansi? Are you alright?" the voice said, and Hansi felt the weight lift in an instantaneous spasm. He sucked in hard. The stench was awful. The gash in his leg throbbed to life.

"What happened to you?"

Hansi recognized the voice and the face in the same instant.

He opened his mouth in warning. The German, covered in filth, stood over them. The knife was out of sight.

"Release him, sir," he said. "The boy is in my custody."

"Oh really? It doesn't look that way. What has he done?"

"He has been caught trespassing and needs to be questioned in connection with the threat to the railway system," the German said, impatient. Then he added, "And if you obstruct any further, I'll have you arrested as well."

"Arrested? Who are you?"

"I'm Heinrich Schlinge with the German Security Service," he said, retrieving an identity card from his pocket. "And who are you that you obstruct an official investigation?"

"I'm the boy's father, Alain Broussard."

"Then you might be interested to know that your son has been informing for certain terrorist groups known to be operating right here in your capital city," Schlinge said, recovering his official tone.

"Even if that were to be true, you have no authority here in Luxembourg," Hansi's father said.

"I have authorization from your own Ministry of Public Safety to assist in the investigation of suspected communist cells operating in your country seeking to overthrow your government." Schlinge retrieved another set of papers. "And I have full authority, from your own government, to detain for questioning any person I deem necessary for these investigations."

"That's ridiculous," Hansi's father said. "There are no communist cells in Luxembourg trying to overthrow our government. Those are lies spread by Nazis like you, hoping to scare us into submission. It won't work here like it did in Austria. Come on, Hansi, let's go."

He pulled Hansi to his feet, unaware of the intense pain in his thigh. He positioned himself between Hansi and Schlinge and raised his arm to place around Hansi's shoulder. Turning, Hansi saw Schlinge reach his hand in his pocket.

"He's got a knife!" Hansi shouted. His father spun around, flinging Hansi out of the way. As he fell, he saw the flash of the blade swinging upward.

In the next instant, everything disappeared in a tremendous explosion. In a singular moment, the sound ripped Hansi's ears and vibrated through his bones. The shock wave smacked him from head to toe, with the force of a giant sledgehammer. His view was swallowed by a dense gray cloud.

As he lay on the floor, stunned, deaf, and blind, a shower of fine debris rained down on him. He lifted his head off the floor. He wasn't completely deaf because his ears were ringing. And not blind, just in a thick fog of dust.

A moment later, his hearing returned. The first cry rose from the terminal. Then more followed: moaning and sobbing and calls for loved ones or simply for help. Then sirens. Then a cry that pierced all the others—more animal than human.

"Papa!" he called. "Are you there?"

Hansi rose to his knees and winced from the shards of debris that cut into them. "Papa?"

Gaining his feet, he stepped forward cautiously in the retreating fog. He came to a man lying on the floor clutching his face. Not Papa.

Straining to see through the cloud, he called Papa again. It was impossible to find his way.

His eye caught a reflection on the floor, and he stopped. The knife lay alone on the tile and beyond it a motionless hand stretched out from a black sleeve. Hansi followed the arm up to the body crumpled awkwardly on the floor. There was a pool of blood forming around the slumped head, and Hansi looked away. Then something made Hansi pick up the knife. He held it, feeling its weight for a moment. He closed it and put it in his pocket before moving away.

A few steps further Hansi bumped into a black shoe.

"Hansi?" his father groaned. "Is that you?"

"Yes, Papa, I'm here!" Hansi said, kneeling beside him. His father was lying on his side. Hansi examined his face. Miraculously there were only a few cuts. "Are you alright?"

"I think so," his father said. He tried to sit up but recoiled at the pain and clutched his ribcage. "We've got to get out of here," his father said, trying again.

"Don't worry," Hansi said. "I think Schlinge is dead. He's over there."

"Still, we've got to go," his father said. "The terminal is not safe." His father struggled to stand, and Hansi crouched under his arm to help. They stood together and took a few tentative steps. Hansi felt raindrops and realized some of the roof must have collapsed. Despite the pain in his thigh, he hobbled forward, following his father.

Ambulances had arrived and men and women, angelic in their white uniforms, spread through the terminal.

As they pushed toward the exit, stepping over people and debris, Hansi remembered Karin and Madame Dumont with a shock. The terminal office was but a pile of rubble. If Karin had taken Madame Dumont there for help, he couldn't bear the thought of what might have happened to them.

"I need to look for someone," Hansi said, stopping suddenly.

"It's not safe here, Hansi. We've got to go," his father insisted.

"But I can't leave them," Hansi said.

"Who?"

"I was waiting with an old woman and a girl. The woman's son was supposed to be on your train. Instead, the gendarmes arrested him for the bombing."

Papa was suddenly interested. "Who was it? Who did they arrest?"

"His name was Dieter," Hansi said. "Dieter Dumont."

When he said the name, the blood rushed from his father's face.

"Do you know him? What did he do?" Hansi asked.

"I'll explain later. Let's go, Hansi. Now."

The urgency in his voice and look on his face was clear—the discussion was over. Karin and Madame Dumont were on their own.

They crossed the terminal through intermittent sheets of rain pouring in through the gashes in the ceiling. The dust cloud from the explosion was mostly gone now, converted to a paste of red grime that covered everything.

Hansi gripped his father's arm and tried not to look as they passed through the mass of travelers just beginning to recover. Other than being knocked down by the blast, many people were unhurt. But others were still on the floor, moaning, bleeding, pleading for help. He tried not to look.

The front wall of the Gare was still intact. The exit was jammed with people desperate to escape.

Hansi wanted to close his eyes and tear this scene from his memory. He couldn't. There was no escape from the excruciating pain, and not just in his body. How could he abandon Karin and Madame Dumont? Why wasn't Papa helping the injured?

Behind them, another sharp whistle shrieked. The crowd parted. A pair of medical aids were struggling with a stretcher. When Hansi saw the figure they carried, he leapt to its side.

"Madame Dumont! Wake up!" He begged.

She didn't respond. The rear stretcher-bearer shook his head.

Hansi's legs gave out. Madame Dumont was dead.

CHAPTER SIX

The trip home was like a bad dream. He remembered floating through the panicked mob outside the terminal beneath the streetlamps and rain that pelted his face. He remembered, too, sharp throbs in his leg from Schlinge's knife. And the image of Madame Dumont, dead on the stretcher, was seared forever in his mind.

He awoke at home to sunshine streaming through the window and thoughts of Karin. The memory of abandoning her tormented him. She had not been with Madame Dumont when they carried the old woman away and he blamed himself. Was she buried beneath the rubble?

He drew the sheet back to see the bandage wrapped tightly from the top of his thigh to just above the knee.

Maman poked her head through the crack in the doorway. She smiled, came in, and sat down on the bed beside him.

"I'm so glad you're awake, dear one. Are you feeling better?" She rested her hand on Hansi's shoulder.

"Papa." It merely croaked out. "Is he here? I must talk to him."

"He went to the mill, like always," she said with a tone that betrayed a touch of disappointment. "He'll be home any minute."

"What time is it? What day is it?"

He had slept all day.

"So Papa's alright, then?"

"Only a few scratches on his face, thank God. But how are you feeling?"

Hansi tried to sit up. His thigh protested with a spasm of pain.

"Easy, dear," Maman said, trying to help him. "The doctor said you need to stay in bed."

Hansi started to swing his legs off the side. "But I want to see Papa the minute he comes home."

"Of course, dear," she said. "In the meantime, let me get you some tea."

She returned with a hot cup, a buttered piece of bread, and a jar of jam. She sat down on a chair beside him and looked at him with a smile.

He recognized the smile. It was the one he could always count on—when he scraped his elbows on the playground, brought an injured sparrow home, or lost a fight under the bridge.

He told her about Karin and Madame Dumont, leaving out the encounter with Schlinge. It helped the torment but left a knot in his throat.

"It's all right, dear," she said, taking him in her arms.

I'm too old for this, he told himself, though some part of him wanted to let go and cry, to give in to the guilt and grief he felt. But he couldn't.

They were interrupted by a noise in the hallway and in the next instant, Hansi's father appeared in the doorway.

His broad smile was framed by two small bandages on his forehead and another one on his chin. He gave Maman a kiss and a squeeze and then knelt beside Hansi's bed.

"How's the patient?" he asked.

"Still a bit groggy," she said with a smile. "But at least he's safe and sound. He just woke up."

Maman excused herself. "I'll finish supper and let you two talk," she said, eyeing Papa a moment longer than normal. Hansi wondered what silent thoughts passed between them. "We're having Ardennes ham, Hansi. Your favorite." She was gone a moment later and they were alone.

"I need to know everything," Papa said. "Everything."

Hansi told him as much as he could remember, from the conversation he and Karin heard at the air-raid shelter, to running from Schlinge at the Casemates and fleeing on the tram, to meeting Madame Dumont, to Dieter's arrest, and finally, to the second escape from Schlinge in the washroom.

"What did you want to tell me yesterday?" Hansi asked.

His father looked down and rubbed his hands together. It seemed like he had planned to get to this place in their conversation all along, but now that he was there, didn't want to go on.

"We need to make certain preparations, son," he said.

Hansi shifted to sit more upright in the bed and winced at the pain. He knew what "preparations" meant.

"For the war?"

His father nodded.

Hansi's mind took off. "You said the Germans were looking east, to Russia. You said they weren't strong enough to face France and Britain in the west," he argued.

"Yes, that's what I believed. But things are changing. And quickly. You're seeing them yourself. Last night was an example."

Hansi was confused. "Last night? What does that have to do with the war? What's going on?"

"The Germans in black, the man that tried to hurt you—what was his name—Schlinge? He says he's with the German State Police—the Gestapo for short. He said he is investigating terrorist groups in Luxembourg. He accused you of being an informant for them."

"You don't believe him, do you?" Hansi asked.

"Of course not, Hansi. Nothing could be farther from the truth. But that's just it, son. They're starting it here just like they did in Austria and Czechoslovakia."

"Starting what?"

"The rumors, the plots. They enter these smaller countries offering help to find terrorists, but the help is worse than if they never came."

"What do you mean?"

"I think they're behind the terrorist plots themselves."

"They blew up the Gare themselves?"

"Yes."

Hansi thought about this for a moment. "So, in the tunnel, Karin and I overheard them making plans to blow up the Gare?"

"Possibly," his father answered.

"But what about Dieter Dumont? They arrested him for it. Is he innocent?"

His father paused for a moment to consider this question, and then said slowly, "Perhaps."

Hansi shook his head, unable to clear the fog that lingered. "But what are they up to? What do the Germans hope will come from all of this?"

"They want Luxembourg," his father said. The sentence hung there between them, floating like dust particles, visible in the light yet impossible to fully grasp.

"Then why don't they simply invade us?" Hansi asked. "What could we possibly do to stop them?"

"I don't know, Hansi. Maybe they're not ready just yet. Or maybe they're still afraid of France or Britain. Maybe they just get some strange pleasure out of playing with their prey until we beg for mercy and invite them in. I'm not sure, but there is one thing I am sure of: if they come, it will be terrible."

His father sighed deeply and rubbed his face slowly with both hands, as if he were trying to wipe the stress off. Hansi couldn't believe it.

"This war won't be like the last one," his father continued. "You remember those newsreels we saw at the cinema of the Spanish Civil War? That was the testing ground for the new German weapons. They have tanks, dive-bombers, armored vehicles. They've perfected a new kind of warfare that strikes like lightning and sweeps through the enemy defenses. The cities won't be safe."

Hansi couldn't forget the German Stukas, hawk-like warplanes falling from the skies, slinging bombs from their open bellies. Buildings crumbling in billowing clouds of dust. Endless streams of people wandering country roads.

"What are we going to do?" he asked quietly.

"We want you to move to your Aunt Milly's," His father said, looking up.

It took a moment for Hansi to register the meaning. Aunt Milly lived in a tiny village north near the Belgian border in the Ardennes Forest.

"Without you and Maman?"

"Yes, Hansi," his father answered. "Until I can make other arrangements."

The answer pressed the center of Hansi's chest and didn't let up.

"Other arrangements?" He wasn't sure he wanted to know.

"You may have to leave Luxembourg."

"Leave Luxembourg? What do you mean? Why?"

"And take Maman with you," he said. "I'm making plans for you and Maman to flee the country."

The questions erupting in Hansi's mind were dizzying. "But why?"

"It's too dangerous to stay here. Aunt Milly's might not be safe enough either. When the Germans come, they'll smash our necks under their heels. No one will be safe from their goons."

Hansi felt a heavy weight in his stomach. He couldn't take it all in. Then finally, terrified of the answer he already knew, he asked, "But why can't you leave with us?"

His father took another deep breath, reached out, and took hold of Hansi by the shoulders.

"Some of us men at the mill and others—all across the country—have been preparing already for the war. We're a tiny nation. Our army can't stop Hitler's panzer tanks. We know it. But still, we cling to the motto handed down to us by our fathers from their fathers, and from their fathers before them: Mir wëlle bleiwe wat mir sinn!"

Hansi knew immediately what his father was saying. The old motto of Luxembourg: We will remain what we are.

"We're forming an organization ahead of the invasion that will work behind the scenes, underground some people say, that will resist and disrupt the German occupation. I've been a part of it. I've been forming a group at the mill."

Hansi lingered over his words. "Is that why you can't go with us? Because you've joined this group?"

"We've named it the Red Lion Brigade. Groups are forming all over, and my part in it is why you and Maman will need to leave the country. Once the Germans come, if they suspect me of being part of it, you and Maman will never be safe. Not in the Grund, not in the Ardennes, not anywhere in Luxembourg. Perhaps not even in all of Europe."

Hansi was shaking now.

"Why must you join this Red Lion Brigade?" Hansi asked, but he knew the answer. "And where will we go?"

His father took him by both shoulders.

"Dear boy, I don't expect you'll understand me. But Luxembourg is our home. Our tiny nation has lived through countless invasions throughout the centuries, from both east and west, and yet our people, our language, and our gentle and quiet way of life has remained. I want it to be here for you and your children and for your grandchildren. Someone must fight for it, and I'm too old to join the army. This is my way to help. And until it's safe here in Luxembourg, I hope to find you and Maman somewhere that is. France first, then perhaps Switzerland. Perhaps even America if I can arrange it."

"America? Really? But we don't know anyone there."

"You're right, Hansi, we don't. But I've got to find somewhere safe for you and Maman. No one knows if anywhere in Europe will be safe once Germany goes to war."

Hansi could not begin to imagine what his father was saying. It was inconceivable to him that he could move next door, let alone to a country or, worse yet, a continent away. And he couldn't imagine how Maman could accept this either.

"Have you told Maman yet?"

His father paused and it seemed to Hansi there was something he wouldn't say. Then finally he answered. "Not yet. I don't know if she can bear it just now. But I will tell her, dear boy, I promise." Hansi waited, not sure what to say next. His father was noticeably shaken, holding his hands together tightly as if to keep them from shaking. Then he looked right at Hansi.

"If anything were to happen to me," he said in a soft voice, measuring out each word carefully, "I need you to promise me you'll follow through on the plan."

The words rocked Hansi. "Plan?" he croaked.

"I've been saving money for your journey and working on the arrangements. If anything should happen to me, anything Hansi, I want you to go to our friend, Manolo. He will know what to do."

"What are you saying, Papa? What do you mean by anything?"

His father swallowed hard and blinked repeatedly. There were tears welling up in his eyes, something Hansi had never seen.

"Our work is very dangerous, Hansi," he said. "Promise me you'll go to Manolo."

Hansi was numb and couldn't speak.

"Remember my words and promise me, Hansi. You'll go to Manolo, yes?"

Hansi was completely spent. This was worse than anything he could have imagined the day before, waiting on the Casemates. Compared to what his father just told him, he cared nothing about what his father knew about Dieter, whether the Gestapo was after his father already, or what happened to Karin. All the facts and questions Hansi tried to organize were scattered like the bricks of the Gare.

It occurred to Hansi there might be something else his father was trying to say. Was he hinting about what might happen to him that he didn't want to tell Hansi? Hansi had thought the previous night had been a nightmare, running from Schlinge, seeing Madame Dumont alive and then dead, enduring a bomb blast in the Gare, and abandoning Karin. That was nothing compared to the terror he felt at this moment.

"Hansi, you promise me? You'll go to Manolo?"

The room was in deep shadow now, the sun having slipped beneath the skyline in the west, and evening was upon them. His father sat completely still, like a statue, except for glistening eyes fixed on Hansi.

"Yes, Papa, I promise," Hansi muttered, slumping down onto his bed. He was beyond understanding now, far past his capacity to reason. There would be no supper of Ardennes ham he could enjoy tonight, no warm bread or cold milk to wash it down. Just a dark room and empty hours between now and an uncertain morning.

CHAPTER SEVEN

In the last two weeks of August, life returned to normal. Hansi's leg healed steadily and got strong from walking up the valley road to the Casemates. He found enjoyment in his sketches with the help of a new sketchbook, a replacement of the one lost in the bombing of the Gare. Plans to move to Aunt Milly's had faded, he was glad, in part due to reports on Radio Telegraphie Luxembourg, RTL, that the major terrorist groups had been rounded up but also because of encouraging news of peace talks between Britain and Germany. Invasion did not seem as imminent as it had two weeks earlier. His father spoke no more of trouble at the mill, Dieter's arrest, or secret plans to flee the country. For his part, Hansi had not seen a black-coated Gestapo agent since the night of the bombing. Thoughts of Madame Dumont and Karin were never far, but the sting he had felt from leaving them had begun to fade too, both by the passage of time and by his own desire to return to the carefree life he'd known earlier in the summer. By the last night of August, Hansi was looking forward to the one event he anticipated all year: the Schueberfouer, or Shepherds' Fair, which marked the traditional end of summer just before the start of school.

Hansi's custom was to go to the fair with his best friend Georges, and two others, Peter and Paul, whom they nicknamed "the Apostles," not only because of their names but also because they were inseparable and not above the occasional argument. But when Hansi arrived at St. John's School to walk the rest of the way together, only Georges and Peter were waiting for him.

"Where's Paul?" Hansi asked, looking at Peter.

"Where have you been lately?" he answered, disgusted.

Hansi was confused.

"Paul's gone," Georges answered.

"Gone? Where?"

Peter sneered. "No one knows. Or no one's saying." Peter said.

"What are you talking about?"

"His parents sent him away," Georges said. "They're not saying where, but he mentioned once he had a cousin in Brussels. I bet they sent him there."

"Because of the war?" Hansi asked, shocked at the news.

"He's not the only one," Georges said. "My cousin in Bonnevoie told me two boys in his class left. Their parents sent them to France."

"It's stupid," Peter said. "I don't know what his parents are afraid of. People act like the Germans are hiding behind every tree waiting to snatch up their children and eat them or something. It's ridiculous."

"So he's gone, just like that? Not going to school this year?" Hansi asked.

"It's like he vanished," Peter said. "I wonder if he even knew it was coming. When I saw him two days ago, up on the Casemates like always, he didn't say anything about it. Then yesterday I went by his place and his mother said he wouldn't be coming back. At least for a long time." He let out a long sigh. "Come on, let's get going. There's a fried cake at the fair with my name on it, and I don't want to keep it waiting."

"Wait a minute," Hansi said. "His mother wouldn't tell you where he is? An address? Somewhere to write to him?"

"No. Not so much as a hint. Something happened to her. She would hardly speak to me."

"I can't believe it," Hansi said.

"Forget it. It was about time Paul grew up. Maybe he'll be better off somewhere else anyway."

Peter took off at a quick pace to separate himself from the other two, but Hansi caught up with him and grabbed Peter by the arm.

"What are you talking about? You and Paul are best friends."

"Look, do you want to go to the fair or interview me for the *Lëtzebuerger Zeitung*?"

Hansi looked back at Georges and mouthed silently, "What happened?" Georges shook his head as if to signal Hansi to leave things alone. They continued on, Peter by himself, in silence, well ahead of the other two.

The Limpertsberg district of the old city was the center of the universe that night. Having outgrown its original space in the Old Market Square, the fair sprawled across the playground and soccer field behind the Limpertsberg School. The spectacle of flashing lights, spinning rides, and mechanical merry-go-round melodies was perfumed to every corner by cotton candy, roasted pecans, and freshly baked pastries.

The three boys started down a broad circular path through the center of the fairground, past the rides, food, and sideshows to a branch full of carnival games.

Hansi's favorite was a throwing game whose object was to knock down a pyramid of three bottles. The boys' usual custom was for the four of them to compete to knock down the most bottles, the winner not only taking whatever prize he won at the booth, but also getting an ice cream cone at the expense of the losers. Paul's absence would be felt immediately—they played matches of one on one, the winners of the first round competing in an epic final.

The booth, no more than a white-washed wooden frame covered with canvas and a string of lights, was managed by a slender mustached man with a leathery face and sunken eyes. "Knock the bottles! Knock the bottles! Three throws for a franc!" he called to everyone passing by.

"Hello, boys! Welcome, welcome! Hansi, my friend, you've grown again!" the man said, then laughed. It was the same greeting every year.

"How's the carnival business, Joseph?" Hansi asked, following their annual unwritten script.

"Picking up, my boy, picking up," Joseph answered, as if on cue. "Georges, you think you can beat Hansi this year? And Peter, you are growing too fast for your arm. I think the bottles will be safe this year." He laughed at himself and then stopped suddenly. "Where is Paul? Is he tired of losing to you, Peter?"

Peter looked away.

"Paul's sick," Georges lied.

"Who ever heard of a boy being sick for Schueberfouer? Heh heh, did you poison him so you wouldn't lose to him?" He laughed again.

"Very funny, Joseph. Would you please just set up another set?" Peter said, slamming his franc down on the railing. Joseph slid off his stool, muttering mock apologies like he had offended the Grand Duchess herself, and quickly arranged a third set of bottles beside the other two.

"How are we going to do this?" Georges asked.

"We'll throw together the first round," Peter said. "Top two advance for the final competition." Hansi and Georges nodded in assent and put their francs down on the railing. Joseph handed out three balls each. They agreed in the first round to throw in the order of youngest to oldest: Georges would throw first, Hansi second, and Peter last.

Georges' first throw missed high. Hansi knocked the top bottle of the other two. Peter missed left and swore.

"Take it easy," Georges said.

"Mind your own business and throw," Peter snapped back.

On his second, Georges missed low. Hansi knocked the right bottle over, his second, and Peter matched him by hitting the right bottle, which took the top one with it.

On the final throw, Georges missed left and was eliminated. Hansi missed his last bottle, and so did Peter, swearing again, but they advanced to face each other in the final round. They put their coins down, Joseph reset two stacks, and they decided on the throwing order with a quick game of rock-paper-scissors. Hansi won and decided to throw last.

Peter's first throw knocked off the top bottle. Hansi missed right.

Peter's second throw was so wide it nearly hit Hansi's stack. He struck his fist on the railing and swore once more. Hansi missed right again, halving the width of the first miss.

Peter's final throw struck the railing below his stack with a CRACK! and spun harmlessly in the dirt below, leaving two bottles standing. He spun around and kicked the ground with all his might, sending up an explosion of straw and dirt. "Stupid game is rigged!" he said.

The explosion caught George's full force. "What's wrong with you?!" he sputtered.

The question lit Peter's fuse. He jumped at Georges and in an instant had him by the collar.

"Peter!" Hansi yelled, grabbing him from behind.

The three of them struggled for a moment before Peter let go.

"Leave me alone," he said, shaking himself free. "I just missed, that's all."

"Are you sure you're alright?" Hansi asked, and then saw Georges behind Peter, silently telling him to drop it. Hansi nodded.

Hansi turned back to the booth and eyed his stack of bottles downrange. He needed two to win, a difficult but certainly not impossible task. Just last year he needed a perfect triple just to tie Paul, and he did it. He could do it again.

Peter's back was turned when Hansi winked at Georges, coiled, and threw. The ball sailed wildly left and disappeared behind the railing. Hansi smacked his hands together and turned around. "You win, Peter."

Peter flew at Hansi and smacked him against the railing. The entire booth shuddered. "What are you doing?"

"Huh?" Hansi lifted his hands in surrender.

"You think you're so clever, do you, missing on purpose?" Peter shoved Hansi harder, and the booth quaked again.

Joseph jumped off his stool and grabbed both boys by the collar. "Take your fight somewhere else, boys! I'll not have my respectable game ruined by a couple of ruffians." He pulled them out into the middle of the path, away from his booth, and gave them a shove. "Away with you! Go on!"

Hansi faced Peter, whose face looked like it would burst into flames, and asked, "What's got into you?"

"Nothing! I just can't hit anything tonight."

"We're all upset about Paul," Hansi said.

"Look, I don't need your charity." Peter turned and left.

Georges stepped to follow, but Hansi touched him on the arm.

"Let him be," Hansi said. "He'll cool off."

Hansi and Georges watched Peter disappear into the crowd and then Hansi's gaze caught movement at a nearby booth. A group of girls about their age were tossing rings at glass bottles, laughing and teasing each other. A blonde ponytail bounced up and down, causing Hansi's heart to jump. It was Karin.

CHAPTER EIGHT

At first, he was relieved—Karin appeared to be as fit as the last time he saw her. Laughing with her friends, she was once again the girl at the railing whose hair danced on the breeze. But the longer he stared, the stronger the memory he had worked so hard to deny took hold. He had abandoned her with Madame Dumont—that was the truth—and it riveted him to the pavement.

Georges seemed to have changed his mind about letting Peter cool off and had started off when he realized Hansi wasn't following him.

"Come on! We can't just let him go like this."

Hansi heard Georges but could not take his eyes off Karin.

"What are you staring at?" Georges asked, retreating.

"I know her," Hansi said.

Georges followed Hansi's gaze. "Who? Which one?"

"The one with the blonde ponytail. There."

"Is now the time to spy out the girls? Peter is disappearing and we can't lose him. I've never seen him this upset."

Hansi agreed but still didn't move. "You go after him," he finally said. "Meet me at Manolo's in ten minutes."

"You can't be serious!"

"I've got to talk to her, Georges."

"You've never approached a girl in your life! Let me get Peter. He's going to want to see this."

"It's not what you think," Hansi said. "I'll explain later. Now go on."

Hansi pushed Georges away. Georges shook his head and took off at a run.

Then Hansi looked back to the ring toss. A bolt of panic shot through him. The girls were gone.

He rushed over to the booth and looked in every direction. A narrow path between it and the balloon dart game led deeper into the fair. He followed it, came to another row of games, and surveyed the crowd. They had vanished.

To the right, the row ended at a wide open space full of kids, adults, performers, and vendors, and at its center, the giant Ferris wheel. With every passing second his heart thundered.

He ran there and circled the giant wheel, scanning the faces. The crowd was thick, and progress was too slow. Every step was blocked by someone moving in a random direction. Every moment took Karin further and further away.

Overwhelmed, he withdrew to a calm space beside a cart selling roasted nuts. The throng surged past. Boys, girls, couples, families, gendarmes, priests, nuns—everyone smiling, laughing, sharing food, relishing the moment. He closed his eyes. The chance was lost. He had been a fool.

Someone touched his shoulder.

When he looked up, Karin's eyes were round and full, her expression cautious.

"Are you looking for me?" she said, then added, "Finally?"

It was an arrow in his heart. "Yes—er, no."

"Oh, so you're not looking for me. Stupid of me to think so."

"No, Karin. It's not that. It's just that I didn't expect to see you here."

"A rather inconvenient surprise for you then," she said.

"No! No! Nothing like that." His brain seemed to have swollen to the sides of his skull. "What I meant was I wasn't sure I'd ever see you again."

"And now that you have?"

"Were you hurt?

"Not by the explosion, if that's what you're asking."

Another stab of guilt.

"Karin, I'm really sorry about what happened at the Gare," he said. "I wanted to come back, I really did. In fact, I tried, but I couldn't find you."

She didn't respond.

"I came as soon as I could, after I was sure they'd gone. I saw them take Dieter away in a car," Hansi replied. "But then I ran into him."

"Who?"

"The German. He called himself Schlinge. He claimed to be with some sort of German security service. He said he's working for our government to track down terrorists."

"You know, Hansi, I've had time to think about things. Why were we so afraid of him? Maybe that day we should have just talked to him. We didn't do anything wrong. In fact, running from him made us more suspicious."

"He tried to kill me," Hansi said calmly. "Yes, he wanted to know what we heard in the air-raid tunnel. When I told him we didn't hear anything, he didn't believe me. So, he put a knife to my throat. When I tried to get away, he took a swipe. So whatever we heard in the tunnel was not meant to be heard."

Karin's expression changed.

"Just a slice in my leg, but it's better now. I got away and found my father. Just before the explosion. It got him."

"Your father?"

"Schlinge. It killed him. I saw him lying there. Then my father made sure we got out quickly. That's when I saw—" Hansi closed his eyes. "Madame Dumont."

"Madame Dumont? You saw her?"

"There was nothing I could do. They were carrying her out on a stretcher and said she was dead. I don't remember much after that." Hansi couldn't look at Karin, whose expression had transformed from suspicion to sympathy. She looked at him with soft blue eyes, and he couldn't look back, unsure of what would happen if he looked directly into them. "I'm really sorry, Karin," he said.

Just then three girls appeared at her side. "We're going on the Ferris wheel," a girl with red curls said, glancing inquisitively at Hansi. He forced a smile.

"This is Hansi," Karin said. "Hansi, this is Margaretta, Lilie, and Marie."

"Nice to meet you," they said, and then Marie, the red-headed one said, "Are you ready, Karin?"

Karin seemed suddenly torn, paused a moment, then brightened. "You want to come, too, Hansi? Only three can cram in a seat, so we need someone else to ride with us."

Karin's offer came as a shock. Except for his cousins, whom he rarely saw, Hansi had not spent much time with girls at all, much less ride the Ferris wheel with one so pretty as Karin. He made a quick scan of the area for Georges and Peter. They were nowhere in sight. He wanted to ask Karin what had happened to her at the Gare. He smiled and said, "Sure. It's my favorite ride."

The three girls locked arms as they strolled out in front, whispering, snickering, and alternating glances back at Hansi and Karin. Hansi's cheeks went hot when he heard Marie not so discreetly whisper, "He's cute."

CHAPTER NINE

In line for the Ferris wheel, Karin told Hansi her story of what happened at the Gare.

"After you fled, they dragged Dieter out of the terminal, and we were alone. A woman helped me get Madame Dumont to the superintendent's office where they called for an ambulance. That's where we were when the bomb went off."

"Were you hurt?" Hansi asked.

"Barely a scratch," she answered.

"I thought for sure the office was flattened."

"All around us, yes. A man told me afterward the inside walls saved us."

"But if the blast didn't kill Madame Dumont, what happened?"

"The medics said it was her heart. Seeing Dieter like that was too much. Poor thing. Perhaps it was a blessing she was gone before the bomb even went off. I'm sorry, Hansi."

He found no comfort in the news.

"I'm sorry I couldn't get back to you," he said. "How did you get home?"

"I called Fritz and he picked me up," Karin said, and then added, "Our manservant."

"Your parents must have been terrified."

"They never knew," she said flatly.

"You didn't tell them?"

"Father was away on business, to Trier or someplace, and I could never tell Mother something like this. She'd never let me out of the house again."

"Wouldn't your, uh—manservant tell them?"

"I swore him to secrecy. I wouldn't have been allowed to come here tonight if he hadn't," Karin said, with a sly smile.

They came to the front of the line, paid the operator, and climbed onto the empty chair that rocked gently at the top of the ramp. When Hansi took his seat beside Karin, memories of the Gare and worries for Georges and Peter disappeared beneath the giant wheel.

They ascended chair by chair, side by side, and then began to pick up speed. Karin let out a cry of delight when they soared over the top and flew down toward the eager crowd below. They swept through the canyon of yellow lights that striped the steel frame and rose again, each rotation more perfect than the one before. They were spinning in a moment he wanted to last forever.

"It always ends too soon," Karin said with a frown when the wheel began to slow.

"I know what you mean," Hansi said. "But my favorite part is coming up."

"What's that?" she asked.

"Stopping at the top, while they're unloading."

"Why do you like it so much?" Karin asked.

"You'll see," Hansi said.

The wheel unloaded chairs one by one, stopping only long enough for the man to unlatch the metal bar and let passengers off. At the highest point, Hansi slid far into the corner of the seat and waited for Karin's reaction.

"What's that?"

"The Notre Dame. And over there's the Palace."

"It's beautiful," she said.

Hansi drank in the view, letting his eyes drift up to the stars and crescent moon above. He wanted to take Karin's hand, slip out of the seat, and soar together above everything—the city, the valley, the missing Paul, the rubble of the Gare, the body of Madame Dumont. They would fly fast, toward the western horizon, fast enough to catch and overtake the setting sun. The day would begin again, and they'd be far away from ruins and rumors of war. Hansi closed his eyes and inhaled deeply.

The wheel started up again. They would be returning to earth, too soon. But before they did, something caught his eye at the far edge of the festival. On a nearby alleyway, a brown paneled truck nosed slowly out from the edge of darkness, headlights off.

"Hansi?" Karin said, her voice soft.

He glanced quickly to her and then back to the truck.

"I know what you mean," she said.

The sound of her words vibrated his eardrums but didn't penetrate. His heart jumped out of his chest when he saw two men in wide-brimmed hats and black trench coats get out of the truck.

"Hansi?" Karin said.

"Look!"

"What is it?"

"See that truck in the alleyway?" The two men had disappeared.

"The brown one? What about it?"

"I just saw it roll up. It didn't have its lights on."

The Ferris wheel moved again, and now he could just barely see the top of the truck beyond the roof of a game booth.

"There!" he called, pointing. Deep in the shadows beyond the truck they could see dark figures moving in the alley. But before they could focus, the wheel rotated again, and the view was lost.

"Who are they?" Karin asked, now also straining to see.

"I don't know," Hansi said, "But I saw two men get out. They were dressed like Schlinge and the Germans we saw holding Dieter," Hansi said.

"What would they be doing here at the fair?"

"I don't think they're here for the rides."

The man unlatched the bar and swung it open before the chair stopped, and Hansi and Karin jumped out.

At the end of the wooden ramp, Hansi hesitated and looked back at the giant wheel shimmering against the night sky. Letting out a slow and heavy sigh he wished, more than ever, he could return to the chair and swing between the skyline and the stars. It was a foolish thought. The next step would leave the fair far behind, and there was nothing Hansi could do but touch down on the cold, hard pavement with Karin at his side.

CHAPTER TEN

The girls were waiting for them, still whispering and giggling.

"Did you two have fun up there?" Lilie asked with raised eyebrows.

"I don't think they saw much of the scenery," Marie answered, elbowing Margaretta. Everyone laughed but Hansi and Karin.

"Be nice to him," Margaretta said.

"Why should I?" Marie answered through a wide grin.

"Maybe he'll introduce us to his friends," said Margaretta, which brought a round of laughs from the other two. Even Karin smiled at that one.

"What shall we ride next?" she asked.

They talked about whether to try something faster, or another game, or something silly like the carousel. Hansi was distracted, looking past them for the German agents.

"What do you want to do?" Marie asked him, but he wasn't paying attention.

"Hansi?" Karin said. "You're coming too, aren't you?"

"Oh, sorry. I promised my friends I'd catch up with them."

"Ah, he does have friends!" Margaretta said.

Hansi felt torn again. "I told them I'd meet them at Manolo's after this."

"Manolo's?" Lilie asked.

"A friend of mine. He runs a food stand. Sausages, frites, fried cakes, that sort of thing."

"Sounds wonderful," Lilie said.

Karin asked, "Would they mind, Hansi?"

Hansi could only imagine how Georges and Peter would react when he walked up with four girls! He'd be a hero except for Peter's sour mood. Still, Hansi would have done almost anything to spend more time with Karin. And maybe the girls would cheer Peter up a bit.

"Come on," he said.

Every year, Manolo set up a collection of mismatched wooden tables around a worn-out trailer with a propane stove to serve up a mix of boiled sausages, deep-fried potato frites, dark beer, mineral water, and a deep-fried cake that he sprinkled with sugar. Hansi chose Manolo's stand over both ice cream and candy.

"Hansi, my boy, so good to see you! And welcome to your friends! Peter and Georges wait for you just now. Please come. Sit down, sit down!"

Georges was just finishing a fried cake while Peter's lay untouched on the plate in front of him. When Georges looked up, relief swept across his face. Peter scowled.

"Sorry I'm late, boys," Hansi said, trying to sound cheerful. "I've got some friends I want you to meet."

The girls huddled together behind him and took some coaxing to step forward. "This is Lilie," he said, indicating a petite, black-haired girl.

She dipped slightly and said, "Moyen."

"And this is Margaretta," he continued, pointing to Marie.

"Margaretta is the smart one," Marie corrected. "I'm the pretty one," she finished, tossing back her fiery red hair. The girls stifled a burst of giggles. Georges grinned but Peter rolled his eyes.

"Oh, sorry," Hansi said. "This is Marie. That's Margaretta."

Marie stuck her hand out toward Georges and Peter, as if she expected them to kiss it. They sat frozen.

"Marie!" Margaretta scolded. Marie doubled over with laughter.

"And this is Karin," Hansi finished, but no one was paying attention.

Then came an awkward pause while everyone except Peter stared at Hansi. Georges raised his eyebrows at him.

"Oh, of course. This is Georges, and this is Peter."

"Very nice to meet you," Georges said, almost before Hansi had finished.

Just then Manolo appeared behind them. "Boys! Girls! Please, sit down! Manolo make you something delicioso!" They slid a second table over, gathered more chairs, and sat down, girls on one side, Georges and Hansi on the other. Peter didn't move.

Manolo delivered a pile of fried cakes and orange sodas on a tray, then refused everyone's offers to pay. "Please, for you, my friends, no money tonight!" he said, waving his hands and pretending not to see the bills they waved at him. "Tonight is most beautiful night! Last night of the fair!" He winked at Hansi and left them alone. They dug into the cakes, a flattened flour delicacy deep-fried to a golden brown and smothered with sugar, still warm on the plate. Their sweet aroma filled the air all around them, pushing the memory of what Hansi had seen on the Ferris wheel to the back of his mind. If only Peter would snap out of his sour mood, Hansi thought, Manolo's proclamation might be true.

Georges was eager to talk with the girls and soon had a conversation going. He found out that they attended St. Bernadette's girl's school near the Grand Ducal Palace. He was finding out where they all lived when Peter finally spoke up.

"Where are you from?" he asked with a suspicious tone, looking at Karin.

"I'm from Germany," she said.

"I knew it," he said with a huff and turned away. The girls quieted.

"What's that supposed to mean?" Hansi asked, irritated.

"I could tell by her accent. She's not a Luxembourger."

"So what?" Hansi said. "You don't have to be so rude about it."

"It's all right," Karin said quietly.

"No, it's not. He's been in a bad mood all night. Leave her alone."

Peter shot up out of his chair. "Why did you bring them over here in the first place?"

Hansi rose to meet him. "Take it easy, Peter. I thought you and Georges might like to meet them. They're fun."

"Maybe we should go," said Karin, signaling to the girls, who looked genuinely disappointed, though not as much as Georges.

"Don't bother," Peter said. "We're leaving. Come on, Georges." Peter pushed past Hansi, not too careful.

"Come on," he repeated, glaring at Georges, who remained seated across from Marie. "Let Hansi entertain the Germans by himself."

Hansi leaned in close. "That's enough, Peter!"

Margaretta stood up. "Come on girls, let's get out of here." Lilie and Marie got up.

"Wait, don't go!" Georges said, also on his feet now.

"Obviously we're not wanted here," Marie said, tossing her hair back.

"That's right," Peter muttered.

The girls gathered themselves together and started to leave.

"Don't go," Hansi said to Karin.

"I don't think this was such a good idea," she said.

"It was a great idea if it weren't for Peter."

"Don't worry about me," Peter interjected. "We're leaving. Come on, Georges!"

The party ended before it started.

"Karin, are you coming?" Margaretta said, hands propped on her hips. Karin hesitated; her expression pained.

Peter stepped around Hansi and grabbed Georges by the shirt. "Let's go try the bumper cars. I feel like crashing into something."

Georges pleaded silently with Hansi.

"You two go on," he said. "I've had enough for one night."

Georges at his side, Peter stormed up the path in one direction while the girls left in the other.

"Are you coming or not, Karin?" Margaretta said, slumping her shoulders impatiently.

Karin looked at them, then back at Hansi, with the same tortured look as before. "Why don't you join us?" she asked.

"You go ahead," he said. "I'm going to see if Manolo needs my help before I head home. It's getting late."

"Karin, come on!" Marie called, "Or we're going to leave you!"

Karin ran over to the girls and Hansi's heart sank. But he couldn't bring himself to follow her. Their lightheartedness highlighted the opposite feelings inside him. But if she left, would she be gone forever?

He didn't understand the feelings at war inside. Then a voice rose to scold him.

What business does a Luxembourger have making friends with a German girl?

Theirs had been a chance meeting on the Casemates, a brief but dangerous flight to the Gare, escape, and separation for almost three weeks during which he was starting to forget her. And now another chance meeting. His feelings were like the Ferris wheel, starting, stopping; rising and falling; and then over too soon. Perhaps Peter was right, if even for the wrong reason.

He was about to turn away when he realized the girls hadn't moved. They stood there, beyond his hearing, Karin saying something to them. Then, before he knew it, Lilie, Margaretta, and Marie moved on up the path, leaving Karin alone. She turned to Hansi and let a smile spread across her face. In the next instant she was right in front of him.

CHAPTER ELEVEN

"I didn't want to go," Karin said softly.

"I didn't want you to either," Hansi replied, instantly transported back to the top of the Ferris wheel. They sat down at a nearby table and, as if by magic, a fresh tray of fried cakes and soda appeared, compliments of Manolo. In silence, they ate and drank beneath the soft yellow lights strung along Manolo's booth, but it was the only time in Hansi's memory he had no appetite.

"I'm really sorry about Peter," he said finally and then proceeded to tell her about Paul.

"Are Luxembourgers so afraid of Germany that they send their children away in secret?"

"After what happened at the Gare, everyone seems to be on edge." He didn't mention his own parents' plan.

"But wasn't the bomber, Madame Dumont's son, a Luxembourger?"

"Yes," Hansi said, "but there are many people who think the Germans were somehow behind it."

"How?"

"They planted the bomb and made it look like Dieter did it."

"That makes no sense. If German agents planted the bomb, why wouldn't they—well, find it first and then arrest Dieter?

Why risk their lives arresting a man knowing the bomb is ticking nearby?

She had a point. "I don't know," he answered.

"The fact that the bomb actually went off proves to me German agents had nothing to do with it. It doesn't look very good for the German agents to arrest a bombing suspect if it turns out the bomb is real, does it?"

"I suppose it depends on who you ask."

Karin was perplexed. "What do you mean?"

Hansi paused for a moment, considering his words carefully. "Look at what happened. The bomb killed nineteen people. What's been the reaction? Some people are more afraid of war now and people are sending their children away in hiding. Perhaps that's exactly what Germany wants."

"Are you serious? You really think the Germans would kill innocent people, like Madame Dumont, just to intimidate your country?"

Hansi didn't answer.

"That's ridiculous," Karin huffed, rising from the table. "I thought you were different."

"Karin, please, sit down. I'm not Peter."

"But you're suggesting my countrymen—these German agents—have some strange, twisted goal of killing people and frightening your country. What on earth for?"

"I don't know," Hansi said. "But they want something. Something very badly. Please, don't go."

They were interrupted by the sound of a piercing scream, an explosion of plates, and then the hiss of hot steam. Behind them, a group of about ten young men stood over Manolo's overturned cart and proceeded to smash it up with wooden clubs. More screams and people started running. Sprawled on the pavement lay Manolo.

Hansi ran to him. His eyes were rolling toward the back of his head and his mouth was full of blood. Plate shards clattered off his apron as he struggled to sit up.

"Be still," Hansi said, trying but failing to hold Manolo down. The man had the strength of a beast and shook the confusion away with a snort.

Karin pressed a cloth napkin against Manolo's bleeding mouth.

"You're not welcome here, you swine!"

The boy, no more than twenty years old, wore a brown shirt with a diagonal belt over one shoulder for a uniform. He spit at Manolo and shook his club in the air. His companions, all dressed alike, shouted in agreement.

The leader took a step forward. Eyes rabid, he warned, "If you know what's good for you, you'll pack up and leave. For good! Luxembourg is for Luxembourgers!"

"But he is a Luxembourger!" Hansi had stepped between Manolo and the mob.

The leader eyed him for a moment and then laughed. With a nod, Hansi was in the grip of one of the others, a tall boy with arms like Hansi's thighs. Hansi started flailing wildly until another one joined in and seized him with a fistful of hair on the back of his head. The pain was excruciating.

"Look here, boys! A piglet trying to protect the pig! Let's see if he squeals!" He punched Hansi in the side with the butt of his club and laughed again.

"Stop it! Stop it at once!" It was Karin.

"No!" Hansi's warning was cut off by a shot to the stomach that took his wind away.

The leader turned to face Karin. "Ah ha! Who do we have here? A little sow chasing after the piglet. It's a regular barnyard here!"

"Release him at once or I'll call the police!" she said.

"Oh, you will? Please, fraulein, don't do that. We wouldn't want to get in trouble with the police, would we boys?" His mocking evoked more laughter from the mob. He touched Karin on the shoulder and rubbed a fold of her sweater between his fingers. "What's a pretty little tart like you doing, sticking up for this dirty piglet and his swine of a big brother?"

The leader's touch set off an explosion of rage that Hansi had never known. He jumped at him, but his captors held on. They crashed to the pavement in one frenzied mass and wrestled for a moment until everything went black in a sharp crack to the side of his head.

When Hansi opened his eyes, he observed the scene as through the wrong end of a telescope.

The leader had clamped one hand on Karin's arm. Struggling to free herself, Karin was shouting something at him. He raised his club to strike. Trapped by a body that seemed to weigh a thousand pounds, Hansi let out a silent scream.

The club reached its apex when something diverted the leader's attention. His eyes narrowed. The club returned to his side.

Before releasing her, he jerked Karin close and whispered something in her ear. An instant later the gang was gone.

Pain awoke in Hansi's forehead. Sounds of the fair returned. Karin's face appeared above him, her hair spilling softly around her neck, glowing from the festival lights.

"Hansi," she breathed.

Her voice lifted him. He blinked the haze away and brought his fingertips to the throbbing lump on his forehead.

"Are you hurt?" he asked.

"I'm fine," she said. "But that's quite a knot. We need to get you some help."

"Manolo," Hansi said.

With Karin's help, Hansi managed to stand up. The scene reminded him of the Gare. The cart was a crumpled lump of splintered wood and twisted metal in a pool of steaming meat and mud. Broken plates and shattered glass covered everything. Of the upturned tables and chairs, a single chair remained upright—upon which a dazed Manolo sat dabbing his lip with a napkin.

"I'll take you to my house," Karin told Hansi, tugging at him. "Fritz will call a doctor."

Hansi staggered to Manolo.

"We've got to go, Hansi." Her voice was urgent. "The leader said they'd be back."

Hansi leaned down to Manolo, who waved him away.

"Not the first time they try to scare me. I'm not afraid." He shook his fist weakly in the air.

"We need to get you some help," Hansi said, looking at Karin.

"No, Hansi, no. It's all right. Help comes."

Hansi didn't understand. Manolo was all alone.

"Maria goes for help," he added. "She brings friends. Big friends." His eyes brightened. I'm not afraid of little boys with sticks."

Karin pulled at Hansi again.

"Go, Hansi! Quickly now!"

CHAPTER TWELVE

Beyond the border of bright lights, motion, and noise, Karin led them along a dark and quiet street.

"What happened?" Hansi asked. "Why did they leave?"

"We had help. From a German agent."

"The one I saw getting out of the truck."

"He broke it up just in time."

"Why?"

Karin stopped. "What do you mean, why? You're not going to start up on the German agents again, are you? Are you about to suggest that the agent back there was hoping you'd get beat up and was glad Manolo's booth was destroyed?" She huffed and started walking again.

Trailing behind, Hansi offered, "It does make a kind of sense, Karin. I saw him getting out of the truck, right?"

She said nothing.

"Then I saw him go around the back and open the doors."

"So?"

"There were others behind the truck with him, but I couldn't make them out."

"What are you saying?"

"He was making a delivery."

"What are you talking about?" she asked, growing more irritated.

"He was delivering a truckload of thugs in brown shirts."

"That's crazy."

"Is it? Then answer a question. Did those thugs look like the fair-going types?"

"I've not been to many fairs. I wouldn't know."

"Then I'll try another one. Wasn't it awfully convenient that a German agent was nearby just when we needed him to rescue us?"

She remained silent.

"And did you find it the least bit odd that the thugs ran off so quickly once he got involved?"

Karin stopped again, not far from the upcoming intersection. Her eyes narrowed as she seemed to contemplate his words.

"There's one thing I don't understand," Hansi continued. "If he was, in fact, willing to see them bust up Manolo's booth—and Manolo with it, by the way—and if he didn't mind me getting cracked on the head, then why did he change his mind?"

Her eyes widened. "Maybe he didn't care to spare us," she said. "Maybe he only cared to spare me."

Her answer clanged between the throbs.

"What were you shouting at the leader?"

She swallowed hard. "I told him who I am. Or rather, who my father is."

"But he didn't care, did he?"

She shook her head. "But the agent—"

"He overheard you," Hansi said. "He knows your father. He called them off."

Karin put a hand to her face. "How could I be so stupid?"

"You want to think the best of your fellow Germans, I understand," he said, touching her arm.

"It's not that. I missed it completely. The leader told me."

"What?"

"Just before he let go, he whispered, 'I'll be back, without my German nanny.' I didn't know what he meant until just now. Oh Hansi, what are we going to do?"

"Get you home, of course. Isn't that where you're heading?"

"What are we going to do if these agents really are trying to hurt and scare people?"

The question caught him by surprise. It never occurred to him to do anything at all. "I have no idea," he said, "except that we need to get you home before they find you."

"It's too late," Karin said, looking over Hansi's shoulder. At the far end of the street, bathed in the harsh light of the streetlamp, stood a group of figures whose long shadows stretched eerily toward them. "They already have."

CHAPTER THIRTEEN

"How far to your house?" Hansi asked, eyes trained on the intersection ahead where the group of thugs stood in the middle of the street.

"About two blocks more. At the end of this street, you make a left then a quick right. That's my street."

Hansi knew this neighborhood a little, but not well enough to map in his head a route around the group. The leader stepped toward them, out of the circle of light into the darkness of the street. The group followed.

"This way!" Hansi said sharply, grabbing Karin's hand and reversing direction. They took off together in a run, leaving the shouts and clatter of shoes behind. At the intersection he turned left, jerking Karin behind. The street, not much wider than an alley, was unlit and empty, curving out of sight to the right beyond the next block.

They ran as fast as they could, Hansi glad that the wound on his leg had healed. And grateful that Karin was fast, indeed faster than he, as demonstrated at the Casemates. She was pulling ahead when he saw, on his left, an opening between two buildings.

"In here!" he called in a loud whisper, grabbing a drainpipe to slow himself. Karin slid to a stop and turned around. He peered into the dark crevasse between the buildings, just wide enough for them to slide in, one at a time, sideways. Until his eyes adjusted, he couldn't see far in the blackness. The damp brick scraped at his palms as he fell forward, but there was little time. Calculating they couldn't outrun the older boys, he hoped they could hide here until they passed. But the farther he slid, the greater the regret. The thunder of steps rumbled up the empty street.

Hansi's hand came to the edge of the wall they were facing. He pulled forward to discover, with a surge of hope, a small niche where the two buildings joined. They were at the end. But there was enough space to turn his body around. He pulled Karin through and felt the dimensions with his hands. An idea sprang to life.

The footsteps neared.

He pulled Karin close.

She gasped.

The percussion of footfalls rose as the thugs passed and then faded as they ran on. Hansi held his breath, hoping the ruse worked.

Fear of the gang was replaced by fear of another kind. Pressed tightly against the wall, Karin in his arms, Hansi was for the first time aware that they were alone.

They didn't move. His heartbeat thundered loud in his chest—she was sure to feel it. He turned his face a quarter turn from the wall. The radiant light was soft on her face. She looked back at him with wide, trusting eyes. His fear dissolved.

They lingered in silence, straining their ears for even the smallest sound. The gang was gone, probably following the street past the curve, or perhaps splitting up at the next intersecting street. The moment teetered between the danger just past and the danger that might yet come. It brought Hansi a strange feeling that surprised him. Something stronger than fear, something he had not felt before, something very alive. All from just being with her.

"They're bound to realize they were fooled," he whispered, "and so we don't want to be found here. Trust me."

"I do," she said, looking directly into his eyes. Her response startled him.

Hansi exited first to confirm that the street was clear and quiet. Karin joined him and together they took a few careful steps.

Stars dusted the black sky. The cool breeze carried the tension away. Midway to the corner, Karin slipped her arm inside his—in an instant becoming his only attachment to the earth.

The diplomatic quarter, just north of the central city, was unfamiliar to Hansi. The wide, tree-lined boulevard was uncommonly spacious compared to the narrow streets of the Grund. Its stately stone mansions, each a towering fortress, were nestled among meticulously manicured lawns and shrubbery, guarded by tall iron fences. Crossing from his world to hers, he hesitated.

"This is your street?" he asked.

"Yes, but it's much prettier in the daytime."

He couldn't imagine. And was surprised at the sudden discomfort.

"How much farther?"

"Not far. Just up there. I want to introduce you to Fritz."

"I should probably get going."

Before she could respond, a shadow moved from behind a tree up ahead and they froze.

"Well, if it isn't the Piglet and his little tart." The gang leader stepped into the light. Behind them, the gang emerged from behind the row of trees. They had walked right past them. In his bliss, he had let his guard down, and now they would pay.

CHAPTER FOURTEEN

The leader took a last swig on a bottle and hurled it into the street, where it shattered in a wet explosion. He wiped his mouth with the back of his hand and took a deep breath. Hansi sensed it—he was afraid.

"You shouldn't have told me who your father is," he said, tapping the club on the sidewalk. "Every diplomat lives on this street."

"You're a fool," Karin said. "You touch me, and you'll regret it."

Moving closer, he spread his stance in a show of toughness, or maybe just to steady himself. They could smell the beer on him. His eyes darted nervously to his comrades. A tooth was missing in the yellow sneer. The club twitched in his hand. His gaze turned to Hansi.

"Who says we're after you, fraulein? Your nanny may not be here, but he's always somewhere, isn't he? And soon we're all going to be one greater Reich. Cousins. Friends, even."

Something inside Hansi passed beyond fear. Surrounded as they were by this pack of dogs, he knew somehow, he couldn't simply wait for the disaster to come. Instinct rose above reason.

"Run, Karin!" he yelled. At the same instant, he swung his leg up sharply in a kick that would have sent a football over the spire of St. John's. His ankle burst in pain but found its mark, squarely between the leader's legs.

Karin ran.

The boy shrieked and collapsed to the concrete.

Hansi tried to jump. His ankle could not bear the weight and he stumbled. The leader flailed wildly and caught him with his club. Hansi went down. The pack was upon him.

BANG! Hansi expected sharp pain to accompany the blow—but felt nothing. The sound was far sharper and louder than any wooden club.

No one touched him. He looked up and saw why.

A tall man in a tuxedo stood three meters down the sidewalk, smoke rising from a raised pistol. Karin stood behind him. He was slim, lean-faced, with chiseled features highlighted by the shadows. Older than Hansi expected for Karin's father.

"Hände hoch!" he commanded, now lowering it straight at the heart of the leader.

The boys complied. Then one, whom Hansi hadn't noticed before, emerged from the group. He was red-faced, with a cap cocked sideways over his blonde licks that dangled between intense eyes. He leaned forward and grinned.

"Take it easy, old man,"

BANG!

The boy dropped to the pavement, howling from the bullet in his foot.

"Next?" the man asked, searching the faces in the shadows. No one moved.

He told Karin to go inside. Then, a nod to Hansi to do the same.

"Raus hier!" he commanded. The gang snatched their wounded by the shirts and dragged them off.

The large, tiled foyer of Karin's house reminded Hansi of a school tour of the Grand Ducal Palace. A curved marble staircase swept up to the second floor, shimmering under the light of an enormous crystal chandelier.

Oddly, the house was alive with activity. They seemed to have stepped into a party. The rooms adjoining both sides of the entryway teemed with tuxedoed men and sparkling women—talking, laughing, clinking glasses. All beneath a fine haze of tobacco smoke.

Karin halted just inside the door, as surprised as Hansi.

A couple shuffled in from the hallway next to the stairs—a man with a woman draped heavily over his shoulder. At first, they were unaware of Karin and Hansi's presence at the door. But seeing Karin she stopped, flashed a hint of alarm, and then forced a giggle when her champagne sloshed onto her dress and the floor.

"Karin, you're back. How wonderful!" She took a swig, let her arm slide off the man, and then looked at Hansi. "Well, hello there!"

"Guten abend, Mother," Karin said, without emotion. "This is Hansi."

Hansi realized now his mistake. The man outside was not Karin's father. But this one, short and round, with small gray eyes lost in the glistening puffiness of his face, seemed even farther from his expectation.

"Guten abend, Frau Blik," Hansi said, offering his hand. "Guten abend, Herr Blik."

Karin's mother blasted a champagne-filled snort. The man let out a chirp of a cough.

"This is not my father," Karin said with emphasis.

"This is Herr—," her mother began. "Oh, never mind. Yes, well it's nice to meet you—Hansel. Have you heard the news?"

She raised her glass in the air, sloshing what was left in her glass. "The German Army crossed the Polish border! The war has begun! Isn't it wonderful?"

Hansi felt a sharp pain in his heart. War!

Germany's invasion would certainly trigger France, Belgium, and Britain. Tiny Luxembourg would get caught in the middle. His father would put the plan into effect.

He looked at Karin, unable to speak, and then back at her mother, who was swinging around the stair rail post. From the room to their left, they heard a burst of laughter and her ears perked up as if she were missing something. She spun back around, dropping her glass. It popped against the marble steps. She shrugged, then flung herself toward the excitement, the pudgy man in tow.

Hansi and Karin stood silent, unable to move.

"I'm sorry, Hansi. I'm really sorry," Karin began, but Hansi didn't want any part of her pity. He turned toward the door and then remembered. He was trapped.

"Is there a back door?" he asked, voice trembling. "I've got to get home."

"This way," she said. "But you can't leave until Fritz comes in and tells us it's safe." She led Hansi down the hallway to an enormous kitchen at the back of the house. They sat in silence at the worktable while servants buzzed around them, refilling silver trays of food and drink.

When Fritz appeared, Hansi realized now who had saved them. The pistol was gone. His expression bore no evidence of what happened outside. Karin spoke to him and then explained to Hansi that Fritz would drive him home. Considering everything, Hansi didn't refuse.

Safe in the back of the long sedan was little relief. At least he was out of that evil house and all it stood for. Karin sat beside him in silence. He should have been grateful for Fritz's rescue. But instead, he was overwhelmed by the contempt he felt towards them all—and for himself. He had been a fool to think he and Karin could be friends. The war would leave no room for this kind of friendship, which had shown nearly impossible even in a single night of peacetime. Loyalties would be tested. And, as his father said, things would be made clear like a blast furnace makes clear—through fire.

As the car descended into the Grund and another world, Hansi stared out the window. The wide valley was peaceful, sleepy, and seemingly unaware of the news heralded by the drunk Frau Blik. He wondered what would become of this quiet city, the gentle valley, and most of all, his own family. He braced himself for what surely awaited him at home: Papa's announcement that they were leaving.

They stopped in front of his building along the Rue du Grund. This was goodbye, but he wanted to scream. Or cry, he wasn't sure. He said nothing and simply stepped out onto the curb.

As they pulled away, he could only watch as Karin's face faded into darkness, her eyes straining to pass a sympathetic message Hansi was unwilling to receive. His gaze continued up the valley to the top of the Casemates where the spire of the Cathédrale d'Notre Dame was bathed in warm light. Beyond glowed the fair, where people played and ate and laughed without care. A lifetime ago.

The door of his flat was cracked open, allowing light to spill into the dim hallway. Hansi pushed in and noticed at once that Papa's coat and hat were not on their hooks.

He flew into the front room. The man on the couch was not his father, but Father Jean, Hansi's teacher and the family priest. Beside him sat Maman, who was as distraught as when Hansi revealed his story. When he entered, out gushed a wave of sobs.

"What is it?" he asked, looking back and forth at them both. "What's happened? Where's Papa?"

His mother raised her head slowly. She was quivering at the edge of control. "He's been arrested," she said, then let her head fall back into her hands.

Hansi would have preferred a club to the head.

CHAPTER FIFTEEN

Tired as he was, Hansi could not sleep that night. And not very well the next night, nor many nights after that. When Papa had not come home by his regular time of six o'clock that Friday night, Maman called the mill. The superintendent told her Papa left at his normal time. Fearing the worst, Maman called the hospital in Differdange and then the gendarmes. The hospital knew nothing and neither did the gendarmes, at least at first. The way Maman told it, the first person to answer the phone at the station was a junior officer, who, when she asked about Papa, set the phone down and consulted with his superior. When he returned, he said "I am not permitted to say," an obvious blunder. Maman demanded to speak with his superior immediately. The lieutenant in charge came on the phone and reluctantly admitted Papa was there, but he was not permitted to discuss any of the circumstances with her. They argued for several minutes before she finally gave up and hung up on him. That's when she called Father Jean, and together they took the train to Differdange to press for Papa's release.

Their visit surprised the gendarmes, according to Maman. Father Jean's threat to take up the injustice with his brother, Captain Bertrand, Commander of the Luxembourg National Guard and hero of the Great War, sent the gendarmes scurrying.

Urgent calls rang superiors in Luxembourg City. When it became clear that Maman and Father Jean were not leaving without information, the senior lieutenant finally took them into his office, closed the door behind him, and admitted that Papa was under arrest in connection with the bombing at the Gare. Despite the very strict orders from his superiors, he risked his "long and distinguished" career, as he put it, to grant them a two-minute visit with Papa. But only after extracting a promise from Maman, guaranteed by Father Jean, that they leave for home immediately afterward. She only agreed after Father Jean convinced her there was nothing more to be done, not without a lawyer. The gendarmes let her leave a woolen overcoat and parcel of food behind, but only the steady arm of Father Jean could pull Maman from the station.

Back in the Grund, Father Jean called retired lawyer Monsieur Pfaffenschneider, an old friend and member of the board of advisors at St. John's, who immediately pledged his help. But there was nothing more anyone could do Friday night. Nothing but pray, according to Father Jean. And as Hansi saw, weep.

Papa spent the night in jail. Friday night became the weekend, the weekend grew into the next week, and the next week stretched until the end of September. Maman made a trip to Differdange every day, rising before dawn to prepare a parcel of food and change of clothes, attend early morning mass at St. John's, give an update to Father Jean, walk twenty minutes to the Gare, ride forty minutes on the train, and wait an hour or more at the gendarmerie for a thirty-minute visit with Papa. After that, she'd turn around and head back to the city, finish shopping, return home, call Monsieur Pfaffenschneider, cook supper, clean house, wash clothes, and fall into bed after dark, exhausted.

Hansi began to think Monsieur Pfaffenschneider was a fool. Days piled on one another with no news, and it seemed he always had an excuse. In the early days, he said the government was preparing charges of such a sensitive nature they could not discuss them. Then he said they were gathering evidence against other conspirators to put them on trial together and to be patient because these things take time. Finally, he attributed the government's silence to "national security concerns." By the end of the month, the government had not brought a single charge against Papa. And though Monsieur Pfaffenschneider claimed to protest what everyone agreed was an illegal detention without trial, Hansi wondered whether Monsieur Pfaffenschneider had spoken to anyone in the government above the level of a janitor.

Maman seemed content enough to wait, which soon became a growing source of frustration for Hansi. Perhaps it was due to the influence and guidance of Father Jean and the church. Interpreting Papa's arrest as a trial of her faith, she seemed to gain perspective through the lighting of candles, quiet meditation, and the daily mass. It wasn't that Hansi didn't believe, or even that he didn't like Father Jean; it was just that instead of merely folding his hands and nodding understandingly, Hansi preferred that Father Jean actually do something.

St. John's, the all-boys school in the Grund, started in September and Hansi felt like he was sleepwalking through it. Normally a top student, he watched his early marks slip, reflecting minimal effort, but both Father Jean and Maman seemed uncharacteristically forgiving. Even Georges and Peter let go of the jealousy left over from the fair when they found out about his father. But after-school romps on the casemate walls lost all their promise—the last thing Hansi wanted to do was pretend to be a brave knight fighting barbarians in the twelfth century when real barbarians in his own century were amassing their armies twenty kilometers to the east!

Memory of Karin faded except for the faint question that tiptoed in the far back of his mind—would her father, the diplomat, be able to help? Officially the Luxembourg government maintained a public face of neutrality, but rumors persisted all the same. Even news reports on RTL said German diplomats were prodding Luxembourg into an alliance with the Nazi regime. Hansi had seen for himself. The Gestapo men had led the gendarmes by the nose when Dieter Dumont was arrested—perhaps Karin's father could make a phone call to see what they knew about his father's arrest. Could Hansi trust him? As the days passed, the idea of asking Karin crept closer and closer, moving steadily forward through the frustration and inaction of September. By month's end, it strode noisily to the front of his mind and knocked on the door. He decided to open it.

CHAPTER SIXTEEN

Because he was young, Hansi was permitted to visit Papa only on Sundays. Though he was glad to see him, he couldn't exactly say he looked forward to the visits. Maman insisted they attend mass at St. John's together, which normally Hansi didn't mind. But word spread that his father was arrested in connection with the bombing, resulting in a range of reactions, from sympathy to scorn. Hansi hated to admit it, but even after only a few Sundays the visits started to blur together in his mind. Always under the careful eye of a sour-faced gendarme, he and Maman sat on the opposite side of a wide table from Papa, crammed between other family members and their captive loved ones, forced to talk about anything but the one thing they wanted to—his arrest and what he knew about the conspiracy to blow up the Gare. Hansi never doubted Papa's innocence, but because of their conversation the night of the bombing, about Papa knowing Dieter and about the new Resistance movement, Hansi wanted to find out what Papa knew about everything. And it was impossible.

Papa seemed to be holding up far better than Maman. He was the best-fed, best-dressed prisoner Differdange had ever seen, thanks to her. But the schedule took its toll. By the end of September, she looked pale and seemed to be disappearing inside her blue cotton dress. She let out longer and longer sighs at times she didn't think Hansi noticed.

On the last Sunday of September, the dull gray of the sun hid behind a lumpy blanket of clouds. The flat was cold and dark and unusually quiet for the one day of the week he accompanied Maman to Differdange.

He padded across the cold tile in the hallway. The kitchen was still dark. Maman's door was cracked open, and to his surprise, she was still in bed. He couldn't remember the last time he slept later than her, and certainly never on a Sunday.

He crossed the floor quietly and approached the bedside. Maman was lying on her side, her back toward him, so he had to lean over her to see her face. It was white, and when he touched her forehead, she was burning up.

"Maman?" he whispered. She stirred. "Are you alright?" She groaned and rolled over.

"What time is it?" she asked.

"Just past eight," he said.

"Oh dear," she said, hardly moving. "I wanted to go to early mass."

"No, Maman, don't get up," Hansi said. "You're on fire. I'll call for the doctor."

"No, Hansi," she protested. "I'm just tired. I need to get to mass and take the things to Papa."

"But you're burning up," Hansi said. "You shouldn't go anywhere today. You've exhausted yourself and need to get some rest."

"But I've got to get to mass and light a candle for Papa. Father Jean will be expecting me."

"Don't worry about that, Maman. Let me get you some tea."

"But who will go? Your father needs us. We can't leave him—"

"Don't worry, Maman. He'll understand if you don't come this one time. You can rest today and go tomorrow when you feel better."

"No, Hansi, I can't." She tried to rise but struggled to free herself from the sheets. Her face was taut with worry, as though she hadn't slept at all.

"I'll go," Hansi said. "I'll go to mass and take the things to Papa in Differdange myself."

Maman considered it. "But all that way, by yourself? I'll call George's father and ask him to take you."

"No, Maman, please. Don't worry. I know the way. I've been there enough, I could do it blindfolded. I'll be fine. You can stay in bed and rest, knowing that I'll take care of everything. Don't worry."

She exhaled and smiled faintly from the pillow. "So eager to be a man already. And a fine one you're making, just like your Papa. His clothes are in a bag under the hooks in the hall. The food is in the kitchen. You promise me you'll go to mass first and light a candle?"

"I promise, Maman," Hansi said, "on one condition."

"What is it?"

"You promise me you'll rest."

"I will. I promise."

Hansi dressed quickly, gathered the food Maman had prepared the night before—a baguette, a slab of butter, cold ham, a jar of currant jam, a tin of fish, and a Belgian chocolate bar, and put it in the leather satchel with the change of clothes. He put on his own gray cotton jacket and black felt beret and headed out the door, determined not only to keep his promise to Maman but to do what he could on his own to help his father.

The courtyard was empty when Hansi jumped up the smooth granite steps of the chapel at St. John's. Adorned with rugged stone, a short spire, and a steep slate roof, St. John's possessed a practical elegance that matched the Grund's character. Hansi pushed open a crack between the two heavy oak doors and slipped into the dim light of the sanctuary. The service had already begun.

Not wanting to attract attention, Hansi avoided the center aisle and took a corridor along the far wall to his left. Making his way quietly along the rows, he came to a small niche about halfway up the aisle leading to the front of the church. Inside, on tables arranged in a U-shape along the walls, was a congregation of small votive candles flickering in the cold drafts. Hansi stepped into the soft glow, dropped a coin in the box, and crossed himself. He bowed his head, closed his eyes, and thought for a moment. *What should I pray? I've never done this before.* He thought for a moment and then mouthed a short prayer: *Please help Maman feel better.* That was simple enough, he thought. And then another one came to mind: *And help me free Papa.*

He lit the candle. *Help me free Papa.* On second thought, that prayer seemed rather bold. What could he really do? And then he wondered, *Can I make two prayers with one candle? Or will only the first prayer count? If that's true, then I didn't really pray for Papa.* Hansi hesitated, pondering whether he should light another one. To do this, he would have to use another coin, which he might need later for the phone or if he got hungry. After wrestling with it for a moment, he made his decision. One candle would have to do.

The back row afforded the closest seat to the exit. After the service, Hansi could beat the crowd and leave unhindered. He sat down at the end of the row beside an older couple. The woman smiled at him. He smiled back and looked up to the front, where Father Jean's voice echoed throughout the sanctuary.

"Today we celebrate Saint Jerome, patron saint of students and scholars. He taught us to believe, both with our hearts and our minds."

Much like at school lately, Hansi had trouble concentrating. So when the service concluded, he was the first one out of his row. At the back of the chapel, he came around a stone pillar and realized he wasn't the only one interested in leaving quickly. Some paused to greet Father Jean. Hansi joined the group heading straight.

Hansi wedged himself between a pair of plump old women snug in their winter wool coats already. He was nearly at the doorway when he felt a strong hand on his shoulder. "Trying to sneak past me, son?" It was Father Jean.

"No, sir—I mean, no Father. It's just that I'm in a hurry."

"I can see that from the time you spent in the prayer niche," he said, more as a gentle joke than a scold. "Is your mother alright, Hansi? It's not like her to miss Sunday mass."

"She's not feeling well this morning, Father. But I promised her I'd come and say a prayer for Papa and her."

"That's a fine thing for a son to do. Your mother is exhausted, no doubt, with all that travel. Is there anything I can do?"

"Thank you, Father, but I think she just needs some rest. I really should get home to her now, thank you." He took a half step toward the door.

"Yes, of course," Father Jean said. "But you look like you're dressed for a journey today." He was looking at the satchel.

"I need to run an errand, first," Hansi said, inching forward.

"I see. All the same, I think I might send Sister Elaine by to check on her later, if you don't mind."

"Yes, Father, thank you. Maman would appreciate that."

Hansi took this as permission to leave and turned to the doorway.

"Hansi," Father Jean's tone was different, lower, and more serious.

"Yes, Father?"

"You know my brother Gerard is captain of the National Guard. I've spoken to him about your father's situation, and he is very interested. Very. He tells me he will look into it personally and do whatever he can."

"Thank you, Father." Hansi's tone was more serious too. As he stepped out of the darkness of the church into the light of the courtyard, he wondered what "very interested" meant. He would have to find out later. He would need the rest of the day for his errand.

CHAPTER SEVENTEEN

Hansi's memory of Karin's street was that of a canyon of stone fortresses protected by iron barricades. In the daylight, they couldn't have looked more different. Beyond the fences lay groomed lawns, manicured trees, and lavish gardens. At Karin's house, the red Nazi flag ruined the otherwise pastoral effect. When Hansi passed through the front gate, the chill of that night returned. Even in his own city, he was far away from home.

He pressed the buzzer and stepped back, hoping against hope that Karin would answer the door. He wasn't eager to meet Fritz again or Karin's mother either.

Footsteps sounded inside, a click of the latch, and then the door swung open. Hansi's chest clamped tight. Before him stood an athletic-looking man in a silk jacket. His blonde hair had been greased straight back originally, but much of it now fell haphazardly over cold blue eyes. He wiped it roughly out of the way, squinted at Hansi, and took a long drag on his cigarette. This must be Karin's father.

"Guten Morgen," Hansi said.

"Not really," the man said. "Who are you?"

Hansi swallowed hard. "I'm Hansi. Perhaps Karin told you about me." He was going to continue but Herr Blik cut him off.

"No, she didn't. What do you want?"

This was not easy. "I was with her the night of the fair. I brought her home that night. I was hoping to speak with her."

"Ah yes, the Luxembourger," he said. "Fritz told me. A misunderstanding with some local patriots. You could have avoided the whole mess if you'd only made your loyalties known to them, boy."

It wasn't exactly the "thank you" Hansi might have hoped for. He couldn't imagine how the thugs who cracked him in the head could be called patriots. And what loyalties was Herr Blik talking about? To the Germans in black coats?

"Is Karin here?" he asked.

Hansi had to dodge Herr Blik's cigarette that he flicked into the front yard. "Not at the moment. She's taking her morning walk. You can wait for her if you like." Suddenly he was gone from the doorway, leaving Hansi standing in front of the open door.

Hansi hesitated.

"Close the door, will you?" came the voice from inside. Hansi stepped tentatively over the threshold and pulled the door closed behind him. Herr Blik was gone, leaving Hansi alone with the steady tick-tick-tick coming from a clock in a room to his left.

"In here," Herr Blik finally said, the voice coming from the direction of the clock. Hansi took a few tentative steps and stretched his neck through the doorway. Herr Blik was slouched on a velvet sofa in a large sitting room with a new cigarette. "Sit down," he grunted, sweeping the first puff away.

Hansi entered and was struck by the enormous dimensions of the room. His entire flat could fit inside with space to spare. The marble fireplace behind Herr Blik sparkled in the light of a crystal chandelier. Polished bookcases lined the walls, so tall there was a ladder to reach them.

Herr Blik pointed to a high-backed chair near the sofa. Hansi sat down and took in the leather smell. It was like a museum—no, the Grand Ducal Palace. Or what he imagined, except for the occupant opposite him on the sofa. He gave Hansi the impression of a man who was not happy to be up this morning, nor perhaps any morning.

Hansi wondered how he might bring up the subject of his father's arrest, but Herr Blik seemed in no mood to discuss anything at all. Perhaps when Karin returned, she could help. So, while he waited, he left her father alone and found a book to stare at.

"Hansi is a German name, is it not?" Herr Blik rubbed his day-old beard.

"Yes, sir," Hansi said. His name was the diminutive form of Hans or John.

"So your family is German?"

"My grandparents were German. From the Saar region."

"What about you? Do you consider yourself to be German?"

The question made Hansi uncomfortable. "We are Luxembourgers, sir. My parents and I were born here."

"You stubborn Luxembourgers," Herr Blik said, wagging his head back and forth. "So proud of your neutrality. Stubborn in your belief in a separate national and cultural identity. If you're so independent, why do your diplomats insist I speak French to them? Yet your shopkeepers speak German, and the newspaper comes in German. I don't understand it. Which do you speak at home?"

"Luxembourgish, sir."

"Luxembourgish? Is it a real language? Isn't it just a German dialect?

"I don't think so, sir. Luxembourgish has its own grammar, even though we borrow occasionally from both French and German."

"And yet at school, you learn French and German, am I correct?"

Hansi had the impression Herr Blik already knew the answer. "Yes, sir," he replied.

"And which do you prefer?" Herr Blik put his cigarette down, blew out a long cloud, and watched Hansi carefully, the edge of his mouth turning up in a slight grin. It felt like a trick.

"Luxembourgish, sir," Hansi said.

Herr Blik raised an eyebrow. "Very well, Hansi," he said, moving away from the sofa. "But I'd suggest you pay attention in German class. And what's more, I'd suggest your people pay more careful attention to the lessons of history."

"Sir?"

"It seems to me you could have saved yourselves a great deal of misery throughout your history by simply recognizing the obvious—your so-called independence has always been worthless unless you ally yourselves with a great power. You have no power in yourselves to protect that which you love the most. I mean no disrespect, Hansi, but it's absurd."

Hansi shifted nervously in his chair. "I'm not sure I understand you, sir."

Herr Blik crushed his cigarette in the ashtray and turned back, aiming his bloodshot eyes right at Hansi. "Your nation needs to recognize its historic bond with Germany before it's too late."

Hansi felt goosebumps growing on the back of his neck as if Herr Blik had threatened him personally.

"War is coming, Hansi, and tiny Luxembourg will not be granted the luxury of neutrality like Switzerland. You have no Alps to keep anyone out, no banks to hide the money of the war profiteers, no experience in the dangerous dance of letting select refugees in, spies through, all the while keeping the armies out. But your people have a strong Germanic work ethic, rich farms, forests, and vineyards, and another commodity very important to Germany."

Hansi's curiosity overcame his fear of Herr Blik. "What commodity?"

"Steel."

Hansi sat frozen.

Herr Blik wasn't finished.

"Soon you will come to the biggest decision of your young life, Hansi—a decision upon which that life will depend." It was clear now that Herr Blik derived pleasure from frightening him.

"War is coming, Hansi, and you must decide with whom you will fight. If you join with Germany, you will live and be part of a new empire, whose glories will last a thousand years. But if you keep insisting on this foolish independence, or sillier yet, ally with France—indeed, even if you do nothing, you'll be crushed beneath an unstoppable tidal wave, such as history has never seen!"

Herr Blik's blood-rippled eyes twitched and then he fell back into the sofa. He sucked heavily on his cigarette and leaned his head back as if exhausted from his speech.

Hansi changed his focus to a crease in the carpet. And for the second time, he wished he had never ventured down Karin's street.

Just in time, Karin appeared, silhouetted in the entryway.

"What are you doing here?" she asked with a wide-mouthed smile between cherry-red cheeks.

Hansi jumped up only to realize he hadn't planned for this moment. "I was out on an errand for my mother, who is ill, and I wondered if you'd like to come with me." He wondered if his explanation sounded plausible, considering he hadn't seen Karin in nearly a month. Her eyes widened above the smile.

"If it's all right, I mean," he added, glancing back and forth between Herr Blik and Karin. "I've been very busy since that night of the fair, with school starting and everything. But I was thinking perhaps I could show you more of the sights of the city."

Karin blinked and grinned and bounced on her toes.

"May I, Father?" she asked.

Herr Blik was resting his head on the back of the sofa and massaging his forehead with his fingers. "Haven't you had enough walking for one day?"

Karin ran over and plopped on his lap. "Oh, Father, very funny. You know how I love to sightsee. Remember the time you took me to Paris with you? I wore you out walking up and down the Champs Élysées. Why don't you come with us? It looks like the air could do you good."

Hansi's heart jumped.

"Now you're the one not being very funny," Herr Blik said. "You two go on. Hansi and I have already had a pleasant time getting to know each other. So why don't you go before something terrible happens." His evil grin was back, widened to reveal tobacco-stained teeth.

Karin jumped up, the joy on her face replaced by a look of shock. "What are you talking about, Father?"

Herr Blik chuckled, which became a cough, and then rose to a fit before drifting away like a truck unable to stop its engine. "Now the joke's on you," he said. "I meant you should go before you cut off the circulation in my legs."

Karin's shoulders relaxed and the grin broke out again.

"Let's go then," Hansi said, jumping up from the sofa.

Hansi couldn't get away quickly enough. Outside, he made straight for the gate. Karin bounded off the porch and then half-skipped, half-walked. At the gate post, she hooked her arm and made a carefree arc toward him. With some distance between himself and the gate, he finally relaxed and let out a grin.

"You're in quite a hurry this morning. Have you got a train to catch?" she asked with a chuckle.

"Actually, we do."

"Very funny," she said. "Where are we going today? With these clouds, perhaps we should go to a museum, don't you think? Luxembourg has museums, doesn't it?"

"I don't like museums," he said without looking at her, missing the frown that he caused.

"Can you slow down, please? I thought we were out for a leisurely walk and tour of the city sights."

"We've got to hurry."

Karin surged forward again to stay even with him. "Hansi, did something happen between you and my Father?"

"I think he threatened me," Hansi said, still looking straight ahead.

"How? What did he say?"

"Basically, he said the war is coming. Here to Luxembourg. And I need to choose now whose side I'll be on."

"Oh, Hansi."

"Only the way he put it; I really don't have much of a choice."

"What do you mean?"

"It's quite simple. 'Join Germany or be crushed!' he said. It was quite a speech. I wish you could have been there."

"Oh, Hansi, I am sorry."

"Me too," Hansi said, stopping. They were at the corner at the end of her street. "I was hoping to ask him something."

"What, Hansi? About Schlinge? Or about that boy that Fritz shot?"

"No, about my father. He's been arrested. You said your father was a diplomat. I was going to ask him for help."

Karin's eyes registered the news with alarm, and then her face softened. She placed a hand on his shoulder.

Hansi began to tremble and couldn't look at her.

"What happened?" she asked softly.

Hansi hesitated, a sudden wave of emotion rising quickly inside. Then he turned away and began to walk again.

"We need to hurry," he said.

She jogged a few steps to catch up. "You're not joking. Where are we going?"

"The Gare. We really do have a train to catch."

CHAPTER EIGHTEEN

From the outside, the Gare Centrale showed few signs of the bombing a month earlier. All the blown-out windows had been replaced except for one which was draped with canvas to cover the work being done. Karin and Hansi mixed easily with the light Sunday crowd enjoying a very Luxembourgish tradition of taking to the country for a hike.

Inside, canvas could not hide the damage. Scaffolding covered the back wall around the administrative offices and ticket windows where repairs were still in progress. The new brick was a brighter shade of yellow that would take years to fade into the old. Wooden barriers channeled ticket buyers into narrow crowded lines.

"We'll buy our tickets on the train," Hansi said, leading Karin past all the repairs and through the tunnels to the last track and an uncovered platform. A single-compartment, olive-drab electric commuter train was waiting, more trolley than train, humming like a fat insect whose antennae rubbed against the overhead high-voltage wire.

They sat in back, away from the only other passengers, a young couple and an old man reading a newspaper, none of whom even looked up. A white-haired CFL engineer stepped on and began punching tickets. "Two for Differdange with returns," Hansi said, handing him two francs.

"What's in Differdange?" Karin asked.

"Nothing but steel and smoke, I'm afraid, mademoiselle," the engineer said and then passed the punched tickets back to Hansi.

Karin frowned and looked at Hansi. The engineer moved forward to the cab.

A sharp bell rang, the doors slid shut, and then the cab lurched forward. It jerked sideways and clunked over a switch joint in the yard before gaining speed and settling down on the main line.

"Hansi, what's going on? Why did you come to my father for help? What kind of trouble is your father in?"

"The authorities think he had something to do with the bombing."

"What do the police say your father did?"

"They aren't saying. They won't tell us anything."

"Do you think he had anything to do with it?" Karin asked.

"With the bombing? No, absolutely not. My father is a great patriot. He fought in the Great War."

"For Germany? Your father fought for Germany?"

"No, of course not! He hates—I mean, back in 1914 Luxembourg tried to keep out of the war, like now, but the Germans invaded anyway. He fled to France and fought for them."

"Oh, I just assumed…"

"That Luxembourgers are German. Well, we're not. Ask your mother, she should know."

Karin slid away to the edge of the seat and shot Hansi a look like she smelled something bad. "Excuse me, I didn't know. Look, I wasn't trying to be rude. My mother never says much about growing up in Luxembourg. It upsets Father enough when she speaks Luxembourgish to me."

Hansi exhaled heavily. "I'm sorry, I guess I was assuming, too."

"That I'm like my father? Then we're even. I'm not."

The tram was moving faster now, rocking them gently back and forth. The line headed west toward Paris. They would change trains in twenty minutes and head south into steel country. Ten minutes more and they would arrive in Differdange.

"Karin, do you know why your father's here in Luxembourg?"

"I told you, he's a diplomat. He's trying to improve trade between Germany and Luxembourg."

"Are you sure?"

"What's that supposed to mean?"

"You said he knew Schlinge. How well did he know him?"

"I don't know. Despite what you might think, there aren't that many Germans in Luxembourg. But they do tend to stick together. They probably met at a dinner party or some other gathering. But it doesn't mean my father is a member of the Gestapo."

"Was Schlinge at your—I don't know what to call it—your Invade-Poland Party?"

"It wasn't my party. And how could he be? You said he was dead."

"I did. That is, I thought he was."

"Well, I haven't seen him, and I don't like what you're suggesting. I went straight to bed after we dropped you off. Look, if you decided not to ask my father for help, then why did you invite me to come with you?"

Hansi was caught. "To see the sights," he finally said.

"Differdange? Aren't you taking me to the jail?"

"I know it's not a very interesting destination, but the weather's no good for a hike. I thought you might like to get out of the house."

"Well then, thanks for feeling sorry for me."

"No, it's not that."

"Then what is it?"

Hansi was unprepared for the question. His feelings for her were new and unfamiliar. Had he wanted her help or just her company? His head answered for the former, but seeing her again cast the deciding vote for the latter. Memories of their time together at the Schueberfouer were pleasant—for the most part. But was he right to bring her along to visit his father? In jail? Something in him hoped they could just ride the train to Differdange, see his father, and then ride back. Now he had to explain something he didn't understand himself.

"I don't know," he said. "It's just that everything changed so fast—that night at the fair."

Karin's voice softened. "Yes, I know."

After changing to the southbound spur, their train wandered deep into the countryside, stopping at every village big enough for a platform. They rode in silence, lulled by the rails and sleepy fields and farms. Hansi lost himself out the window. He saw a boy, about his age, leading a cow by a rope along the fence. The boy looked up at the passing train and caught Hansi's eye. For an instant, Hansi wished they could trade places.

The engineer announced Differdange and Hansi came back. Karin was watching him with soft, clear eyes that took him by surprise. Her voice was gentle.

"Hansi, I know you don't believe this, but my father could help you."

"I think you're right," he said.

"You do?"

"You're right in that I don't believe it."

She looked hurt. "Stop it. As a German, he may represent everything that's evil in the world to you. But as my father, if I ask him, he will help you. I know it."

Without thinking, Hansi took Karin by both shoulders. "Listen to me. You've seen everything I have. First, there's Schlinge, a member of the Gestapo, very interested in what we heard in the casemate tunnel the day we first met. Very interested in getting me to talk—I have a scar on my leg to prove it. Second, those Gestapo men at the Gare, the ones that arrested Madame Dumont's son, were not taking orders from the gendarmes, they were giving them. Third, do you really think that Gestapo man was at the fair to have fun? Didn't it seem convenient to you that he just happened to be nearby when those thugs destroyed Manolo's booth and split his head open? Did he seem concerned when one of them tried to split my head open?"

She broke away. "What are you saying, Hansi? That my father works for the Gestapo? If that's it, then you're saying he's just pretending to be a trade diplomat. Is that it? My father is a liar?"

"I'm not saying that Karin, please believe me. I'm not. But if you admit that the Gestapo is connected to the bombing arrests, then surely they know something about my father. And maybe they want to keep him quiet. If I ask your father for help, and he starts making inquiries, it may alert those who want my father to stay quiet. And then who knows what might happen to him."

"Wait a minute," Karin said. "Are you suggesting that the Gestapo wanted the bomb to go off at the Gare?"

Hansi took a breath. "Don't be upset when I say this, Karin, but think about it for a minute. What was the first thing you felt when you heard the announcement that the trains had been stopped 'due to national security concerns'?"

"I don't understand."

"What did you feel?"

She looked away.

"Tell me."

"I was afraid."

Hansi's voice softened. "And suppose for a moment that's what they wanted. A frightened child runs to its mother. A frightened nation runs too. I think they want Luxembourg to run to Germany."

Karin stiffened. "That's ridiculous."

"Is it? Some people say it's the German way. Look at Austria. The Sudetenland. It's not a big secret. If you invent enemies, you have someone to blame. It draws more people to your side."

"I think you've been listening to too many radio dramas, Hansi. And still, you haven't answered the basic question: why are you so sure my father can't help you? He's no Gestapo stooge, believe me. He could make some calls, talk to some people, quietly if you like."

The train slowed as it entered the sprawling Differdange yard. The tiny station was dwarfed by the tall stacks beyond, belching gray smoke that merged with the gray sky above the town.

"I'm sorry, Karin, but after what happened this morning, I don't trust him," he said, with more resignation than protest in his voice.

"Then trust me," she said.

They were nearly at the platform. Hansi leaned forward and lowered his voice.

"I'm sorry, but before we get off this train, you must promise me you won't speak a word of this to your father."

"But Hansi…"

"You must promise, or I won't step a foot off this platform. We'll turn around and go home. I'm sorry, but you must promise me. Please."

Karin didn't answer.

"Please!" he repeated, softly, with a tone neither angry nor demanding.

The brakes squealed and they lurched forward. Hansi's eyes were fixed on Karin's as the train slowed to a stop. The doors slid open and the speaker squawked "Differdange."

"Okay," she said.

CHAPTER NINETEEN

The town of Differdange sat at the base of a line of hills that miners first clawed before the time of Christ. Now a network of iron-rich mineshafts, mounds, and refineries across the southern third of Luxembourg gave rise to the country's nickname, The Land of the Red Earth. The ARBED steel works, built in the middle of the nineteenth century, produced huge steel beams used in buildings and bridges. Massive rollers took lumps of glowing dough in one end, then rolled and stretched them as they cooled, spitting I-shaped beams out the other end. These beams were sought by all of Europe, both east and west, and could be found supporting both Parisian skyscrapers and great German bridges across the Rhine.

The Differdange Gare, blackened by years of exposure to soot and smoke, sat at the head of a broad freight yard that spread over the valley like a vast river delta. Smokestacks of the massive ARBED complex stretched to the sky like reeds in a swamp.

Stepping onto the platform, Hansi and Karin were greeted immediately by a heavy smell of burning ore, its sulfuric scent like rotten eggs. Gray smoke hung over the town, casting it in gray monochrome even when the sun was out. Along the Sunday streets, red-faced miners from Italy and France mixed with black-faced German steelworkers and white-faced French and Belgian managers—all working together with Luxembourgers, their might and minds combining to produce some of Europe's finest steel. But compared to the beautiful majesty of Luxembourg City, Hansi could hardly believe he was in the same country.

He looked at Karin. Her face was contorted when she came alongside him at the first corner. She swallowed hard and put her hand over her nose. "Is it always like this?"

"Some days are worse than others," Hansi said. "There is not much breeze today, so the smoke gets hemmed in by the hills."

"I can hardly breathe."

"You'll get used to it. Come on, the gendarmerie is this way."

The Gendarmerie de Differdange was near the center of town away from the bustle of the Gare. The three-story brick building framed by two iron lampposts sat across from the only living things in the town, a line of trees in a small park. Hansi and Karin joined the small crowd of people already gathered on the top step. A lone officer blocking the door pretended to look above them.

"What are all those people doing?" Karin asked.

"Same as us. Sunday is a popular day for visitors."

They waited on the sidewalk for a few minutes until there was a sharp rap on the door, the signal to the officer outside that he could let the visitors in. He disappeared inside and it was like someone had pulled the plug on a drain—the crowd jostled and pressed together, everyone shoving to get inside first.

Hansi and Karin let the pressure subside before joining the others. Inside everyone knew to gather along the wall where a folding table had been set up to process the visitors. A pair of officers sat behind it, indifferent to the jostling in front of them.

Flipping casually through lists on their clipboards, they directed people down one of the hallways at the far end of the large foyer.

When it was Hansi's turn, he told a puffy-faced officer his father's name, just like Maman had countless times. The officer thumbed the page and looked up over his spectacles with a start.

"Who'd you say?"

"Alain Broussard, my father."

The officer rifled through the papers in his clipboard and then those of the officer with him before returning to the page he first consulted. Then he set the clipboard down and looked up at Hansi with a crease on his forehead.

"You won't be able to see your father today," he said matter-of-factly.

Hansi was stunned. "Why not?"

"He's ill."

"He was fine yesterday. There can't be a better-fed prisoner in the entire country. What's wrong with him?"

"Watch your tone, young man. I'm just telling you what it says here: Ill. No visitors."

Hansi looked at Karin, and then back at the officer.

"There must be some mistake. My father never gets sick."

"Well, son, things change. Move along now. Come back tomorrow, or next week if you like." He waved the next person forward.

Hansi was undeterred. "You don't understand. I must see him. I need to make sure he's alright."

"And his mother sent food and a change of clothes," Karin added.

The officer looked at Karin like he didn't appreciate her contribution. "Give them to me," he snorted. "I'll see that he gets them."

Hansi leaned over the table. "No. I'm going to see him."

The officer's face matched the color of the Ardennes ham Hansi had in his bag. "Look here, boy! I'm not going to say this again—there's a line of people already waiting their turn to see the healthy prisoners, and I told you, your father is not among them. There are no visitors for him today—lieutenant's orders."

"Where is he?"

"The lieutenant? He can't be bothered just now. So, for the last time, move along. Or I'll have you removed."

Karin stepped forward.

"Excuse me, sir, but he has the right to see his father, ill or not. As you can see, he's not leaving until he sees his father. Or speaks to the lieutenant. So, I think you should get the lieutenant."

"Who are you?"

"My name is Karin. I'm his friend."

"Now look here, you two. I don't know what you're up to, but nobody just walks in here, on the one day a week when half the town's here waiting to bail the family drunk out of jail and starts giving orders to an officer of the law."

"What's going on here, Didier? Why is the line not moving?"

The old officer spun around and nearly fell out of his chair. Behind him stood a taller officer whose build, unlike that of the older one, was suited to the dark blue gendarme uniform. His square face reminded Hansi of a rocky crag along the Casemates. He stood there, feet apart, his arms folded across his chest.

"Excuse me, lieutenant, but these two…"

"I need to see my father!"

"You won't speak to the lieutenant like that—"

The lieutenant raised his hand for calm.

"Come with me," he said.

The old officer couldn't help himself. "I beg your pardon, sir, but these two have shown nothing but disrespect for this uniform."

"Never mind that, Didier. Get those people through the line and be quick about it."

The lieutenant led them down the hallway to an office at the end of the corridor. They sat down on gray metal chairs while the officer took up position behind his gray metal desk. Along the wall stood a row of gray metal file cabinets beneath the lone window, so dirty as to be nearly opaque. The officer placed both hands on the top of his desk and looked up.

"Alain Broussard is not here," he said.

CHAPTER TWENTY

"Where is he?" Hansi asked.

The officer ignored the question, instead thumbing some papers on his clipboard.

"What's your name, son?"

"Hansi Broussard."

"Is this your sister?"

"No," he replied. "My friend."

"Name?"

"I'm Karin Blik."

The lieutenant's steel blue eyes flashed recognition.

"Does your father know you're here today?"

"Of course," she lied.

Hansi shifted to the front of his seat.

"My father! Where is he?"

The lieutenant put the clipboard down and drilled his eyes into Hansi's.

"I was hoping you might tell me," he said.

"What? I don't understand."

"I think you do."

The answer confused Hansi but also set off a warning.

"Truly, sir, I don't know what you're talking about. I come to visit every Sunday with my mother. Your list probably shows that."

"And where is she then?"

"Ill. She wears herself out visiting him. The cell is damp and cold, you hardly feed him."

The lieutenant lifted an eyebrow.

"We just come to visit, that's all. What happened to him?"

The lieutenant pressed his lips together. "He escaped."

Hansi felt a surge of hope. *Papa, escaped? Where did he go? Had he fled to France already?* Why wouldn't he have contacted them? It was confusing but also too good to be true.

"When? What happened?"

"Then he hasn't contacted you? Or your family?"

Hansi shook his head.

"Are you sure? He was arrested for his part in the bombing of the Gare in Luxembourg City. If you're lying to me and have helped him in any way, or are withholding knowledge of where he is, you will be charged in the conspiracy." He looked at Karin. "Well, not you, because of your father. But you," he said, bearing down on Hansi.

"Excuse me, sir," Karin interrupted, "but how could his father have escaped? Aren't there gendarmes here at all times, even through the night?"

"M'selle, this is not your concern. Monsieur Hansi here— now he's the missing button." He leaned forward. "If you don't want trouble, you had better tell me what you know, son."

Karin's cheeks flushed as she stiffened in her chair. Then she leaned sideways, intercepting his gaze.

"I know this," she said. "Monsieur Broussard has been arrested and no one seems to know why. And now he's escaped, and no one seems to know how. And as for trouble, I should think that there would be plenty of it to pass around a gendarmerie that lets a prisoner escape."

Hansi's eyes bugged in amazement. The officer's face swelled as he rose to his feet. Hansi might have laughed, if not for the officer's exploding rage. He took his stand behind the desk, his head framed by the window and gray sky behind him, as if girded for battle.

Hansi was startled by urgent raps on the door.

"I'm busy here!" the lieutenant barked, but the knocking continued.

"What is it?"

A younger officer entered.

"Excuse the interruption, sir, but there are some gentlemen here that wish to see you and they say it's extremely urgent and cannot wait."

"What gentlemen?" the officer asked, perturbed.

The younger officer glanced at Hansi and Karin and then back at the officer. "I think you'd better see for yourself, sir. They're from Luxembourg City. It's about last night."

Hansi and Karin's eyes met hopefully, but they said nothing. In the meantime, the officer stepped quickly from behind his desk.

"I'm not finished here," he growled, looking right at Hansi before he left, closing the door behind him. His steps echoed up the hallway a short distance and stopped. The silhouette of the younger officer standing guard filled the frame of the translucent pane of the door.

"What's going on?" Karin whispered urgently.

"I wish I knew," Hansi answered, still standing, his eyes sweeping the room. "But I have a feeling I know who those gentlemen are."

They heard muffled voices outside in the corridor. Hansi climbed up on his chair and carefully peered through the open transom above the door.

"We've got to get out of here, Karin, and now," he said, climbing down, his voice firm but urgent.

"Why? Who is it?"

"Our German friends," Hansi answered. "Looks like the Gestapo are interested in what happened last night too."

Hansi leaned over the desk and began to shuffle through the papers.

"What are you doing?" Karin asked.

"The officer forgot his clipboard," Hansi answered, and, reaching across the top, picked it up. "Here," he said, handing it to Karin. Then Hansi picked up his chair, very slowly and very carefully. "Look through the papers," he said, never taking his eyes off the silhouette.

"What am I looking for?" Karin asked as she began to thumb through the sheets on the clipboard.

"I'm not sure," Hansi said, moving the chair slowly toward the door, "but I'm hoping there is something interesting—notes, records of Papa's activity, anything that might help us."

Karin thumbed through the papers while Hansi positioned the chair back at a careful angle beneath the door handle.

"What are you doing?" Karin repeated.

"We can't stay here," Hansi said, "and we need some time."

"These notes mean nothing to me," Karin said.

"Don't worry," Hansi said, still holding the chair for good measure. "See if you can climb up on the cabinets back there and open the window."

Hansi didn't see the look of alarm that appeared on Karin's face as she realized what he was saying. But she complied and used the officer's desk chair to climb up on the file cabinet and reach the window. She grabbed the handle and twisted hard. It started to squeak.

"Slowly!" Hansi whispered sharply. Karin tried again and the latch came free.

"Open it!"

"It's stuck!"

"Hurry!"

She pulled harder, and the result was near disaster. The desk chair she was standing on slid out from under her, banging hard against the officer's desk. The clipboard sailed across the desk and rattled off the back of Hansi's chair, sending its contents everywhere. The officer, reacting to the commotion, turned and grabbed the door handle.

"Hey! Open up in there!" he shouted, but Hansi's chair held.

"Go, Karin—now!" Hansi called, leaning hard against the chair and the door. The officer outside pushed again, but Hansi held on.

Karin climbed through the window, looked down to the alley, and then disappeared with a shriek.

"What's going on in there? Open up!"

Hansi heard rapid footsteps in the hallway and had to go. He gauged the distance between himself and the window and visualized how he would leap up the chair, onto the cabinets, and out the window. And it was then that strangely, almost miraculously, something caught his eye.

The missing button echoed in his mind.

On the floor beside the desk, among the mess of papers strewn about, there was one that seemed different. It was folded in half and almost blank in comparison to the well-filled notes and lists. Something in the handwriting, even from two meters away, was recognizable. As his body jerked from the officer's latest assault on the door, Hansi caught a glimpse of the only thing that, short of seeing his father, made the entire trip worthwhile. There, in the center of the floor, on the folded paper, was Papa's unmistakable script: For Marie.

In a flash of instinct, Hansi let go of the chair, swept up the note, and leaped onto the chair. His barricade took one more blow from the officer, giving Hansi enough time to ascend the cabinet, pitch himself through the frame, and fall to the gravel below. They were down the alley and gone before anyone reached the window. Within minutes they had weaved their way through the dirty side streets back to the Gare, where it was easy to disappear among the Sunday travelers headed back to Luxembourg City.

Only after the doors closed and the train was moving was it safe for Hansi to read the note.

The train clunked over the rail and switch joints as it headed north out of town. Moments later, it slowed for its first stop, a small platform on the north edge of Differdange called Niederkorn. Hansi grabbed Karin's wrist and shot up and out from the bench. They slid through the doors just before they slammed shut.

"What are you doing?" Karin asked. "Don't we need to get away?"

"We've got another stop to make," Hansi said, waving the letter in front of her.

"Where?"

"The mill," Hansi replied, pointing south to the tall billowing stacks. "Papa's left us a clue."

CHAPTER TWENTY-ONE

Alone on the Niederkorn platform, Hansi read the letter to Karin.

Dear Marie,

I'm sorry for this letter but please don't worry. I am well and certain I'll be back in your arms soon. Tell Hansi not to worry. I have his birthday present in my locker at the mill. There is also a jar of jam he can give to his dear old grandmother.

Yours always,

Alain

When Hansi finished reading, he folded the letter and returned it to his pocket.

Karin looked perplexed.

"Are you telling me we jumped off this train because you want to go back to the mill for your birthday present?"

"Of course not," he replied. "It's some kind of clue."

"How do you know?"

Hansi stood up. "Two reasons. First, my birthday was in June. My father is trying to send us a message. There's something at the mill he wants me to find."

He walked to the end of the platform and surveyed the horizon to the south. The railway cut a gentle curve for about a kilometer back to the Differdange. Just before the Gare, a soot-stained bridge lined with trucks connected the dingy town on the right to the massive ARBED steel complex on the left. Iron fence works protected the perimeter of the plant in both directions, broken only by a brick archway where the road from Differdange passed through. Red- and white-striped poles guarded the entrance to the mill.

"There," Hansi pointed. "We can enter through that gate. We just need to get across the bridge. Come on, Karin."

"What about the gendarmes?"

"As far as our officer knows, we're snug on the train back to Luxembourg City. As long as we're careful to keep clear of the Gare, I don't think they'll have any idea."

They descended a set of stairs near the end of the platform to a gravel pathway. They followed the trail to a road that led into a group of soot-stained tenements. Soon the buildings pressed in close, along with the foul smells of stale garbage strewn along the base of the walls. Somewhere an angry dog barked.

"Is this safe?" Karin asked, moving close.

"I think so," Hansi said, without confidence in his voice. "Just act like you've been here before," he added. Without Hansi offering it, Karin took his arm, and they moved quickly past a section of the building where the windows were boarded over. They continued along mostly quiet streets, except for a sprinkling of children playing with their dogs, jumping rope, or throwing rocks at tin cans. They paid them little attention. After a few blocks, Hansi found a cross street that he hoped led to the tracks.

His sense of direction proved correct. Beyond the shadow of the last building, the street joined another running south along the tracks. The bridge lay half a kilometer away, and when they saw it, they both stopped. On the Differdange side, headed for the mill, the line of vehicles stretched as far as they could see back toward the center of town. None of them were moving.

As they drew closer, they saw that the first vehicle was a brown paneled truck surrounded by four gendarme officers. One officer stood in the road blocking the way across the bridge, a second was opening the cargo door in the rear, the third had knelt to look underneath the truck, and the fourth was talking to the driver, examining papers.

"We'd better avoid the gendarmes," Hansi said, looking back. "But maybe there's a crossing somewhere up this way." He started back the way they had come, scanning the never-ending fence for a break.

"Hansi look!"

A motorcycle rolled onto the bridge from the mill side, its engine sputtering above the rumble of idling trucks. It stopped by the truck the gendarmes were inspecting. A man climbed off, wearing a black trench coat, motorcycle cap, and dark goggles, which he pulled off to speak to the lead officer.

"Do you think it's—?"

"Gestapo," Hansi said.

"I don't understand. Do you think the gendarmes knew your father's clue?"

"How could they? I'm hardly sure of it myself. But I need to see that locker."

Karin's stare had shifted to a spot across the street, where a trail was worn in the grass toward the tracks.

"I have an idea." She took off running.

He followed through a line of bushes to the edge of the slope down to the tracks. The chain-linked fence stood nearly twice their height.

"How are you at climbing?" Karin asked.

"That fence? Are you serious?"

"I am if you are," she answered.

His eyes were locked on the jagged wires along the top of the fence. He cleared his throat.

"What about your skirt?"

"Turn your back," Karin replied, already reaching up. "I'll tell you when it's all right to look."

He was surprised at her agility up the fence until he realized he should be looking away.

"That's not what I'm worried about," he said, moving up the fence. "What if you don't have a skirt when you get down?"

"Then you'll just have to bring it down for me, won't you?" The chain links rattled. A moment later, a thump on the ground.

"You can look now," she said.

Hansi turned to see her broad smile, flushed cheeks, and undisturbed skirt. Her beauty surprised him, and he looked down.

"To think we were going to waste time walking across the bridge," he said.

Gears ground behind them, followed by the roar of an engine approaching.

Hansi grasped the fence above his head, crammed the tip of his shoe in a link of the fence, and began to pull himself up. He was not as skilled as Karin but was determined not to embarrass himself either. He climbed steadily, carefully, his arms burning from the effort.

At the top, the fence wobbled under his weight. Swinging a leg over he scraped his inner thigh going over and fought not to react. At least he had missed the most sensitive spot.

The truck rushed past, sending a cloud of dust down the bank. He tensed. It kept on.

He swung the other leg over, anxious to descend. Gravity took hold, in a battle with the fence, which bit his jacket under the arm with an audible rip.

A moment later he let go, too high. His feet hit the ground and he tumbled forward into Karin. They landed on their backs looking up at the gray sky.

Karin sat up, her hair spilling across her face. She was laughing.

"How do you know I haven't broken my leg?" he asked.

"You were so worried about my skirt. Let me see what happened to you."

Hansi twisted.

"I guess we're even," she said. "Your jacket and my skirt the night of the fair."

He wanted to say they made a good pair. That he was ready to go anywhere with her. All he could manage was, "You're right."

"I guess I should expect getting dirty and ruining my clothes when I'm with you," she said.

"You look great—er, fine."

"But we're not finished. There's a fence on the other side too. Come on."

He rose and dusted himself off. Karin let him resume the lead down the embankment through a patch of high weeds along the tracks. Energized by their success, he bounded forward.

He let himself accelerate down the slope, stretching his stride with every step. For an instant, he thought he might lose his balance. Then, nearing the bottom, he saw a dark blur flash before him. A shaft sliced into the path and CRACK! Hansi went airborne. He rolled through the last of the weeds and skidded to a stop on a bed of sharp stones.

When he looked up, a figure stood over him, arm raised holding a long stick. Ready to strike.

CHAPTER TWENTY-TWO

"No trespassin' down here!"

Hansi sat up and saw a grisly man in a worn-out coat. His weapon turned out to be a well-placed but unimpressive walking stick.

"Thought you'd sneak past ol' Jean, did you? Well, I may not be as fast as I used to be, but I can still take care of myself down here, yes, I can!" He shook the stick in the air as he spoke, his bloodshot eyes glaring from the sunken gray holes in his unshaven face.

Karin appeared behind him.

"Hansi!"

The man spun around with his stick, missing wildly, and then staggered sideways. He fought to hold his balance and then tumbled onto the weeds along the bank.

Karin ran to Hansi. "Are you hurt? Can you move?"

"Wait," he said, getting up. "He might be hurt."

"He might have hurt us!" Karin said.

Hansi approached the man slumped over on the bank. He reeked of cheap wine and other smells Hansi didn't want to think about. Hansi touched him on the arm. "Are you hurt, Monsieur?"

The old man tried to get up, but he was too weak and stumbled back again.

"Take it easy," Hansi said. The old man blinked a few times and sputtered something unintelligible. Hansi pulled the water bottle from his bag and gave the man a sip. Much of it spilled over the man's rough face and onto his soiled shirt, but he seemed eager to drink it. He reached for the bottle with quaking hands. Hansi helped steady it.

"My bag," he said to Karin. "There's bread."

Karin hesitated.

"Go on," Hansi said. "It's all right."

Hansi tore off a small piece from the baguette and held it up to the old man's mouth. He took it and chomped down ravenously, sending an avalanche of crumbs down his front. Some of them stuck to the wet stubble of his beard and others tumbled like tiny boulders off his craggy chin.

"He's probably starving." After a few more bites, the man's eyes grew steadier and began to brighten.

"Let's try the cheese," Hansi said, pulling it from the bag.

Soon the man had regained enough strength to sit upright on the bank. A tear rolled down his face. Watching him devour the food, Hansi realized the man was not so much drunk as weak and hungry.

Karin watched in silence.

"Forgive me, boy," the man said after a moment. And then, turning to Karin, "Are you hurt, my dear?" He looked down. "I suppose not. I can't swing like I used to. Better for your sake and mine. Such a pretty girl you are." Then back to Hansi, "I thought you were one of those strange characters snooping around here lately."

"Are you alright now, Monsieur...?"

"Please, call me Jean. Jean Pétain. Yes, I'm feeling better now. Thank you both for your kindness." He thrust out his bony hand and Hansi took hold of it, scraping Jean's long fingernails.

"I'm Hansi, and this is Karin."

"We didn't mean to startle you," Karin said. "We didn't expect to see anyone down here."

"No, I suppose not. But you two better take care. This is a dangerous place for a couple of kids who don't know their way around. So, what are you doing down here?"

"We're trying to cross over to the mill," Hansi replied, "and, well, we preferred not to use the bridge."

Jean Pétain rubbed his chin. "Ah, I see. Well, yes, ol' Jean sees lots of characters interested in avoiding that bridge lately. Enough that they're starting to attract attention from the gendarmes. Usually picking up or delivering. What's your errand?"

Hansi looked at Karin, wondering if she understood the old man.

"I'm talking about smugglers," Jean said.

"Smugglers? What are they smuggling?"

"Ol' Jean hasn't seen it firsthand, but the rumor is that over there at the mill, they're losing track of some of their explosives."

"Explosives, here?" Karin asked.

Jean chuckled. "I can see by your pretty curls you aren't from around here. They use explosives down in the big mine in Thillenberg. To blast through the rock deep in there to get at the rich coal seams. Lately, it's been disappearing."

"Who's stealing it?" Hansi asked.

"I don't know," Jean replied.

"How many are there?" Hansi asked.

"A handful. Young lads. Not the smudge-faced types you normally see making trouble down here. My guess is they're working for somebody in the city. Can't be sure, though, and believe me, I'm not about to ask."

"Do you think these smugglers were involved with the bombing of the Gare? Perhaps they stole the explosives for that," Hansi said.

"Who knows," replied Jean. "The word is they've smuggled enough for a hundred train stations. That's what you'd think by the activity of the gendarmes around here lately. They've been trying to get ol' Jean involved in it all."

"How?" Karin asked.

"They want me to snitch for them. To find out what these smugglers are up to. But I think it might be time for ol' Jean to move on from these parts. Things have been too busy along here, and I just need a nice quiet place along the rails to stretch my legs. Don't want any trouble."

Karin stepped forward. "If you thought the smugglers might be involved in the bombing of the Gare, why wouldn't you help the gendarmes?"

Hansi shot Karin a look to stop, but it was too late. Under normal circumstances, it would have been a good question, but Hansi wondered how Jean would react.

"Who can you trust these days? Some say the Germans are behind this smuggling, others say the Resistance. It's obvious you two aren't anxious to see the gendarmes or you'd be up on that bridge now instead of down here with ol' Jean."

Remembering the conversation with his father from weeks ago, about the new Resistance movement forming, Hansi was suddenly troubled. To think his father might have been involved in smuggling explosives was too close to the thought that the Resistance really had been involved in the bombing.

"Why would the Resistance want to blow up the Gare?" he asked.

"What are you talking about, this 'Resistance'?" Karin asked.

Jean was quick to answer. "The Resistance is those Luxembourgers, true patriots they are, who are getting ready," Jean said.

"Getting ready for what?" Karin asked.

"Getting ready for war," Jean answered, and pulled up his pant leg, revealing a shrunken, shriveled calf. Karin drew back. Hansi winced.

"The Germans did this to me in the last war. I was lucky, if you want to call it that, when a shell hit our trench. I lost the use of my leg. My mates weren't so lucky."

"I'm sorry," Hansi said.

"When the Germans come this next time, ol' Jean won't be much help. It'll be up to the young ones like you two I'm afraid," he continued.

A look of horror came over Karin's face. "Herr Hitler promised to respect Luxembourg's neutrality."

"Words are just words. Germany thinks of Luxembourg as its long-lost cousin. They want us to rejoin the family, you might say. But in Germany's eyes, we've run off and married Belgium and taken France as a mistress. That's who Germany is really upset with. They'd prefer we rejoin the family quietly, so to speak, but either way, they'll come through Luxembourg on the way to France."

"Then what is this Resistance going to do about it?" Karin asked.

"Our little country can't stand up to Germany on our own. We're no match for them. Who knows if even France and Belgium can stand up to them? Maybe the British can, or the Americans. But not the tiny Grand Duchy. The Resistance are everyday Luxembourgers getting ready to fight the Germans—but after they invade. They'll fight—in the shadows, you might say."

"The Resistance could be hiding the explosives to use in the future," Hansi said, though he didn't like the thought.

"That's right, Hansi," Jean said, pulling himself to his feet. He leaned on his weapon, which in reality was just his cane. "Now, I'm sure you two didn't come down here to talk politics. You need to make that crossing before the next patrol."

"Patrol?" Karin asked, looking around suddenly.

"The gendarmes patrol on foot down here. With dogs. Me they leave alone, but you two clean-faced city kids are sure to be interesting to them."

"When is the next patrol?" Hansi asked.

Jean chuckled. "They aren't trains, my boy, and don't exactly publish their schedule. They just show up, among the cars in the yard over there. I can take you through the north end of the yard if you like. Not as many patrols this far up. The smuggling's back at the Differdange end of the yard where there's more freight cars. I can take you as far as the main line and you can make a run for it there."

"Would you?" Karin asked.

"Tell me something first," Jean said. "What business have you got at the mill? And why are you so interested in avoiding the gendarmes?"

Hansi looked at Karin, not wanting to answer.

"Tell him," she said. "Tell him, Hansi."

"My father works at the mill. The gendarmes arrested him a month ago, thinking he had something to do with the bombing of the Gare in Luxembourg City. He didn't, but I need some proof, and I think it's at the mill."

"You sure about that, Hansi?" Jean asked. "Sometimes people aren't who they seem to be, you know."

Hansi bristled. "My father is. I'm sure of it."

Jean shrugged. "Let's get going then," he said, hobbling forward. He staggered past both Hansi and Karin and led them along the ditch to a place where the slope up to the tracks was not so steep. Hansi was glad they were moving because if Jean or Karin had looked hard into his face, they would have seen how unsure he really was.

CHAPTER TWENTY-THREE

"Give ol' Jean a hand, if you please."

Hansi, already up the slope, turned back around to help. They were at the head of the yard where, on a half dozen lonely sidings, a sparse collection of worn out and abandoned coal and flat cars waited for recycling in a blast furnace. It was more junkyard than freight yard.

They worked their way over the tracks, pausing in the shadows of the rusting hulks until Jean was satisfied that no one, whether on the bridge, patrolling the yard, or watching from the yard tower nearby had seen them. Only then they would move to the next car, inching their way across the yard. Had they been on their own, Hansi and Karin would have covered the distance quickly, though running would have surely attracted attention. But Jean was experienced, and though his feet were slow and shaky, his eyes were steady, and soon they were on the other side with only the main lines to cross.

Jean paused in the shadow of a wooden toolshed to catch his breath. A whistle blew in the distance. "I leave you here, my dears," he said with a gentle smile. And then, tapping his cane on his leg, added, "I'm afraid I don't cross the main line myself anymore. But if you two hurry, you'll have plenty of time to get across before that freighter that just blew."

Karin stepped forward and embraced him. "Thank you for your help, Monsieur Pétain," she said.

"For everything," Hansi added, extending his hand.

The whistle blasted again, nearer, and approaching from Differdange.

"It is I who thanks you both," Jean said, pressing his hands together and bowing low. "For your kindness to an old man."

Just then the sharp bark of a dog echoed through the metal canyon. Karin grabbed Hansi's arm. Jean leaned around the corner and peered back toward the bridge.

"We must go, now!" he said in a raspy whisper. With the dogs closing in, Jean seemed to have suddenly changed his mind; he was going to cross with them. Hobbling forward, he led them out from the shadow of the toolshed and moved toward the tracks, careful to keep the shed between them and the direction of the barking. Hansi took Jean's arm and helped him across a slight dip and over the first rail of the first track. Down the line in Differdange a bell was ringing, the gates were closing at the road crossing, and beyond the line of buildings that curved along the track, a plume of smoke puffed above the rooftops.

Karin, having already run across both tracks, turned to look back. "Hurry, it's coming!" she shouted. Hansi and Jean were just crossing the second rail of the first line.

The dog barked again. It was so close now that Hansi had to look. Muscular and black, the beast was rounding the corner from behind the toolshed, hacking at the end of its leash as it dragged a gendarme officer.

"You there, on the tracks! Stop!"

The whistle blasted again. The black locomotive had rounded the curve and was thundering toward the crossing, snorting steam sideways along the track bed. Hansi squeezed Jean's arm more tightly and dragged him down into the shallow ditch that separated the two tracks.

"Stop, I say! I command you to stop!" The first track was all that separated Hansi and Jean from the officer and the snapping jaws. The officer retrieved a whistle from his pocket and puffed his cheeks to blow. It was lost in the storm of the locomotive's whistle.

Hansi pulled Jean out of the ditch and up the bank to the second track. He couldn't tell which line the locomotive was coming on. Either they were already safe or in imminent danger. But it was no time to guess.

"Faster!" Karin urged, jumping up and down, but Hansi and Jean were already moving as quickly as they could. Jean stepped over the first rail of the second line and then hobbled over to the second. Jean was huffing like the locomotive bearing down on them.

Hansi looked again and his heart jumped. The train was on their track. The locomotive was well past the crossing now, thundering closer, enveloping the bridge in an explosion of steam and smoke and cinders. The timbers below them quaked and the whistle blasted an angry warning, making mute both the officer and the dog.

Hansi stepped over the second rail and caught a glimpse of Karin, standing in the shallow ditch beyond the tracks, her face contorted with horror. Jean stepped with his good leg but caught his toe on the top of the rail. He stumbled and hurtled forward, sending Hansi tumbling into the ditch. But Jean fell over where he stood, with his bad leg hanging across the rail. The thunder of the locomotive and its whistle drowned out both Karin's scream and Jean's shriek.

It was seconds away.

In the deafening roar, Hansi scrambled to his feet and clawed his way up the gravel to Jean. Karin was already there, reaching out to Jean. They each grabbed an arm and together yanked as hard as they could, making one last desperate effort to clear the track. Hansi met eyes with Karin for the flash of an instant and he saw not terror but amazing calm. Then came a tremendous shockwave of sound, steam, smoke, and cinders. Hansi tumbled down the bank in a strange silence, unable to see, no longer holding Jean.

When the world came alive again, the first thing he realized was that he was lying in the dirt rather than the crushed stone right next to the track. He didn't get up, but instead, immediately covered his ears as best he could. The ground shook beneath him and he was pelted by wave after wave of debris. The air was hot and metallic and threatened to choke him. He held his eyes shut, ground his face into the ditch, and hoped he wouldn't get sucked under the thundering monster.

The whistle screamed a scold and then faded away. The storm cloud of smoke and steam roared past and subsided. Tiny flecks of black cinder rained down on Hansi, but gently now. And like a sudden summer storm, the locomotive swept past. In its wake came the groaning rails and clicking joints, rhythmic and gentle by comparison.

Hansi lifted his head and watched the train cars flick by. Through the flashes of light between them he could see both the dog and the officer on the other side. With the train stretched well beyond Differdange, they would have at least two minutes before the massive rolling barrier would be gone. He stood up, sore but not hurt.

Further up the ditch, Karin and Jean lay on the ground. Karin rose slowly. Her face was smudged with dirt made into mud from her tears, but she was smiling. Jean hadn't moved.

Karin reached him first and touched him on the shoulder. "Monsieur Pétain? Are you all right?"

There was no response, and a cold chill came over Hansi. He knelt and started to roll Jean on his back. Then suddenly came a grunt, and then a rattling cough. Jean rolled onto his back and blinked. His face was black, and blood oozed from his bottom lip.

"Are you alright?" Hansi repeated.

"I think so," he said, grunting again, and then spit out a mouthful of blood and dirt.

Karin helped Jean to sit up and pressed a handkerchief to Jean's mouth. Hansi looked down and then across the tracks. "The end of the train is at Differdange, and that officer is right across the tracks, waiting for it to clear. We've got to keep going. Jean, are you hurt? Can you move?"

Jean tried to shift his weight forward to stand but winced. "My leg," he groaned.

"Can we carry you?" Hansi asked with a nod to Karin. Without waiting for the answer, he took hold under Jean's arm, and together he and Karin lifted him to his feet. Had Hansi known before how light Jean was, they could have carried him in the first place and avoided all this trouble. But now, as the last freight car came into view, they took advantage of their strength and moved quickly beyond the tracks into the brush along the far side of the main line.

"The mill is just up the bank, Jean," Hansi said. "They've got a clinic there and a doctor will help you."

Jean stiffened. "No! No doctor, no clinic. Down there! Down there!"

He was pointing toward the bridge to the ditch that ran along this side, a ditch deeper and wider than the one where Hansi and Karin had first met Jean, where from a large conduit sticking out of the embankment, water streamed out and ran through a brick culvert. They ducked into a line of bushes and found a path leading down toward it. The rhythm of the rails faded, and they could hear the faint hack of the dog again.

"In there, Hansi. Quickly!"

They carried Jean down the path to the conduit, an arched opening large enough for them to walk in.

Karin's eyes grew wide.

"Go! Go!" Jean urged.

There was no time to discuss it. Hansi and Karin stepped into the steady flow, still supporting Jean between them. Hansi was surprised to find the water warm and then remembered his father explaining how huge pipes delivered cool water for the blast furnaces. *This must be the runoff*, he thought as they shuffled through the opening and moved in beyond the light.

"A little further," Jean said, urging them deeper into the darkness. When only a sliver of light remained sparkling on the water, Jean directed them to turn down another branch of what Hansi figured was a vast drain system that ran under the mill.

"Stop here," Jean said, and they were glad to oblige. Hansi was breathing hard and felt his heart in his throat. He turned around and tried to get his bearings.

"Shhhhh," Jean whispered, and they waited.

The drainage tunnel was quiet except for the gentle rush of water running along the bottom of the chamber. After a moment they could hear the dog barking in the distance. It grew louder and louder and distorted sharply as it echoed up the tunnel. Then suddenly it stopped.

No one breathed. It was quiet again, and then Hansi thought he heard another sound above that of the water, almost like waves hitting the shore. He strained to interpret it and then it hit him—the dog was taking a drink where the water spilled out of the drain.

They waited for another moment and heard the officer speak. "Come on, boy. Maybe next time." And then the solitary sound of the water returned.

After another few minutes, Jean thought it was safe enough to go back outside. "The dog would have come," he told them as they carried him out. "But the gendarmes are afraid. They never follow anyone in here."

"Why not?" Hansi asked.

"The gangs," Jean said. "I don't mean to scare you, but some of them are pretty tough. The gendarmes don't confront them unless they come in force and with more than one dog. And that's only every so often."

"Do you come here often?" Karin asked.

"Not anymore," Jean replied. "But it's a favorite route for the smugglers. These tunnels lead to places in the mill. The gendarmes are focused on the bridge and road above. They ignore the road below."

Outside, they set Jean down on a grassy spot on the embankment.

"Let me see your leg," Hansi said.

"It's fine, I'm sure," Jean said. "The warm water felt good on it. I just can't move like I used to." He pulled up the leg of his worn pants, revealing the injury again, for which Hansi was still unprepared.

"Ol' Jean was lucky again," he said, smiling. "But I wasn't counting on such adventure on my morning walk." He smoothed his pants back down and pushed himself off the bank. "Now where have I put my cane?" he asked, looking around.

"I think you're going to need a new one," Hansi answered. "Last I saw it was on the main line. It's probably tinder now."

Jean let out a throaty laugh and took a couple of short steps back up the path. "You two better get going before the dog comes back and brings his master. Ol' Jean will draw 'em off for you. Not to worry."

"Monsieur Pétain," Hansi said. "Here. Take this." He gave Jean the bag with the rest of the food in it along with the change of clothes originally intended for his father.

"You've got some room to grow into them," Hansi said with a grin as Jean discovered the pair of pants and shirt, "But eventually I think you'll fill them just fine."

Tears ran down Jean's soot-covered cheeks, revealing light skin underneath. He hobbled over to Karin and took hold of her by the arms.

"You both have been very kind to this old man," Jean said, wiping his eyes with a dirty rag from his pocket. "That's not the normal way of things down here. I'd forgotten that it's still possible. Thank you, my dear," he said, and then turned to Hansi.

"There's strange characters about, so be careful, my boy." His dark eyes penetrated for a long look. Then, with a click of his tongue, he turned away and started up the path. As before, his movement was labored and sluggish. He was about to disappear over the crest of the knoll when he paused, turned back, and dipped his head in a final farewell.

CHAPTER TWENTY-FOUR

Hansi and Karin had just moved out of the shadow of the drain and started climbing the bank that led up to the mill when they heard a truck braking on the road above them. In the next instant, a tall, brown-paneled truck was backing down the slope right toward them. Hansi and Karin retreated to the cover of the taller bushes along the ditch at the bottom and watched from their bellies.

The truck, gears grinding on the way down, came to a stop almost even with the drain opening, not twenty meters away. The back doors swung open and four young men jumped out, joined by the driver from up front. Hansi and Karin locked eyes in recognition. These were some of the same brown-shirted thugs Hansi first saw at the fair. But this time there was no Gestapo handler in sight. They gathered at the mouth of the drain, spoke briefly, and then disappeared inside.

Hansi leaned close and whispered, "Let's go before they come back."

Leaving the cover of the bushes, Hansi turned toward the truck. Karin jerked him back.

"I want to see what they're smuggling," Hansi said.

"Didn't you hear Jean?" Karin whispered. "He said these men are dangerous." Unpersuaded, Hansi dragged Karin toward the truck. But near the back corner, she broke free. Hansi continued around back and when he looked inside, jumped.

A dark, hunched figure stood in the doorway between the front seats, waving a pistol. Hansi instinctively raised his hands. Karin froze.

"Don't move," the man said in a gravelly voice, "or I'll put one right in your gut."

Hansi didn't need the instruction—fear had already anchored him to the ground.

"I'm sorry," he stammered. "I didn't mean to startle you. I'm just passing through."

The man's head bobbed strangely as Hansi spoke, as if he wasn't just listening but also smelling the air like a dog.

"Are you alone?"

"Yes," Hansi replied. "I'm just on my way to the mill."

"I see," the man said, a new tremor radiating through his head. His movements seemed somehow unfocused, almost casual for a man aiming a gun.

"Then who's that outside?"

Hansi's heart sank. He had seen Karin after all.

"She's my sister," he lied. "We're alone. That's what I meant."

The man shook the gun again, more wildly, his head mirroring the movements. Hansi wondered if the man was drunk. So random were his movements, so wild his thrashing that now the truck started to rock because of the man's energy. And suddenly a new fear shuddered through Hansi—the man might fire without meaning to.

"Don't lie to me boy!" he growled, his whole body now shaking in the doorway. During one of the flails his head twisted back enough that the light from the cab flashed across his eyes and face. A strange thought flashed in Hansi's mind.

The man stepped from the cab into the cargo compartment, pressing one hand to the roof to steady himself, waving the gun in the other.

Karin stepped forward, despite Hansi's warning, and came alongside him at the back of the truck. "Please, sir, we are only passing over to the mill. We're visiting our father, and he'll be expecting us. If we don't arrive soon, he'll come looking for us."

"I'll let you take that up with the boss when he gets back," the man said. "He'll be glad to know I caught a couple of snitches. In the meantime, you two sit down where you are."

Hansi shot a look at Karin to get her attention. She looked at him, careful not to turn her head suddenly. Hansi swallowed hard and slowly raised his left hand, bringing it close to his face.

"Sit down with your backs turned, so I can tie your hands," the man said, almost shouting now.

Hansi split his fingers in the shape of the letter "V" and pointed to his eyes. Karin registered a mix of confusion and alarm.

The man staggered another step closer and fumbled his hand on a narrow shelf where he found a length of rope. "Now do it!" he roared.

Hansi completed the maneuver, pointing the "V" at the man, then back at himself, shaking his head back and forth. The man took no notice. Hansi pleaded with his expression: *He's blind*.

Karin nodded.

"Okay," Hansi said, carefully taking Karin's hand. "We don't want any trouble." Looking at Karin, he gestured with his head sideways to the left, and then silently mouthed, *one, two*… Karin nodded. On three, they bolted sideways, sending a burst of gravel from under their feet. The man howled when he realized their trick and then fired. The blast echoed in the metal compartment. He was too late.

Hansi and Karin ran as fast as they could away from the truck, up the bank, and across the road. Hearts pounding, they headed for the brick and iron gate ahead. But braving one last glance back at the tracks, Hansi saw, standing in the doorway at the back of the truck in full light now, the man thrashing wildly as he pumped the gun in the air, his eyes blinking and rolling in rhythm with his head.

CHAPTER TWENTY-FIVE

The gate was in view.

"Don't we look like the Grand Duke and Duchess?" Hansi said with a laugh. Karin's white socks were stained an uneven dull brown; her once shiny shoes were so soggy, they squished with every step. Dirt and soot darkened her rosy cheeks and small briars speckled her hair, sweater, and skirt. Her ponytail was coming out and a lock of hair fell over her eye. Still, something about her brought something warm and alive inside Hansi. The feeling was strong and proud. He couldn't imagine being there without her at his side.

"What will you tell your mother?" Karin asked. "Won't she be upset?"

"She's used to it," he replied with a grin, brushing the caked mud on his pants in futility. "I come home like this all the time, from running up on the cliffs or down in the Pétrusse Valley. In fact, I rarely show up at home in clean clothes!"

Karin looked at him and chuckled.

"By the way, I'd love to see the look on your father's face when you show up," he said.

"My parents won't know. I'll sneak in the servants' entrance, change quickly, and have Helga clean my clothes."

"Helga?"

"Our maid. She'll keep the secret. I'll just tell her I've been out exploring the countryside—which is true—and with a wink, my secret's safe. She wants me to grow up like a normal child."

"Ah yes, one can always hope," Hansi said with a sigh and a grin, receiving a playful poke in the ribs in return.

The iron fence they had been following came to an end at ominous brick columns, spanned by a metal archway marked "Gate Number 4." A horizontal wooden pole with red and white stripes blocked the entrance like a military checkpoint.

A square-faced man in a dark blue uniform stepped out from the shadow of the gate and met them. He took up a position with his feet apart and hands on his hips, his bushy moustache twitching back and forth.

"What brings you two street rats to my steel mill today?" he asked from under an equally bushy eyebrow.

"We're here to see the superintendent of Blast Furnace Number Three," Hansi answered as confidently as he could. "It's urgent," he added.

The other eyebrow shot up and he raised a hand to stroke his moustache. "I see. Do you have an appointment?"

"No, sir," Hansi answered, "but it's terribly urgent."

The officer folded his arms.

"Hmmm. Suppose you tell me why it's so urgent? The superintendent doesn't see anyone without an appointment."

Hansi swallowed hard but didn't budge. "I'm Hansi Broussard. I want to speak with the superintendent about my father, Alain Broussard."

At the mention of Hansi's father, the officer's eyebrows dropped and squeezed together at the base of his forehead. He stepped past them and scanned the horizon with an uneasy look.

"Come with me," he said and moved quickly back toward the barricade. He led them through the gate, pausing just inside to take another look back toward the road before continuing. Then he stopped outside the open door of a brick hut. "In here," he said, ushering them past, his gaze still outside the gate.

Once Hansi and Karin were inside, the officer followed, closing the door behind him. He waved them to a pair of wooden chairs while he went straight to the telephone on his desk, dialed, and spoke something Hansi couldn't hear. After only a few words he replaced the receiver and returned to face them.

"Move these chairs away from the window," he commanded, and Hansi and Karin leapt up. They pushed the chairs against the side wall while the officer adjusted the window blind to block the view outside. "The superintendent is on his way, but don't make a sound or move from this spot until I come back for you. Is that clear?"

Hansi and Karin nodded, and the officer moved back to the door. Then, pulling a set of keys from his belt, he disappeared outside and locked the door behind him.

The hut was dark except for the light slipping through the window blinds. Smoke plume shadows danced across the slats like a fast-motion storm sweeping over the mill. A truck thundered outside, rattling the glass as it accelerated past.

A far different scene, Hansi remembered, from the first time his father brought him to the mill. Then, seeing the stacks for the first time and knowing his father helped make steel used for mighty bridges over the Rhine, Hansi felt only pride. But now, entering the mill took on the aura of stepping into a haunted castle—a castle whose drawbridge had been drawn up, trapping them inside.

These thoughts led Hansi back to the night the Gare was bombed and the conversation the following day with his father. He had said there were men at the mill joining the Resistance against Germany. Who were they? Was Dieter Dumont one of them? Papa never told Hansi and said it was better not to know. Why? If Hansi knew, he would know who to ask for help.

If group members' identities were to be kept secret, then there must be others here at the mill opposed to them. Other spies for Germany perhaps? Who could he trust?

He remembered the letter. The reference to the birthday present in the locker seemed clear enough; his father wanted Hansi to come to the mill and find something. But with all the secrets, was he truly safe coming here?

Hansi stole a glance at Karin. She returned the look, her eyes full of concern. For an instant, he was glad that she was with him, but then the feeling gave way to a stronger anxiety that he had led her into something more dangerous than either of them could have imagined. He suddenly felt shame that he had brought her along.

A vehicle screeched to a halt outside. A door slammed and then they heard the slight scuffle of gravel just outside the entrance of the hut. The lock rattled and the officer appeared.

"This way. Quickly." he commanded.

Hansi and Karin got up, crossed the hut, and passed through the doorway. A gray sedan sat outside, a second officer holding the rear door of the car open for them. They climbed in, the officer slammed the door shut behind them, and then he returned to the wheel. With a stomp on the accelerator, the car lurched forward, spraying gravel up against the floor like a hammering hailstorm. The driver spun the car around and tore off deep into the mill.

Without regard for safety, it seemed, they bounced past black brick buildings, crumbling shacks, and stacks of rubble strewn randomly along their path. Losing all reference to the position of the gate behind them, Hansi wondered what kind of new trouble he had gotten Karin into.

CHAPTER TWENTY-SIX

In minutes the car screeched to a stop in front of a two-story building where ARBED, the initials of Aciéries Réunies de Burbach-Eich-Dudelange, United Steel of Burbach-Eich-Dudelange, was cut in stone above the doorway. A smaller, dingy sign beside the door indicated Haut Fourneau 3, L'Operation, Blast Furnace 3, Operations, but to Hansi, it looked more like a prison. Hansi and Karin were glad to leave the car until they met the heat, din, and choking dust outside. The officer whisked them inside and led them up a flight of stairs to an office in the front corner overlooking the massive furnace.

"Sit here," he said, pointing to leather chairs opposite a wide oak desk, which was unoccupied. "The superintendent will be with you in a moment." And then he left them.

The decor of the office was pleasant compared to the industrial landscape outside. On the desk sat a framed picture of a woman holding a round-faced baby. She had a pleasant smile, and the child looked content. In one corner behind the desk, a Luxembourg flag hung proudly; in the other, a brass lamp cast a warm glow across the polished wood floor. A painting of the mill hung on the wall, surrounded on either side by portraits of old bearded men.

"I'm sorry I brought you here, Karin," Hansi said softly.

"There's nothing to be sorry for," she replied. "I wouldn't have come if I didn't want to."

"But I haven't been honest with you," he went on. "At your house, the police station, or the platform in Niederkorn. I've told you practically nothing, and it's not fair to you."

They heard footsteps outside in the hall. "Now's not the time to blame yourself," she said, patting him on the arm. "We can talk about this later."

There was a click. The door swung open, and the superintendent entered then circled around behind his desk to face them. He was a tall, muscular man with black, closely cropped hair and a face that seemed serious without being harsh. He shot a hand out over his desk.

"You must be Hansi," he said, shaking with a strong grip. "I am Superintendent Kruger. And you are?" He extended his hand to Karin.

"This is my friend Karin," Hansi said, hoping his nervousness wouldn't leak into his voice.

"Ah, your friend, of course. I'm relieved to know Alain did not hide from me knowledge of a daughter," he said. "And such a lovely daughter at that. Please, sit down."

Hansi exchanged a quick glance with Karin and smiled awkwardly before sitting down again.

The superintendent forced a smile. "I apologize for the way we rushed you both back here, but, given the circumstances, it's better that we keep your visit today—well, discreet. We don't want to attract undue attention, I'm afraid."

Hansi wondered how the two of them showing up at the mill could cause such concern. Had the gendarmes sent out an alert? Did the officer down at the tracks call the mill to warn them?

The superintendent continued, frowning. "I'm sorry to hear about your father," he said. "It came as quite a shock. Is there any news?"

Hansi didn't know what to answer. What did the superintendent know? "Uh—no news, I'm afraid. We just keep waiting."

"Yes, of course. Well, I'm sure it will work itself out. Just a big misunderstanding, I have no doubt. How is your dear mother? Knowing her, she must be beside herself with worry."

Hansi shifted nervously in his chair. Did the superintendent know nothing of the reasons for Papa's arrest? Did he really think this was a "big misunderstanding?"

"She is upset, of course, but doing the best she can."

"Of course, I understand. It's a terrible thing. Give her my regards. And please tell her that if there's anything I can do, to please call," he said, not entirely convincing.

"Thank you, sir, I will," Hansi said, unable to imagine how he could.

There was an awkward pause. Hansi sucked in his bottom lip and began nibbling at it. The superintendent shifted nervously in his chair, folded his hands together on the desk plotter, and forced a lifeless smile, his glance shifting back and forth between Hansi and Karin.

Nearby a clock ticked. Out the window, a white steam trail drifted alongside a billowy black smoke puff before being swallowed by it. Then a horn sounded somewhere out in the mill and the superintendent shot a glance out the window. Hansi jumped and then inhaled deeply.

"Now… what can I do for you today?" he finally asked.

"We came to get my father's things. Do you have them?"

A look of relief swept across the superintendent's face. "Oh," he said, "from his locker?"

Hansi nodded.

"Yes of course," he said. "I'll send for them at once." He reached for the black phone on his desk and tapped the cradle a few times.

"Excuse me, sir," Karin interrupted, "but will you take us there yourself?"

The superintendent stopped, the phone hanging in midair.

"Given the circumstances," she continued, "I think Hansi would prefer to collect these things, well, personally." She glanced at Hansi.

"Yes, sir," Hansi added, looking down. "It's just that he's got, well, my birthday present in his locker and I'd rather…"

"Oh, of course!" The superintendent said, cutting him off. He set the phone down. "I'm so sorry. I didn't mean to embarrass you. Let's go at once." He stood up and stepped around the front of the desk.

"We'll take my car," he said, leading them out the door.

They climbed back into the same dark sedan and traveled still deeper into the mill, stopping in front of an enormous brick and steel structure that towered above them. Hansi forgot about the tremendous heat that struck them with a slap when they stepped out of the car. Unaffected, the superintendent led them through a side door into a small room.

"Put these on," he said, handing them metal hats from hooks on the wall. He put one on, made sure they did too, and then led them further in. The cavernous building stood five or six stories tall, open to the roof which was made of exposed steel framing. This was easily the largest building Hansi or Karin had ever entered—so big, it seemed, that the entire Gare Centrale Terminal could fit inside.

As they walked along the wall, a massive bucket suspended on a gargantuan frame in the center of the structure slid slowly on its track, radiating wave after wave of heat from the liquid steel inside. It stopped, then slowly began to tip, letting forth a stream of molten metal into a mold below, before releasing another shock wave of heat and shower of sparks that seemed to penetrate Hansi's bones.

Sweat poured off his head and stung his eyes as they turned into a room adjoining the furnace. Inside was a row of lockers along the wall. Superintendent Kruger stepped over to them, pulled a key from a large ring on his belt, and unlocked one of the grey steel doors. Then he stood aside and motioned Hansi forward.

"If you please," he said with a polite smile.

Hansi opened the door and studied the contents carefully before touching anything, hoping to discover some detail, some clue that would be lost once he disturbed the contents.

There was nothing unusual about the locker's appearance. A blue coat hung from a hook in the back and a pair of black leather boots sat in the bottom. Hansi gently moved the coat on the hook to see if there was anything else behind it. There wasn't. A coat and pair of boots, that was all. No box, no bag, no present. No clue.

CHAPTER TWENTY-SEVEN

Hansi retrieved the articles from the locker with a pace that matched his disappointment and placed them in his bag.

The superintendent touched him on the shoulder. "I'm sorry, son."

"Excuse me, sir," Karin said. "Has anyone been to see the locker—that is, since Monsieur Broussard was arrested?"

The superintendent looked down, pressing his lips together. "Now that you mention it, yes."

Hansi looked up.

"There was a search the very next day," the superintendent said, and then frowned. "But they didn't take anything."

"Are you certain?" Karin asked.

"I escorted the gendarmes here myself. I watched them at every moment. They looked through these items just as you have but took nothing. I'm sure of it."

Hansi was at a loss. His father's letter was clear—there was something important in his locker. But what happened to it?

"Is that everything then, son?" the superintendent asked. Hansi took a final look inside the locker and then nodded.

The superintendent led them out of the room, back along the wall past the furnace, and outside to the waiting car. They were soaking wet from the searing heat.

"Can I drive you back to Differdange?" the superintendent offered.

"Thank you," Hansi answered, "But would you mind dropping us by the Niederkorn platform? I'd like to avoid the commotion of the Differdange Gare if you don't mind." Commotion was a flimsy reason, Hansi knew, but he didn't trust the superintendent to tell him the truth about their encounter with the gendarmes in Differdange. He hoped the superintendent wouldn't ask why.

"Of course," the superintendent replied, much to Hansi's relief. "Before that, why don't we stop by my office? You can both freshen up and get a cool drink before your train ride back to the city."

Surprisingly, the air trapped inside the car was cooler than the air outside, and it was refreshing to climb in and drive away. Soon they were speeding back between the drab buildings, flimsy sheds, and rusty machinery.

Just beyond a line of buildings, the operations office came into view. The superintendent hit the brakes and Hansi knew why. Parked in front of the building was an unmistakable black sedan.

"Get down!" the superintendent commanded, spinning the steering wheel hard to the right before gunning the engine.

Hansi and Karin were slammed together for an instant until they clambered to the floor and crouched down below the level of the windows. The only view left to them was the electric poles and smoke plumes whizzing by.

"What is it?" Karin asked, squeezed tightly between the seats.

"The gendarmes are back," the superintendent said. "Perhaps you were followed after all. We'll have to take a detour. Hold on."

They sped off in a new direction. The superintendent let them return to their seats, only to see the car fling a plume of red dust behind as they flew through a small rail yard where mine cars, filled to overflowing with shiny black coal, lined up to deliver coal to the furnaces. The black-faced workers looked up from their shovels in amazement as the car whizzed past, bouncing over the narrow rails. Within minutes they rejoined the main road again and saw Gate Number Four come into view. When the bushy-mustached officer saw the approaching car, he raised the barricade and waved them past.

Accelerating under the archway, they had no sooner crossed the intersection of the main road to Differdange and the gravel road Hansi and Karin had used from the tracks when the superintendent suddenly hit the brakes again and jerked the wheel, sending the sedan skidding sideways.

The hulk of a truck flashed in front of them, and Karin screamed. The truck roared past, and just as suddenly they were engulfed in a cloud of red dust as the truck disappeared across the bridge.

The superintendent cursed and shook his fist. "That blasted truck! Where the devil did he come from? That old construction road hasn't been used for years. Did you see his number? He has no business down there! The fool almost got us killed!"

Hansi looked to the right, his eyes following the gravel road along the bank down to the tracks. He exchanged a knowing look with Karin—this was the truck they had seen down by the drainpipe. He kept the information to himself.

The superintendent exhaled heavily and let his shoulders drop. "Are you two alright?"

Karin forced a smile, but Hansi saw her rubbing her wrist behind the front seat, out of the superintendent's view. "I'm fine," she said. "Just a bit shaken."

"I'm really sorry about all this. Do you think you can get out of sight again? We've got to cross the bridge, and though it seems the gendarmes aren't paying much attention to the traffic in our direction, I don't think we should take a chance."

Hansi and Karin agreed and returned to their places on the floor. The superintendent eased the car forward and they crossed the bridge without incident.

Arriving at the Niederkorn railway platform, no one was gladder than Hansi to get out. After a quick word of thanks, he started up the walk with Karin.

"Hansi," the superintendent called. Hansi stopped and turned around, leaving Karin further ahead. The superintendent stepped forward and lowered his voice. "I want you to know your father is innocent," he said.

Hansi said nothing.

"Strange things have been happening at the mill, Hansi, and have been for some time. And while I don't fully understand them, I have no doubt that your father was not involved. No matter what happens, you must believe this. You must assure your mother of that as well."

Hansi's mind raced. No matter what happens? What did that mean? If these words were meant as a comfort to Hansi, they fell well short of the mark. Why should he trust the superintendent?

"What's going on?" Hansi asked. "Why was my father arrested? What did he do?"

"Nothing," the superintendent said. "Absolutely nothing."

"Are you sure? Then why did they arrest him?"

The superintendent leaned in close and looked directly into Hansi's eyes. "Listen to me carefully. I make it my business to know everything that goes on in the mill. What I don't see myself, I learn from someone I trust. Your father is that someone. He had been observing things. Some men were up to something. Something terrible, I'm afraid."

"The bombing of the Gare?" Hansi asked.

"Yes."

"Did they arrest others?"

"Only your father and one other," the superintendent said.

"Dieter Dumont?"

The superintendent was taken aback. "You know Dieter Dumont?"

"Not really," Hansi replied. "But I was at the Gare the night of the bombing and saw the police arrest him. Was he part of the group you suspected?"

"That's the problem," the superintendent said, looking down. "He's not."

"Are you sure?"

"Your father seemed sure. At least I thought he was. He never mentioned Dieter—not even once—in any of his discussions about the troublemakers."

"Have you spoken with the gendarmes yourself about this? How do they explain it? Why Dieter? Why my father?"

"They aren't saying anything, and frankly, Hansi, I don't trust them. I've told them as little as possible. Just enough to satisfy their inept investigation and nothing more. I'd advise you to take care around them, Hansi. Be careful what you tell them."

It was advice Hansi had already learned firsthand. "I will, sir."

Behind him, the train squeaked to a stop along the platform, hissed, and slid open its doors. Karin started up the steps to the platform. Hansi followed, taking a step up the walk.

"There's just one thing troubling me," the superintendent said.

"What's that?"

"Your father and Dieter were friends."

Their talk was over. Karin had crossed the platform and was standing in the doorway at the rear of the train, pleading anxiously with her eyes for Hansi to hurry. The superintendent thrust out his hand and Hansi shook it. Letting go, he realized the superintendent had given him a slip of paper. Hansi ran up the walk and crossed the platform just as the engineer was taking his place at the front of the engine.

Hansi stepped through the door.

The engineer rang the bell, signaling he was about to close the doors.

"Hansi!" the superintendent called from the platform. "Please, son. If there's anything I can do to help you—anything— promise me you'll call." Hansi looked at the number scribbled on the slip of paper, and then at the superintendent. The look of fear in the man's eyes sent a wave of despair through him. He could only stare at him, saying nothing. The engineer put his hand on the lever.

"Promise me, Hansi. Promise me." The superintendent said, desperation in his eyes.

"I promise," Hansi lied as the doors slid shut.

The train lurched forward and continued steadily on, leaving the superintendent standing there, the silhouettes of the mill stacks overshadowing him in the afternoon sun.

CHAPTER TWENTY-EIGHT

As the smokestacks shrunk out of sight, a wave of disappointment crashed over Hansi. He was no closer to seeing his father than the moment he left his flat.

Karin was resting her head against the window with her eyes closed. Hansi envied her. If only he could close his eyes and block out the world.

His stare lingered. The train rocked her gently. The grays of the village dissolved into the orange and brown of the autumn countryside. Her ponytail was all but completely undone; most of her golden hair spilled over her shoulders now, still speckled with tiny burrs. Her rosy cheeks were smudged with dirt, but she looked peaceful and at rest.

The train bumped hard, and Karin opened her eyes. She caught Hansi watching her and smiled.

He started to say something and stopped.

"Hansi, don't apologize."

"How did you know I was going to?"

"I can see it on your face," she answered, rubbing her eyes. "Even through the dirt."

Hansi cracked a faint grin. "Still, I shouldn't have brought you here."

"I wanted to come," she said. "I was glad I came. I'm just sorry it worked out this way."

Hansi shook his head. "I don't understand it. Papa was trying to tell me something. I felt sure of it. What else could he have meant by the letter?"

"Perhaps the gendarmes searched his locker before the visit with the superintendent," Karin said.

"That seems too clever of them," Hansi said, "but I suppose it's possible."

His head hurt from thinking. The view out the window was more inviting, the beauty a kind of salve to his bruises. They rolled on, content to watch the farms and fields in silence.

Near the city, Hansi noticed Karin's expression had changed. A pinched brow and darting glances replaced relaxed, drowsy eyes.

"Can I see the letter again?" she asked.

"By all means," he said, more sarcastic than polite.

He retrieved the crumpled page from his pocket and handed it to her.

Karin read it, pouring over the words carefully, mouthing the phrases slowly. Hansi shrugged and returned his attention outside.

"When we were in Niederkorn, you said there were two reasons you knew the letter was a clue. The first one was that your birthday was back in June. What was the second reason?"

Hansi thought for a moment. "I don't remember."

She handed it to him. "Think!"

He read the letter again.

"Here," he said, pointing. "I don't understand it, but this is the reason."

"There's a jar of jam in my locker at the mill for your dear old grandmother," Karin read. "Does your grandmother know something?"

"My dear old grandmother died when I was three," Hansi replied. "I don't remember her much."

"So your father writes about two things—a birthday present when it's not your birthday and your dear old grandmother. They must mean something."

Hansi slumped in his seat. "I told you, Karin. I don't know. I just don't get it."

"Think, Hansi. What was your grandmother's name? Where did she live?"

"Her name was Marie. She lived in the Grund near us."

"Could it be he was trying to tell you to go back home to the Grund?"

"What would be so unusual about that? He wouldn't need to speak in code to say that."

Karin's shoulders fell. "Then what about your birthday? Was there anything unusual about your last birthday? Did you get a special present?"

"I got a new sketchbook and some colored pencils," Hansi answered, shaking his head. "Nice enough but not particularly special. I don't see a secret message in that."

Karin leaned closer, urgency growing in her voice. "But he wanted you to go see his locker at the mill, Hansi. He is very clear about that."

"I know that, Karin. You saw it, same as me. A coat and boots. He wore them every day. Hardly clues to anything." Hansi kicked the bag containing the items.

Karin bent down, grabbed it, and started rummaging inside.

"If the gendarmes thought he was part of the bombing plot, surely they'd search his things once he was arrested. No one would be surprised about that. But your father seemed to have known that too. And still he wanted you to go there. He wanted you to find something."

"Not a birthday present, that's for sure," Hansi answered.

The train was passing through the freight yard south of the station. Passengers stood up in anticipation of arriving at the platform. Karin was examining the boots.

"Check the jacket," Karin said, turning the boots upside down and studying the heels.

Hansi pulled the jacket out of the bag and looked it over. It was a plain, knee-length cotton jacket that his father wore over his clothes to protect them from dirt and grease. It had three wooden buttons down the front and pockets on each side.

"Nothing here," he said. "It's just a jacket."

The train braked, squealed, and turned onto a siding.

"Check the pockets, Hansi. Hurry!" Karin said.

He exhaled slowly through clenched teeth and thrust his hands first in one pocket and then the other. "Nothing!" he said and tossed the jacket onto the wooden seat opposite them. It hit with a faint but discernible clunk!

Karin looked up with a start. "What was that?"

Reaching the jacket first, she ran her fingers over the smooth cloth and squeezed it along the seams. Then suddenly her eyes brightened. "Here!"

She showed Hansi the seam along the bottom of the jacket. Something metal had been sewn into the hem. He found a loose thread, black among the blues of the other seams. He pulled it easily.

The seam opened and the metal chunk fell out. Karin's hand was waiting. She opened her fingers. A brass key.

The train thudded to a stop at the platform. The doors swung open.

"Happy birthday!" Karin said.

CHAPTER TWENTY-NINE

As they walked together, Hansi pondered the key. It was a classic design of brushed brass with three loops for a bow. The cylindrical shaft featured a trio of short teeth.

"Take a look," he said, handing it to Karin.

"I'd say it belongs to a chest or maybe a desk," she offered.

"How do you know?"

"By its size, for one. It's rather small. And the teeth—they're simple notches. I'd expect a door key or a key for a larger lock to have more teeth, and perhaps grooves."

"How do you know so much about keys?" Hansi asked.

"I don't, really. My father has a desk with a rolling top. His key is like this one. Or at least similar. And Fritz carries a ring on his waist for keys to many things—the doors, cabinets, fence gates—all kinds of keys. He loves them."

"I knew it," Hansi said wryly. "Somewhere in his past Fritz must have been a jailer."

Karin ignored him, studying the key again. "This could fit anywhere."

"Wherever it fits, Papa believed he needed to hide it," Hansi said. "You don't sew a key into a seam unless you want to make sure no one finds it."

"No one but you," Karin said. "He counted on you not only finding it but knowing what to do with it. Do you have a desk or chest or anything else at home that it might fit?"

"Not that I know of," Hansi said. "But you can be sure I'll look when I get home."

Outside the terminal into the crowded plaza, they passed a boy selling newspapers, the *Lëtzebuerger Zeitung*. He would tip his cap to the customers dropping their coins into the metal cup that he rattled for attention. Today's headline read: GERMAN ARMY SURROUNDS WARSAW, POLISH CAPITAL NEAR COLLAPSE.

Hansi noticed Karin glance at it and then look away quickly, avoiding eye contact with him. *Just as well*, he thought. *No use spoiling*—and then he caught himself. He was thinking they were having a good time. But how could searching for his father ever be thought to be "a good time?"

At the crowded corner of the Avenue de la Gare, they just missed the crossing light. While they waited, Hansi noticed a young woman in a stylish wool coat crossing toward him, holding tightly onto the arm of a much older woman. The older woman, hunched over her wooden cane, wore a snugly wrapped scarf around her head and face. Arms locked with the young woman, she shuffled across the street as fast as she could, which wasn't fast at all. The pedestrians cleared, leaving the pair alone in the middle of the street, just as the light changed. Impatient drivers surged forward. A car screeched to a stop, others narrowly dodged, and then came the honks. Frightened and embarrassed, they completed the crossing and found the safety of the sidewalk. The event escaped the notice of everyone but Hansi.

"I've got it!" he said.

"Got what?"

"The next clue." Hansi smiled at the two women as they passed by.

Karin eyed him quizzically.

"That old woman reminded me of someone," he said. He retrieved the note from his pocket and studied it again.

"There is also a jar of jam he can give to his dear old grandmother," Hansi read aloud.

"Madame Dumont!" Karin said.

"Yes. I told my father about her the night of the bombing. About how kind she was. And how upset she was to see her son arrested. We saw them carry her out on the stretcher. She's the only old woman I know. She must be my 'dear old grandmother' in his note."

"But why would your father have her key? What does she have to do with all of this?"

"Not her," Hansi said. "But her son. Her son Dieter was arrested. My father knows him. Maybe the key belongs to him."

"How would your father have gotten the key? Do you think Dieter gave it to him?"

"Not unless…" Hansi hesitated.

"Not unless what?" Karin pressed.

Hansi had a pained look on his face. "Not unless they were working together."

"Do you think that's possible?"

"I hope not," he answered, "But I'm going to find out."

He stepped into the street and crossed quickly, forcing Karin to hurry in order to keep up.

CHAPTER THIRTY

Fighting for space between billowing white and gray clouds, the afternoon sun now and then sent bright streaks down onto the city. Hansi strode briskly up the Avenue de la Gare toward the Pont Adolphe. Karin kept up, but every time she drew alongside him, Hansi surged a half step ahead. The new doubt was like a pebble in his shoe. The longer he walked, the more painful the spot was.

They walked several blocks in silence before Hansi realized Karin wasn't keeping up. She had stopped completely, hands on hips in the middle of the sidewalk.

"Aren't you coming?" he called.

"Do you even care?"

"What is that supposed to mean? I thought you were right behind me."

Karin wagged her head, turned, and appeared to take interest in the pastries displayed in the nearby bakery window.

Hansi closed the space between them, but she didn't acknowledge him. So when he spoke, he addressed her reflection in the window.

"What's the matter?" he asked, the accusation gone from his voice.

"Why don't you tell me," she said without looking up.

He exhaled and rubbed his hands together. "Look, I'm just trying to hurry. I need to get you home so there's still time left…"

"What?" Karin said, her voice rising. She turned to him now, wearing a look of mixed frustration and confusion. "Still time for what?"

"I've got to find where this key belongs."

"And where do you hope to find it?" she asked, surprising Hansi with her emphasis.

"West of the city, a village called Strassen. Madame Dumont lived there, and Dieter too before he got arrested. I've got to find out if there's a desk or chest or something this key fits."

Karin returned her gaze to the pastries.

"What?" Hansi said, a bit impatiently. "What's wrong?"

She took a deep breath and turned to him. "I don't understand you, Hansi. What's gotten into you?"

"What are you talking about?"

Karin looked up at him, her chin trembling. "After all that's happened today, you're planning to just drop me off at my house and say goodbye with a pat on the head? Is that it?"

Her words were like arrows in his heart. Delivered without rage, they penetrated deep and exposed the truth that he was intending exactly what she said. He stood there, unable to move or speak, locked on to her gaze. The world passed by in the reflections on the window behind her.

After a moment, Hansi lowered his eyes and his voice. "I'm sorry, Karin."

She was looking at him, her eyes and face frozen, as if she were fighting greatly not to cry.

"But I've been thinking," he continued. "It's my father who's been arrested, not yours, and I'm the one who's got to find him. I don't know where I'll be going or what I'll do when I get there, if I do find him. It's not right to drag you into all of this…"

"I told you, Hansi, I wanted to come. And I still do."

"But this is dangerous, Karin. I've been a fool to think otherwise. It's one thing for me to take the risk on my own, but you…"

She reached out and touched his hand. He stopped speaking and looked into her eyes. Once again, he felt warmth and power in them. In her. He didn't know what to say.

"I want to help you," she said. "And I'm not afraid."

Hansi found it difficult not only to swallow the lump that had suddenly formed in the back of his throat, but to fight back the urge both to cry and shout for joy at the same time. Her hand was warm and soft. Standing together he felt like they were two rocks in the middle of a rushing river, firm and strong. He wanted to embrace her, but something inside wouldn't let him.

Finally, Karin spoke. "But I can tell there's something wrong between us," she said. "And it's not for me to make right. Not by tagging along."

Hansi knew she was right and opened his mouth to protest anyway. He wanted to apologize and beg her to come with him to Strassen. The words didn't come.

"I don't know exactly what you want from me, Hansi, but I don't think it's my help. At least not in the way that's really useful. One word to my father and I think you might be surprised. Then you wouldn't have to do all of this running across the country yourself."

Anger rose in his chest. "I'm not trying to stand between you and your father," he said through clenched teeth, "I'm simply asking you not to say anything about this to him—until I can be sure."

"Sure that he's not a spy?"

"I'm not saying that."

"You don't have to. And perhaps I've been naïve to think we could overcome this, Hansi. You're right on one thing though. We're fools to think that tearing about the countryside together is a weekend holiday. You need help finding your father, help that my father can give. But I can't force you to agree with me. It's your decision. And when you make the choice—if you do, I want to help. You know where I live. And here's my number."

Karin thrust forward a note upon which she had hastily scribbled her phone number. He took it and stared at it without really looking at it. She was right but also wrong. Involving her father was the one thing that gnawed at him, the one thing that was the wedge between them. Even without proof, Hansi had a strong sense that involving her father would be the worst thing he could do. He looked at Karin and swallowed hard.

"Goodbye, Hansi," she said, her chin quivering and her blue eyes luminous with tears.

A knot tightened around his throat, and he remained silent, his feet affixed to the sidewalk as if his shoes had been part of the original concrete. After a brief glance into her eyes, which he could not bear, he returned his gaze to the paper.

Without another word, Karin turned away and ran up the street. Seeing her disappear over the Pont Adolphe, the pressure intensified, squeezing until stinging tears filled his own eyes.

A random car blew its horn, startling him. He had no idea how long he had been standing on the sidewalk staring across the bridge.

The paper was still in his hand. He looked at it once more, imagining the soft hand that formed the numbers, then folded it and thrust it into his pocket. A band of sunlight swept over him as he removed his hand and opened it. He was holding the brass key, lit up now by the streaking rays. The grip on his throat let go. Hansi knew exactly what he had to do.

CHAPTER THIRTY-ONE

Walking up the Rue du Bois in Strassen, Hansi was full of hope until he saw the house, number 43, which he had learned from a telephone directory in the village. It wasn't the look of it—indeed it was a cheery-looking red brick house with a high-pitched slate roof, copper gutters neatly trimming the edges, a chimney running up the side, and flower boxes bursting with orange marigolds below each window. What changed Hansi's mood was the sudden memory of why the house was deserted. Poor Madame Dumont. He imagined her leaving this pleasant home that terrible day, unaware of the dreadful fate that awaited both her and her son. Facing the front door, the memory of that evening fresh in his mind, Hansi felt a rising paralysis, as if he were about to violate a sacred tomb.

Gripping the brass key in his pocket, Hansi took a deep breath, glanced back at the street one last time, and gave the front door latch a try. As expected, it was locked. He quickly retreated, descending the front porch stairs to follow a stone path that led to the back, mindful of the street and upstairs windows of the neighboring house. The back door was also locked—again no surprise. For a split second, he thought of breaking the glass, but the act seemed somehow dishonoring to Madame Dumont.

Deciding to leave this option as a last resort, he moved on to a nearby window.

The large window to the kitchen on the back of the house had a metal frame whose two panes were designed to swing open like double doors. They too were latched shut, but when Hansi pulled on the center of the panes he discovered the latch was worn and allowed considerable movement. He imagined Madame Dumont throwing the window open every morning to take in the fresh air of her garden. He tugged at the window several times, jiggling the latch enough that eventually it fell off and the windows came free. *Perhaps Madame Dumont is helping me, even now.* A moment later he had crawled over the sink and was inside.

He quickly surveyed the kitchen. A loaf of bread, furry with mold, disintegrated on a cutting board on the table. Recalling Karin's suggestion that the key belonged to a desk or chest, he decided to search elsewhere first.

At the front of the house, the room contained a sofa, lamp, fireplace, and bookcase shrouded in relative shadow. But streaming through the front window, catching the dust in the cold and stale air, sunlight spotlighted a yellow pitcher sprouting shriveled brown marigolds stems on a small table. *More death*, he thought.

In the shadowed corner, an ornate cherry cabinet showed promise with its brass keyhole just below the lid.

When he crossed toward it, a board creaked so loudly he stopped with a startle. The sound reminded him he was an invader in a dead woman's house.

He retrieved the key from his pocket and soon realized he needn't have bothered. The lid opened without it, revealing a record labeled *Eine Kleine Nachtmusik* on the turntable of a phonograph. The key didn't fit anyway. The house was not going to give up its secret easily.

He decided to go upstairs where, along with a bathroom, two bedrooms presented opportunities. The smaller of the two, by its plainness, must have been Dieter's. Hansi would try there first.

The room was stark, furnished with only three basic necessities: a bed, a chair, and a wardrobe. The former was unmade while the chair, by its position next to the bed and the lamp missing its shade on the center of the seat, evidently served as a nightstand. The latter held the room's only promise, as the walls held no pictures and the only color was provided by the wool rug in the middle of the floor. Its deep blue fibers and gold trim were completely out of place in what otherwise looked little better than the cells in the Differdange jail.

As before, the first step pressed down on a loose board, reverberating a loud creak off the bare walls. Hansi stretched his stride in the next step, a kind of half jump to avoid the center of the room. In doing so, his weight hit the far edge of the rug, causing it to slide. Hansi nearly fell and in the process of retaining his balance creaked the floor even more. When the moment had passed, he was in the center of the room and the rug was piled in a heap at the foot of the bed.

The wardrobe, little more than a wooden box, had no lock. Hansi rummaged through the few shirts inside, a pair of trousers, a worn suit jacket, and pair of black leather shoes, finding nothing of interest. He was feeling along the boards at the bottom of the wardrobe for hidden compartments, feeling a little foolish for it, when the faint sound of a car caught his attention.

By the sound, faint at first but growing steadily, he imagined a car coming from the Rue d'Arlon up the hill. The car revved as it climbed the slope, and Hansi waited for the sound to fade away as it continued up the hill. Instead, the car slowed and then stopped. Hansi's froze.

Was it out front?

He pondered his options. If someone had come to call on Madame Dumont, he could wait silently upstairs until they realized she wasn't in. But something in the back of his mind didn't let him believe this was just a courtesy visit from an old friend, and suddenly the flicker of nerves burst into the flame of panic.

Hansi stepped away from the wardrobe and turned. The motor went silent. If it came to it, he would jump out the window. But he needed to know for sure first.

Taking a step away from the wardrobe, Hansi's foot came down again on one of the loose boards in the center of the room. This one gave way more than the others—so much that he stumbled and fell to one knee with a sharp knock. That's when the realization hit him. This loose board was not fastened down at all.

In the moments that followed, Hansi worked in a frenzy. The space beneath the floor appeared empty, but a lone loose board among a perfectly good floor had to be significant. Hansi fell flat and reached inside the space. The car door slammed.

Furiously, he swept his hand through the space between the splintery joists. Feeling nothing in one direction he spun around and tried the other. About halfway in, his hand hit something! It had a smooth, hard surface and square corners. Extending his arm all the way, he could reach the far edge and pull it back.

Hansi retrieved his prize—a small metal box covered with chipped black paint and peppered with dings. Checking the key would come later. Right now, he had to see who was outside.

Tucking the box under his arm, Hansi moved to the front bedroom and peered through a slit in the curtains. What he saw made his blood run cold. There, standing on the curb with his back turned as he scanned the street, was the object of Hansi's worst fear: the man in a black trench coat and wide brim hat.

Questions exploded in Hansi's mind as he raced back to Dieter's room. Was it just bad luck that he and the Gestapo had come to the Dumont house at the same time, or had someone tipped them off? Had they been watching the house all along? Was it an observant neighbor? It didn't matter. *I've got to get out of here. Now.*

CHAPTER THIRTY-TWO

Hansi mentally tried to sketch the position of the intruder inside of Madame Dumont's house by sound. Wedged on a narrow slice of roof behind the chimney, Hansi couldn't see the Gestapo man, but he could certainly hear him. The agent's movement inside was loud and boisterous. If Hansi didn't know better, he might have thought the man drunk.

The agent's movements mirrored Hansi's—a brief survey of the ground floor and then upstairs. His steps were like sledgehammer blows. Like Hansi, he came straight to Dieter's room, where his gait became more distinguishable—thump, swoosh—thump, swoosh.

Was he dragging something? Someone?

Hansi fought the fear. The first priority was maintaining his footing on the steep, smooth slate. Then, remaining hidden. For the moment, the street was empty. That could change in an instant. Anyone at a window, front door, or on the street to the south would see him at once.

Hansi worried about Dieter's window. He had climbed through and closed it easily enough but, having no way to latch it from the outside, seemed to have left behind an obvious sign of escape. It couldn't be helped. Hansi was acting on instinct alone.

A crash rumbled from inside. The chair and the lamp? Hansi wondered if he had replaced the rug well enough. Would the agent perceive the creaking floor amidst the racket he was making?

Hansi considered ways to escape. A direct jump to the brick path below would break a leg—or worse. But if the agent had a gun, Hansi would have no choice. The notion was terrifying. He didn't move.

The room inside fell silent. Hansi held his breath. Had he found the board?

Just then a woman appeared in the window of the house next door. Startled, Hansi felt his foot slip on the slate. She looked up and their gaze met. A realization swept over her. The rectangular bulge in the front of his shirt was obvious.

He hoped she saw the desperation on his face. He brought a finger to his lips and pleaded silently for mercy. Instead, her shoulders snapped backward in indignation.

It didn't matter. The window frame squeaked open before the frame banged against the house. Without thinking, Hansi peered around the chimney. The top of the Gestapo agent's hat protruded from the window. He was looking down at the backyard. Hansi was paralyzed.

The woman opened the window. "You there!" she shouted. "How dare you break into that poor woman's house! Shame on you!"

At the sound of her voice, the Gestapo agent jerked his head around, but Hansi didn't wait to see the man's face. Pushing away from the chimney, he clawed higher up the roof, scrambling as fast as he could up the steep slate.

Time for thinking was over. Reaching the peak of the roof, he threw his legs over, sat down, and began to slide down the other side. As his body accelerated, he fixed his eyes on the gutter along the roof's edge, hoping he could stop himself with his heels then hang down by his arms and drop safely to the ground. At least he was not as high as before. If by some miracle he made it to the ground safely, he could flee among the houses on the other side of the street and work his way back home. With the metal box.

At first, sliding down the roof seemed like a good idea. But the roof was quite steep, and Hansi realized too late that he was traveling too fast. He bounced up and down as he hurtled down the slope, the edges of the tiles scraping his back side with a ripping sound. Suddenly there was the gutter, but his heels were in the air. The heavy lip slid hard up the back of his legs, smacked hard on his bottom, and he was over the edge. In a singular jolt that disconnected every other sensation in his body, he smashed to the ground. For a moment, everything was still.

When he came to his senses, he was numb with pain. Something was jabbed in his side. The agony was overwhelming but not as strong as the will to escape. He blinked to clear the fog. He was alive. His mouth was thick with the metallic taste of blood. A maze of branches, broken and twisted, had saved him. He rolled forward out of the bramble to the soft grass and spit out the blood. The feeling on his chest was different. His shirt hung open. Gnarled strands of thread hung where the buttons had been.

The box!

Hansi staggered to his feet and scanned the lawn. He didn't have to look far. On her front sidewalk, not five meters in front of him, stood the woman he had seen in the window. Her jaw was set and her arms wrapped around the metal box as if it were a baby she had just rescued from a burning house.

"This isn't what it looks like, Madame, but I'm afraid I don't have time to explain. But it's very important that you give me that box. I promise you I'm not a thief."

"And I promise you I'm not a fool. How dare you break into that poor woman's house! How could you?"

"Please, Madame, there's no time to explain," Hansi pleaded, arms outstretched. "I'm a friend of Madame Dumont's. You must believe me when I tell you she would want me to have that box." He expected the Gestapo man to burst out the front door at any instant.

The mention of Madame Dumont struck a blow to the stone wall expression on the woman's face; a look of confusion flashed in her eyes before she recovered and set her jaw for battle. "You brute!" she said through clenched teeth. "Anyone can read a name on a mailbox. But imagine stealing from a dead woman! You should be ashamed of yourself!"

"Madame," he said, the blood now trailing from his mouth. "That man inside is a German agent. A spy. He is responsible for Madame Dumont's death."

Her eyes flashed to the house and then back to Hansi. Her expression wavered.

"That box contains evidence that proves what I've just said. I must take it to the Luxembourg authorities at once. I can't tell you how important it is that I leave before that agent arrives. And I must have that box."

The woman thought for another instant, her face trembling as she looked again at the house. She wants the Gestapo man to come, Hansi thought.

Just then came the sound he most dreaded—the click of the latch on Madame Dumont's front door and the squeal of the hinge.

Hansi was not proud of what he did next, but with the Gestapo agent only meters away, it was his only choice.

The woman screamed when Hansi leapt at her, but the sound was cut short when his lowered shoulder hit her in the midsection. Her only defense was a slight twist to brace for the impact. The move helped Hansi more than her because his shoulder clanked on the corner of the box and knocked it free.

They hit the lawn together, but Hansi reacted first. Scrambling on his knees, he collected his prize and jumped to his feet.

"I'm truly sorry, Madame," he said, but the woman, clutching her stomach as she writhed in the grass, just groaned.

Hansi never looked back. The path he saw from the roof was ideal. Within minutes he was well beyond the houses, down the hill, and hidden safely in the thick pines of the Bambësch forest.

Only then did he reach into his pocket. The brass key was warm from the heat of his body. He retrieved it with care and inserted it slowly into the keyhole of the box. It was a perfect fit.

CHAPTER THIRTY-THREE

The sprawling forest preserve north of Strassen hid Hansi from his pursuer. He ran north in silence over the floor of pine needles until he came to a pair of tire ruts across his path. Turning east, he followed the path at a run until he ran out of breath. Only then did he stop and look behind. The forest was empty.

He fought the temptation to look inside the box and continued toward the city at a walk. About a half an hour later, he emerged from the trees just as the sun had found a gap beneath the cloud bank. The city spread out in a golden glow. He would have to hurry to get home before dark.

Climbing the stairs to his flat was like climbing the Matterhorn. But worse to come was at the summit—what would he tell Maman? He couldn't show her the box. If she knew what he'd done to find it, she would never let him out of the flat again.

Maman stood at the end of the hallway when he arrived, trembling as though she had been standing there all day. Eyes fixed forward, Hansi let his bag drop to the floor and slid it sideways with his foot to join the pile of shoes in the corner.

She burst forward and flung her arms around him. "Thank God you're safe!" she cried, squeezing him tightly and nearly collapsing in his arms. Hansi held her the best he could.

"I'm fine, Maman. Just fine."

Her sobs let go, but only for a moment. She wiped her eyes and pulled him toward the front room. To Hansi's surprise, they were not alone. Father Jean stood by the window. The second man was a stranger to Hansi. Almost as round as tall, he sank so deep into the sofa Hansi doubted he could get out by himself. He continually wiped his face and extended forehead with a well-worn handkerchief.

Father Jean introduced Hansi to Monsieur Pfaffenschneider, who didn't hesitate.

"We've spoken with the gendarmes," he explained with another swipe to his head, "And they've explained everything. But we need to ask you a few questions."

Hansi didn't like the man's tone. "Then you know Papa escaped?"

"That's what they may have told you, son, but as it turns out, your father did not. He is still in custody. There seems to have been a mistake."

"But the officer in charge was sure. In fact, he thought I knew something about it."

"He was mistaken," Monsieur Pfaffenschneider cut him off. "He was speaking of someone else, not your father. They mixed up the records."

"Then where is Papa? And where was he when I was at the jail today?" Hansi's voice was rising.

Monsieur Pfaffenschneider rocked forward as if to stand up but failed. He tried again and glanced up for help. Hansi grabbed his arm and pulled him to his feet. His face was bright pink and sweat beaded across his head.

"What did they tell you?"

"They said he was ill. That's what the list said when—"
Hansi glanced at his mother. "When we first arrived."

"Yes, that's right, and it turns out to be true. Indeed, your
father was ill yesterday, and they consulted a doctor. Nothing
serious; perhaps the result of the foul gruel they pass for food
down there. Not to worry. But you bring up another point."

There were worried looks all around, particularly from
Maman.

"The girl," Monsieur Pfaffenschneider said. "Who is she,
and why were you together?"

"She's just a friend," Hansi said. "I met her several weeks
ago." He hesitated again and then finished. "At the Schueberfouer.
Her name is Karin."

"And why were you with her in Differdange?"

Hansi swallowed hard. "Her father works for the German
Trade Mission. He's a diplomat of some kind. I thought he might
be able to help."

"Help?" Maman and Father Jean almost asked in unison.

Unprepared, Hansi lied. "Yes, I thought that since the
Gestapo were involved, perhaps he could help us."

"Hansi, how could you?" his mother said.

"I'm just trying to help," Hansi murmured.

"Indeed," Monsieur Pfaffenschneider said with a grunt.
"From the sound of things, I'd say you're running some kind of
personal investigation."

Hansi's ears flamed hot.

"The officer in charge at Differdange says you left his office
in quite a hurry and, what's more, in quite a mess. The gendarmes
also reported two young people matching your descriptions

down in the freight yard. I don't need to point out that this is a dangerous area known for smuggling and other criminal activities. The report says that when the officer approached the pair, they made a dangerous crossing just ahead of a freighter coming up the valley."

"Oh, dear heavens!" Maman cried.

Hansi regretted the lies but resented the interrogation. And said nothing.

"I know you thought it would be helpful," Father Jean said, playing the peacemaker, "but these matters are left best to the experts, professionals." He looked at Monsieur Pfaffenschneider.

Hansi had had enough. "Like him?" he said. "And what exactly have the professionals done so far?"

"Hansi!" Maman scolded.

Monsieur Pfaffenschneider stepped forward. "I'll tell you what I've done, Hansi. Of course, with what you've done, it all may be for naught. I've been working with top government officials, the Gendarmerie, and the Gestapo in very difficult and delicate conversations, all to secure a temporary release of your father until the formal charges can be drawn up. I've been given assurances by verbal agreement for his release as early as this week. That was yesterday."

"What about the army?" The question was directed at Father Jean. "Did you ask your brother about the Gestapo?"

Monsieur Pfaffenschneider lifted an eyebrow.

"Yes. The official word is that the Germans are here to help the gendarmes investigate suspected terrorists."

"And the 'unofficial' word?"

"He doesn't know yet or won't say. But I know my brother, and he's good at smelling out rats. I trust him to find out soon enough. I'd ask you to do the same."

Hansi looked down. He'd been a fool. Father Jean was right.

"I'm sorry," he said quietly. "I didn't know. But I have no idea what the government is up to. I don't trust the gendarmes—and certainly not the Gestapo. And I didn't speak to Karin's father. He wasn't home. But I wasn't going to sit on my hands and do nothing."

"Children are impatient these days," Monsieur Pfaffenschneider said with a condescending shrug to Father Jean. "Always think they know better than their elders. You should teach more respect in that school of yours, Father. These things take time. We've said what we needed to say and asked our questions. Seeing as I'm late for dinner, I'll wish you a good night."

"Time?" Hansi exploded. "How much time? Look at Maman. Look at her! Papa is gone with no hope of trial, no hope of freedom! The gendarmes are puppets on the strings of the Gestapo. And the government is doing nothing. Maman is exhausted, running back and forth every day to get him some proper food and a clean shirt. All you can do is keep talking and making plans and telling us to be patient. I'm not going to let this kill her. I'm not!"

Maman couldn't bear it any longer. Her sobs could be heard from the hallway.

Hansi turned to follow, but Father Jean stopped him. "There's nothing more you can do. You have to put this in others' hands now."

Hansi snapped back and locked eyes with the priest, angry at him for the homily he thought was coming. Which of them had a loved one in prison? How many trips to jail had they made recently?

"I am not just speaking of trusting God, Hansi. Of course, it's essential. But I also mean trusting others, not only here in this room, but elsewhere. Your father is a good man. Many are concerned for your father, believe in his innocence, and are working for his release."

Monsieur Pfaffenschneider stepped forward.

"And I must insist, young man, that you do the same. Whatever plans you have to investigate this matter on your own must stop. In particular, you must say nothing further to your German friend or her father." He tossed his head to the door. "Let's go, Father."

Hansi stood motionless as the men departed. When the door closed, he closed his eyes and fought the urge to scream. He heard Maman in the hall and then the footsteps stopped. He turned. She stood in the doorway, eyes red, sunk deep in the swollen sockets but dry. And questioning. She was holding Hansi's bag, the flap open so they both could see the corner of the metal box.

CHAPTER THIRTY-FOUR

Maman pulled Papa's blue coat from the bag. "Where did you get these?" she asked.

"I went to the mill, Maman. We spoke to Superintendent Kruger. He gave me the things from Papa's locker."

Maman began to cry again.

Hansi took her by the shoulders. "He believes Papa is innocent. He said to not lose heart, no matter what."

Bringing the coat to her breast, she let the bag fall and ignored the metal clunk when it hit the floor. She shook her head slowly. "He's lost heart himself, Hansi."

"No, Maman, he believes in father. He told me himself."

"He gave you these because he doesn't think Papa is coming back to work."

Hansi carefully slid the bag with his foot and led her back to the sofa where she collapsed in a heap.

"Maman, I didn't mean to upset you. If I'd known Monsieur Pfaffenschneider was so close to getting Papa out, I wouldn't have done what I did. But maybe things will still work out. I'll go to the gendarmes. I'll apologize—anything—please, Maman, don't give up. Maybe they can still get father out. We can go to Aunt Milly's. We can escape to France, the three of us. Please, Maman." Hansi was pleading, begging, and surprised to hear himself say these things. But Maman looked worse than ever—desperate, weak—not at all like she had spent the day in bed. Hansi was worried.

"Your father was very clear, Hansi," she said, an unexpected calmness appearing in her voice. "And I've already spoken to Aunt Milly. Father Jean thinks it's a good idea too. Uncle Pit is going to borrow their neighbor's truck. We'll move on Saturday."

Hansi stood stunned while Maman turned toward the kitchen. "Father Jean brought soup, Bouneschlupp, and the beans are flavored just right. Let me heat it up for you."

"No, Maman," Hansi stammered. "I can do it myself. Why don't you lie down? You need to rest."

"It's no trouble, dear," she said, pausing to rub her eyes as she continued forward. Hansi took her by the arm to steady her across the room. Passing through the doorway Maman's foot hit the bag. There was no ignoring the sound this time.

"What is that box?" she asked.

Hansi didn't stop. "Just some odds and ends from Papa's locker," he said, and then ashamed of his lie, added, "I haven't really looked yet."

In the hallway, Hansi turned his mother away from the kitchen with a tender touch. "You need to rest, Maman, please. Don't worry about me; I'm not really that hungry. Maybe I'll have something later. Don't trouble yourself now."

She relented. He led her to her room where she fell into bed. After pulling the blanket up, Hansi kissed her forehead, turned off the light, and left, closing the door behind him. He went to the kitchen, but not before retrieving his bag from the front room.

The soup could wait.

He opened the box and started with the contents a piece at a time. Photos were mixed with hand-drawn maps. There were pictures of bridges, one of which Hansi recognized as the Wasserbillig-Trier railway bridge over the Moselle River, and others including the Viaduct and Pont Adolphe in Luxembourg City. Then there were the photos of rail crossings, train stations, and famous landmarks including the Gare Centrale, the Place d'Armes, and the Grand Ducal Palace. Any tourist might have taken these. The one that stood out was that of the Differdange steel works. He and Karin had seen the same view today. He pondered it for a moment and realized it was from the bridge facing Gate Number Four. Tourists would have framed the giant stacks that dominated the view, Hansi recalled. This photo featured the tracks they had crossed, the culvert on the far side, the road, the fence works, the gate crossing, and guard shack. As a group, the photos told him nothing.

The second group was hand drawn maps. One showed the rough outline of the country's borders. Various locations were noted along with numbers in parentheses beside the city or town name. Luxembourg City showed the number (150), Diekirch (5), Pétange (6), and so on. About twenty towns and villages were marked this way, and the numbers seemed to be in proportion to what Hansi knew of the towns' sizes. A second map focused on the Differdange steel works, noting locations of the blast furnaces, gated entrances, railroads, truck routes, and the administration building. Some areas were highlighted with circles or check marks; these and other areas had numeric notations. Three locations were marked differently. South of the mill the "Thillenberg Mine" was circled and notated with a (4). A dashed line and arrow pointed on to Gate Number Four (2) and continued inside the mill to a rectangle, presumably a building, marked with an "X" and the notation (6-8). Gate Number Four was also marked with the numbers 13:00, 14:30, 16:00.

Hansi sat back on his chair to think. From all he and Karin had learned that day—from Jean Pétain to Superintendent Kruger—and what he observed himself, Hansi had no doubt that both the map and last photo were connected to smuggling.

His heart sank. Nothing in the box answered the questions firing off in his mind: Was Dieter Dumont observing and mapping suspicious movements of smugglers? Was he himself a smuggler, part of the new Red Lion Brigade, or both? Was Papa Dieter's ally or adversary? And most important of all, what did Papa intend Hansi to learn from these things?

His head hurt from the strain. The last group of items was defined by them failing to fit in the other two groups: a few German and Luxembourgish coins, a broken pencil, and a punched train ticket to Differdange. A more interesting item was a glossy tourist map of Luxembourg City highlighted with hand drawn circles around the Grand Ducal Palace and the Parc du Casemates.

The last item was perhaps the most interesting of all, but also the most perplexing. The leatherbound notebook, designed to fit in a shirt pocket, was full of handwritten notes, each dated like a diary. The earliest notation was January 3, 1939, and the last, about two-thirds of the way through the journal, was August 8th, four days before the bombing of the Gare. The most peculiar part about the entries, however, was not the dates. It was the entries themselves, written in German, in a very small and tight script, with so many abbreviations that it was clearly either a code or a shorthand. "L," for example, could mean Luxembourg and "D" Deutschland. But perhaps it meant Differdange or even Dieter. The possibilities for the frequent "Ts" and "Bs," were endless. A poor enough language student in his native Luxembourgish, he was worse in French and worst of all in German. The last entry was August 8th and the last third of the journal was blank.

Frustrated, Hansi got up and surveyed the objects strewn before him. They may as well have been the pieces of a jigsaw puzzle just dumped onto a table. But unlike the cardboard variety, whose picture on the box served as a guide, the puzzle in front of Hansi had no picture and thus no guide—not even border pieces to start forming a frame. And for all Hansi knew, pieces of the puzzle might be missing.

Overwhelmed and exhausted, Hansi returned everything to the box except the leather journal. He hid the box beneath an old shirt and some dirty socks in the bottom of his wardrobe, not ideal but safe until morning.

He slipped out of his grimy clothes and into a nightshirt. After a quick splash of water on his face, he checked on Maman one last time. She was breathing slowly and deeply. He would soon do the same.

Bed beckoned. His body was giving out, despite the unanswered questions. Tomorrow he'd try again.

He fell into bed and then remembered he'd left the journal on the table. No need for Maman to ask more questions in the morning.

He staggered into the kitchen and flipped on the light. His hand slapped down on the journal and pulled. His fingers were too slow. The journal sailed over the edge and hit the tile floor.

The force expelled something from between the pages, a small piece of paper, gray newsprint. It must have been hidden between the blank pages.

He unfolded it—a receipt with printed lettering at the top: Trier Uniformem, 45 Metzelstraße, Trier.

Reading the name aloud, Hansi's memory sparked a final time—the truck they had seen parked in the culvert below the gate at the mill, the truck with the blind man in back waving the gun at them, the truck that nearly killed them on their way out of the mill was marked Trier Uniformem. These all belonged together, of that he was sure. But why a blank receipt?

Hansi placed the receipt back in the journal, stuffed the journal in his bag, and returned to bed.

Sleep did not come as easily as he hoped, battered by lingering memories and fresh worries. The clues were vague. Papa was still missing.

And Karin. Tussled hair, blush cheeks, hurt in her eyes. *Will I see her again?*

CHAPTER THIRTY-FIVE

School on Monday was nearly unbearable because Hansi thought only of what he was going to do afterwards. Except for art class in the morning, where he started a new sketch of the Casemates, Hansi measured each hour with a doodle in his notebook—an hourglass that he filled with penciled grains of sand. By the sixth hour, German, he found himself staring out the window up at the puffy clouds drifting over the cliffs.

Father Jean made him pay.

"Hansi, conjugate the 'to be' verb, both singular and plural forms." Hansi's heart sank; he had not studied the weekend homework. He adjusted the notebook on the desk, stalling, scrambling to remember before taking his standing in the aisle.

He cleared his throat and recalled the singulars. "Ich bin, du bist, wir sind," he said. I am, you are, we are.

"...all going to be Germans," someone said, loud enough for the class to hear.

Several students stifled laughs unsuccessfully and Hansi stopped. Father Jean, who had been pacing at the front of the room with his back conveniently turned, spun around.

"Who said that?"

The class answered with silent stares.

"I demand to know. Who spoke?"

He waited perfectly still just in front of his desk, at attention like an army officer. Seeing him, Hansi wondered if Father Jean would have been a war hero like his brother had he not gone to seminary. He was a hulk of a man, tall and sturdy.

"Let me make this clear: I will not continue until the person who spoke is identified or comes forward of his own accord. And if the bell rings without us learning who spoke, the entire class will earn detention each day until I find out."

He planted himself at the front of the room and put his hands on his waist with feet apart at parade rest. Hansi didn't move. The class began to squirm. Everyone knew Father Jean would not back down.

Hansi glanced at the clock. He could not bear detention.

Finally, feet shuffled in the back. Father Jean raised the corner of his eyebrow. Peter, his chest puffed out and his chin a little too high, looked to be working hard at being confident.

"Explain yourself, Peter," Father Jean commanded.

Peter stared straight ahead, avoiding Father Jean's eyes as he spoke. "I said, 'We're all going to be Germans.'" This time when he said it, no one laughed. Hansi slipped back into his seat.

"Did you intend this as a joke?" Father Jean asked.

Peter swallowed hard and jutted his chin a little higher.

"Yes and no, sir. I mean Father." Peter's eyes darted back and forth several times and then he started breathing rapidly. "I can explain!" he blurted.

"Then please do," Father Jean said, keeping the pressure on by moving down the aisle toward Peter.

"Well, Father, what I meant was that Germany is soon going to invade us, and then we'll all be forced to become Germans," he answered.

"And how do you know this?" Father Jean pressed.

"My father told me. He says Hitler's armies are almost ready. That's why the city's crawling with Gestapo agents. They're making preparations."

Father Jean's face went red.

"That's what my father says," Peter repeated.

"Enough!" Father Jean snapped. "Take your seat."

Peter seemed only too eager to comply and stumbled into his seat, drawing everyone's attention. Hansi watched an entirely different Father Jean stagger back to his desk.

"Let's pray that that day never comes," he muttered, as if to no one in particular.

Mercifully, the afternoon bell rang. Hansi tossed his books into his bag and left at once, eager to do what he'd been planning. If he hurried, he could just make it in time.

Out the front door and halfway across the front courtyard someone called out to him from behind. He ignored it.

"Hey, Hansi, wait a second!"

Hansi kept going but looked back. Georges caught up to him.

"What's the rush? Where are you off to in such a hurry?" Georges asked. Peter was a few steps behind.

"I've got an errand to run up in the City."

"Us, too."

Hansi would have preferred to be alone but had no reason to be rude.

"What got into Father Jean?" Peter asked, exaggerating his embarrassment as he joined them. "He usually likes a good joke."

"It's not funny," Hansi said flatly.

"Hey, where are you headed?" Georges intervened.

"I'd rather not say," he replied, and then added, "It's about my father."

"You have news?" Georges asked eagerly.

Hansi shook his head.

They crossed the Pétrusse River bridge at the base of the Casemates wall and ascended the steep road that brought them to the south end of the great stone Viaduct bridge. Hansi kept ahead of the pair to avoid conversation.

"Look, boys," Hansi said when they had reached the top, "I'm really sorry, but I guess we'll have to talk later when I've got more time. I've just got a lot on my mind right now. I'd better be going."

"You should come with us," Peter said. "We'll help you get your mind off things."

"I can't."

Georges put his hand on Hansi's shoulder. "I'm really sorry for what's happened with your father, and I wish you wouldn't keep it all to yourself. It's like someone's taken the real Hansi and left behind a ghost."

"There's nothing you can do."

"Perhaps not in the way of finding him," Georges said. "But we're still your friends."

Hansi finally heard him.

"I do feel like a ghost. And I want my old self back, but it feels like it got lost when my father disappeared. Look, I'm sorry, but I've got to go. I'll see you soon."

Hansi started on. He crossed the street and headed toward the heart of the city. The boys continued in the same direction on the opposite side. He quickened his stride and soon had separated himself from the boys. Glancing back on occasion, he saw that they were absorbed in their own conversations. But still they followed.

Several blocks on, Hansi turned the corner and waited out of sight in front of a shoe repair shop. Moments later the boys appeared.

"Where are you going?" they asked simultaneously.

Peter answered first. "The Girls' School."

Hansi's eyes widened.

"You remember those girls we met at the fair?" Peter continued. "They're actually pretty nice."

"If you hadn't been as angry as a spider, you might have had fun that night," Georges teased.

"Hansi, you should come along. There's too many for us!" Peter punched Georges in the arm playfully and laughed.

"I am," Hansi said. "I need to talk to Karin."

It was Peter's turn to react. "Karin? Why?"

"We need to hurry. I think school ends the same time for them as us, and I don't want to miss her," Hansi said. He started on, but Peter stopped him with an arm.

"There's no hurry, Hansi. I'm meeting her."

CHAPTER THIRTY-SIX

Hansi, with a sour stomach, followed Peter and Georges to a three-story stucco building with a high-pitched slate roof on the Rue du Limpertsberg. Girls in white blouses and navy skirts lingered on the broad walk in front—chatting, laughing, making marigold bouquets from the window boxes.

"There's Marie!" Georges said and surged ahead.

Hansi started to follow.

"Let him go," Peter said. "We won't see him until tomorrow. He's helpless. This way."

Peter crossed the street to a small park Hansi hadn't noticed until then. Karin was sitting by herself on a bench beneath a colorful maple, whose fire-orange leaves lit the scene in a warm glow that hurt Hansi with every step.

You fool! Why are you jealous when you should be looking for your father?

Her eyes brightened when she saw Peter—a sword to his soul. But then confusion at his lack of reciprocation. She turned. Did her eyes register embarrassment or rejection?

"Hansi?"

"He says he wanted to talk to you," Peter said before Hansi could speak, as though it was up to him to give permission.

"What about?"

"He wouldn't tell me," Peter answered, though the question was directed at Hansi.

"Can I speak in private?" Hansi asked. "I'll only be a minute, I promise."

"Of course," she said, standing now.

Peter cocked his jaw and let out a slow breath as Karin walked past. Hansi knew the expression. It was the same as when Hansi beat him at the fair.

Hansi let Karin pass so he could turn his back to Peter and block his view.

"Is it your father? Is he alright?" she asked.

"I don't know," Hansi said. "I still haven't found him. But I need to ask you something."

Karin's eyes narrowed.

"Did you tell your father about me going to Madame Dumont's in Strassen yesterday? I need to know."

Her shoulders dropped. "That's what you wanted to ask me?"

"Yes, I need to know. Did you tell him?"

"You came all this way for that question? Because you think I told my father what you were doing?"

"Did you?"

"What do you take me for? I told you. I promised you I wouldn't." She snapped her head away and took a step back toward Peter.

On top of jealous, Hansi felt suddenly stupid. "Wait!"

She stopped.

In the moment he was overcome with a desire that rose above his original request. He wanted to tell her more. How he felt. About his missing father. About her. But the giant vice crushed him again.

Karin waited for him to speak, a flicker of softness in her eyes, while Hansi struggled. He waited, and the silence stretched to the breaking point.

Karin looked at Hansi a moment longer, then a look of sadness replaced the faint hope that had been on her face. Then she slowly turned away. She was nearly back to Peter when the grip eased slightly.

"I need your help," Hansi said.

"Come on, Karin, let's go." Peter said.

Karin hesitated.

"I found where the key belongs. A box. There was a book inside. It's in German, and I need your help to read it."

"Just like in class today, Hansi—your German is—well, *schrecklich*. Find a tutor somewhere else. Come on, Karin."

She didn't move.

"Look Hansi," Peter blared. "I'm really sorry about your father and everything, but fair's fair at the fair, you might say. We got off to a bad start, Karin and me, but that was a long time ago. We have a good time, and with Georges and Marie it's a fun foursome. I suppose in a way we owe it to you; you know—for introducing us. Karin, let's go."

The words seemed to float over Hansi's mind without attaching to his consciousness.

"Stop it, Peter!" Karin said, then, turning to Hansi, "Where is it?"

Hansi looked at Peter, unwilling to say more.

"This is a joke, right?" Peter said to Karin. She didn't answer, offering instead a look of stone. He let his jaw drop. "Oh, is this how it is? You're feeling sorry for him again?" The question pierced Hansi's heart. Peter went on. "That's fine. You go on, have a good time. Let him use you, and then see how long he needs you this time. You'll be calling me in a week, just wait."

"Just go! Please! I'll talk to you later."

Peter stomped off, tossing his hand back dismissively, muttering something to himself.

Hansi showed Karin the journal.

"I can't read the script," he said. "And so many abbreviations. Then there's this." He held out the receipt. "It was tucked in the back. It belongs to the same company whose truck nearly killed us coming out of the mill. The same one that blind man was in. It has to mean something."

Karin studied the receipt and turned a few more pages. Then she closed the journal and tucked it under her arm.

"I'll let you know," she said.

Her expression made it clear their conversation was over.

CHAPTER THIRTY-SEVEN

Three excruciating days and nights later, Hansi was convinced Karin had changed her mind and never intended to speak to him again. But when he opened the front door to leave for school, he was overjoyed at what he found: a gray slip of paper tucked in his doorframe from the outside. He recognized it immediately—the blank receipt, but now no longer blank. In the upper half, just below the printed lettering for Trier Uniformem were pencil smudges across a wide area, revealing a name: Bittendorf. On the lower half, Karin had written a simple note: meet me at the Gare after school. He ran to St. John's.

His excitement was short-lived. Like before, he couldn't concentrate on anything. The seconds ticked by one by one by one. The name on the receipt was strange enough, but oddly he was content to let Karin explain her discovery. What troubled him more was their encounter on the street. He played the scene over and over and could not escape the truth—he was jealous. With the admission came shame, his constant companion. From their first encounter atop the cliffs, he liked her. Abandoning her at the Gare was wrong. The second chance at the fair had been a miracle. But the romance, if even he could call it that, was little more than a half hour of peace that the brown-shirted thugs destroyed. Afterward, when they went to Differdange to search for his father, things got complicated.

No words had ever passed between them about their relationship, and in the end, Hansi realized he was naïve to think a girl like Karin would have the same feelings in return. Any number of boys would pursue her. But Peter? He was the last person Hansi expected. He was tall and confident, to be sure, but arrogant sometimes and absorbed with himself always. And whether it was carnival games, soccer, or school, Hansi—he had to admit it—always beat Peter. This conclusion fueled a new kind of shame, the offspring of pride, that in the end, he was no better.

By the time the afternoon bell rang, he was less eager to meet her now than when the day started. The warm autumn afternoon, deep blue sky, and gold and orange treetops below the Pont Adolphe were lost to him. Still, all his internal arguments came back to the same point: he needed the information.

Karin was waiting on the plaza, waving two tickets when he arrived. Her greeting was cordial. He wanted to be dispassionate, but he studied her expression. Was she glad to see him? What difference did it make?

She led him to the platform and a second-class car marked for Wasserbillig-Trier-Koblenz. The bell rang, the brakes hissed, and the train lurched forward.

"This is Dieter Dumont's journal," she said, holding it up. "And from what I can tell by the entries, he's been playing a dangerous game."

She wasn't wasting time with small talk. Was that a good thing?

"The entries at the beginning of the journal read like a normal diary. For example, here's January 20: 'Took mother to the orchestra for her birthday. She is growing more frail each day.' But after a few pages, everything changes."

Karin flipped to a page with a down-turned corner.

"March 15 – 'met a man, who introduced himself as simply "S". Knows about my circumstances and mother's poor health. Says he will help us if I help him. We agree to meet again.'"

"S, that would be Schlinge."

"That's what I thought," Karin said, turning to the next marked page. "April 9 – 'Our fourth meeting, S slips me an envelope containing 500 francs. Says I can do the 'cause' a great service. Wants to know about things at the mill—locations of warehouses, guard shacks, who's in charge. Asks about AB.'"

"AB. My father, Alain Broussard!" Hansi said. "What does Dieter tell him?"

"He writes, 'S says AB is a suspected terrorist. I told him he's crazy. AB is one of the few fair and honest men I know at the mill. S wants me to report anything suspicious. I tell him he's wasting his time, but how can I say no? I can afford a nurse to help Mama with that kind of money.'"

"What does he learn about my father?"

"Only that your father became increasingly concerned about a German invasion and suspicious of spies operating in the mill."

"Did he suspect Dieter?" Hansi asked.

Karin turned a few pages. "Your father seemed to trust him, at least that's what Dieter thought. May 7 – 'AB admits to me he is organizing a group in the mill to fight against the Germans if they invade. Asks me to join and I agree. When I tell S, he is pleased.'"

"The dangerous game," Hansi said. Karin nodded and kept going.

"S asks Dieter to start skipping work, using the excuse that he has to attend to his sick mother. Instead, S sends him all over Luxembourg. Dieter starts collecting information—the number of gendarmes in various towns, the descriptions and locations of fortifications, rail stations, and things like that. It seems easy enough and the money keeps coming."

"Playing sick a few days for five hundred francs is more than you can earn at the mill in three months!" Hansi said.

"Listen to this: July 22 – 'Found 1000 francs in my mailbox. Met S and this is a big one. They want me to help them steal some explosives. I guess I'm in too deep to refuse now. S assures me he'll protect me and take care of Mama.'"

"When did he steal it?"

"All summer long, I'm afraid. They smuggled explosives in small quantities so no one would notice. Dieter supplied a map of the mill, the locations of the warehouses, the timing of the shipments, guards' schedules—everything. He even faked the records to make it appear nothing had been stolen."

"Does he say anything about what my father knew?"

Karin frowned. "July 8 – 'AB suspects explosives are being stolen. Thinks the Germans are behind it. Our group is going to post constant guard and wants me to help.'"

"I can't believe Papa trusted him."

"Dieter wasn't happy about this. In fact, he seems in over his head. July 24 – 'My turn to guard tomorrow. S wants me to look the other way. He says they're coming for the last time, and they want an entire truckload. How does he expect me to fake that amount?'"

"Poor guy doesn't know what to do," Hansi said with a sneer.

"July 25 – 'S told me not to worry, and now I know why. To protect me, they made it look like I resisted. I've got a nice bruise above the eye to prove it. But AB trusts me now. Says he knows about the Gestapo. Knows they are behind the thefts and are planning something big. I asked S, but he won't tell me. It's better I don't know, and 1000 more francs keeps me from caring.'"

Hansi slowly shook his head. "He fooled my father."

"He didn't," Karin said. "August 4 – 'AB suspects me. Knows I've not been sick. I decided to tell S, who says not to worry, I can lay low for a while. I can travel on weekends, but better to take the box home—it's not safe at the mill anymore.'" She closed the journal. "That's the last entry, two days before the explosion at the Gare."

Beneath the steep slopes and manicured vineyards of the Moselle Valley, Hansi let the facts sink in. "Dieter spied for Schlinge, helped steal explosives to blow up the Gare, and tried to play both sides. When my father got too close, they had him arrested. Pretty simple."

"Except for one thing," Karin said. "If the Germans are behind it all, why arrest Dieter?"

"Maybe they were afraid he would squeal and wanted him out of the way. Schlinge didn't strike me as the type that trusts anyone."

"But now Schlinge is dead," Karin said, "and Dieter and your father are both missing." She put the journal away. "The receipt, please."

Hansi gave it to her.

"That's where this comes in. Bittendorf has something to do with Trier Uniformem. I think that he was among those men we saw going into the culvert under the mill."

Hansi took the receipt and considered it again. "How did you get his name?"

"An old trick," Karin said. "I'm surprised you didn't know this yourself, being an artist."

The word made him smile.

"I studied the paper for a while. The more I examined it, the less it made sense. Why would Dieter hold on to a blank receipt? Finally, I held it up to the light and looked at it with a magnifying glass I borrowed from Fritz. He uses it for his stamp collection. I found indentations."

"The letters?"

"Yes, from a pen with no ink or as if written on the slip above it in the stack. Anyway, whoever wrote it pressed hard enough to impress the letters on this blank slip. If you rub the pencil over it lightly, the letters are revealed."

Hansi grinned. "Very clever of you. I do it all the time in my sketches, but what if it's just a coincidence?"

"Early in the journal, Dieter says this: 'S introduces me to B, a hero of the Great War.'"

"B for Bittendorf," Hansi said.

"We don't have many choices," Karin said. "Bittendorf may be the only one left that can tell us anything. If we find Bittendorf, maybe we can find Dieter."

"But Dieter was arrested…"

"Not necessarily. If they just wanted to get him out of the way or use him as a scapegoat, maybe he's free. I hope Bittendorf will tell us."

Hansi scratched his head. "You suppose we can simply go to Trier, walk up to Bittendorf, and just ask him?"

"Do you have a better idea?"

CHAPTER THIRTY-EIGHT

At Wasserbillig, the last stop in Luxembourg before the line crossed the Moselle River into Germany, German border officers boarded the train. Unlike the friendly Luxembourgish officers, their stern-faced German counterparts in charcoal gray coats, red armbands, stark swastikas, and shoulder-slung machine pistols strode the aisles with deadly seriousness.

"Papieren, bitte," the red-faced officer commanded. Hansi handed him his identification card, something students never had to carry until this year. "Where are you traveling and for what purpose?" the man asked, stone-faced.

Hansi was unprepared. In all his trips to Trier, whether for shopping or sightseeing, not once was he required to explain his purpose for traveling to a border guard. He improvised. "We're going to Trier on a study assignment for school," Hansi said. "We're studying the Roman occupation in the third century. Some of the best ruins are in Trier. The amphitheater, the Porta Nigra—"

"I don't need a history lecture." He handed Hansi's papers back and took Karin's.

"Sind sie Deutsch?" Are you German?

"Ja." Hansi detected nerves.

"Yet you live in Luxembourg?"

"My father is a diplomat," she answered.

An eyebrow went up.

"And he approves of this trip? With this boy?"

"Yes, of course," Karin replied.

If he only knew, Hansi thought.

The officer jutted his chin forward, thinking.

"Is there a problem?"

The officer's grin seemed to indicate pleasure at making Karin nervous. "Nein, Fraulein Blik," he said, thrusting the papers back to her. "Welcome back to the Fatherland."

When the officers passed into the next car, Hansi heard Karin exhale. "Are you alright?" he asked.

"I'm shocked at how different things are now," she replied. "They make my skin crawl."

The train crossed the Moselle River and curved north before stopping at the Hauptbahnhof on the east side of Trier. From the moment they disembarked, the difference between Germany and Luxembourg was immediate and stark. German soldiers outnumbered civilians, on the move around the station and freight yard. Others mingled with the townspeople and tourists along the Christophstraße that led toward the center of town. Terrible swastikas were everywhere, from the pins and armbands on soldiers' uniforms to the red flags on nearly every lamppost and shop.

Hansi and Karin headed for the gateway to the town—the four-story Roman arch known as the Porta Nigra—the Black Gate. Like everything else, it was also adorned with red Nazi banners. Nearby they found the town map mounted on a post, highlighting tourist points like the Basilica and Roman amphitheater.

"Here it is, Metzelstraße ," Karin said, indicating a point not far from the gate.

"We don't have much time," Hansi said. "According to the schedule, we need to be on the five o'clock train back to Luxembourg or we'll be stuck here until ten-thirty. I can't do that to my mother."

"I doubt my parents would even know," Karin said.

Metzelstraße was easy enough to find, and halfway down the block, they found a sign on the plain brick building that confirmed their success: Trier Uniformem.

"Let me do the talking," Karin said as she turned the door handle and stepped in.

"If not for Father Jean's pity, I'd be failing German," he said. "So be my guest."

Inside, a tall counter covered the width of the office. True to its name, row upon row of uniforms hung on racks behind. A middle-aged woman in a matching white coat and cap was moving her pencil back and forth between two lists. She looked up only after reaching the end of a page.

"No beggars here."

"I beg your pardon?" Karin replied.

"Are you lost?"

"No, Fraulein. We're looking for someone."

"Here? Who would that be?"

"Herr Bittendorf."

The woman's face tightened. "Who are you?"

"My name is Karin, and this is Hansi. We have something that belongs to Herr Bittendorf."

Hansi was both surprised and glad that Karin had thought this out.

"What is it?" the woman asked.

"A letter," Karin replied. "From my father."

What was she up to?

"Who is your father?"

"Maximillian Blik."

"We don't know anyone by that name," the woman said. "Give the letter to me."

"My father insists that I deliver it personally," Karin replied. "May I see him, please?"

The woman exhaled with a huff. "It's impossible. He no longer works here."

Just then a boy about Hansi's age stepped out from among the racks of uniforms. He was handsome, with high cheekbones and golden blond hair that curled across his left eye.

"Hallo," he said, tossing his hair back. Karin and Hansi nodded a greeting, but the woman shot him a stern look. "Have you finished tagging the uniforms for the hospital?"

"Almost, Fraulein," he replied.

"Then see to it. You're not to leave until you do."

"Yes, Fraulein," he replied, almost too compliant. He sneaked a smile at Karin before disappearing into the racks.

"When did Herr Bittendorf leave?" Karin asked.

"It's not your business to know," the woman replied.

"But I must deliver the letter," Karin insisted. "Did he leave a forwarding address?"

"No, he did not. Now if you'll excuse me, I have a great deal of work to finish before the day's end. I wish you a Guten Tag."

For the first time, Karin seemed to be at a loss.

"Please, Fraulein, this is very important," Hansi said in his best German accent. "Can you help us find Herr Bittendorf?"

The woman leaned over the counter, ignoring Hansi, to look directly at Karin. "How well does your father know Herr Bittendorf?"

"Very well," Karin lied. "They're old friends in fact."

A look of irritation crossed the woman's face. "Old friends you say?"

"Yes," Karin answered, and then, seeming to feel the woman's stare, added somewhat weakly, "At least that's what my father tells me."

The woman came out from behind the counter and bent down, standing face to face with Karin so that only centimeters separated them. Hansi could see the tremors in Karin's legs.

"I don't know what you're really after here, Meine Kleine Leibchen, but whatever it is, I'm warning you to drop it. You should turn around, take him with you, and return to wherever it is you've come from. Otherwise, you'll find trouble you can't even imagine."

Karin's courage flagged. She retreated a few steps, looking for help in Hansi's eyes.

The woman followed a step.

"And tell your father he's not much of a friend. Herr Bittendorf could never hope to read his letter. He's blind."

The words slapped Karin in the face. Another dead end.

The woman returned to the counter. "The next time I look up, if you're still here, I'm calling the police."

Hansi had to support Karin by the arm as they left.

The beat of drums sounded from town. They moved quickly, saying nothing. At the corner, a mass of people formed a barrier along the sidewalks. The drums grew louder, masking the sounds of footsteps from behind. Hansi strained to see.

Someone tapped Karin on the shoulder.

"Hallo again." It was the boy from the warehouse. "The parade is just starting." Before they could respond, he plunged into a group of people and returned an instant later.

"Take these," he said, handing Karin and Hansi two miniature Nazi flags. Hansi found himself holding it before he could refuse.

"Can't be too careful these days," the boy said. "You never know who might notice, ahem, unpatriotic behavior." He smiled. "I'm Kurt."

"What's going on?" Karin asked.

"Somebody important from Berlin" Kurt replied. "Supposed to be inspecting the defenses along the river in this sector."

"That's cause for a parade?" Hansi asked, his voice rising to match the trumpets now blasting in the street.

"It's easier to discuss what isn't cause for a parade," he said. "It's worth double to me—a proof of loyalty and a break from work." He leaned close. "Smiling on the outside, shaking on the inside."

The band was in the street right in front of them now, playing a brisk march. Behind them came the soldiers, squeezed shoulder to shoulder, curb to curb, arms jutting skyward in the "Heil Hitler" salute, their legs snapping in goosestep march. The crowd surged with adulation, sending an icy tremor down Hansi's back. An instant later he realized he had dropped the flag.

"We've got to get out of here," he shouted into Karin's ear.

"How?" she said, scanning the crowd.

Hansi looked for a way out, but they were pressed in from all sides. Then he turned to Kurt, who was mesmerized by the display in the street.

"We need to catch the train back to Luxembourg. Can you help us?"

Kurt nodded and took Karin by the hand. She took Hansi's. Kurt plowed through the line of cheering and waving people, which, to Hansi's surprise, was not as thick as it first seemed. Once the car passed, the crowd dispersed quickly. In a few minutes, they managed to cross the parade route and put the sounds of drums and horns behind them.

Hansi was eager to say Auf Wiedersehen. Within sight of the Porta Nigra, he stopped and thanked the boy.

"I can help you," Kurt said.

"We know the way now," Hansi said. "But thanks all the same."

"That's not what I meant. I knew Herr Bittendorf."

"Knew?" Karin asked. Hansi missed the German past tense.

The smile left Kurt's face. "Yes. He's dead."

CHAPTER THIRTY-NINE

"Herr Bittendorf worked on a delivery truck. He was making deliveries last week when there was a terrible accident. He was in an unfamiliar place for a new customer in Luxembourg, I think, traveling along a winding road in the hills. A car was coming from the other direction, and the driver of Bittendorf's truck did not see it until it was too late. The truck ran off the road and plunged down a steep bank. They said the truck exploded and Herr Bittendorf, God rest him, was killed instantly."

"That's awful, Kurt. I'm so sorry. Was he your friend?" Karin asked.

"I'd like to think so," Kurt replied. "He trained me—tagging uniforms and preparing them for delivery—a job he had done for years. He was quite good at it, as Frau Gerta is fond of reminding me. But then they moved him onto a truck. I don't know why. I don't think he liked it. Once they put him on that truck something changed, and for the worse. He was tense and cranky to everyone but me. It seemed like someone was forcing him to ride the truck."

Kurt was surely describing the blind man who took a wild shot at them from the back of the truck in Differdange. Kurt seemed to have no idea he was part of the smuggling. How could Bittendorf be forced to participate?

"Do you know how Herr Bittendorf came to be blind?" Hansi asked.

"The Great War," Kurt said. "Story is that some mustard gas blew back on him. Ate his eyes out, or nearly, I think. It's not the kind of thing you can exactly ask about, but some of the other lads at the warehouse told me. Apparently after the war, he went to work in the coal mines, where he didn't need to see, I guess. He felt his way around everywhere. Rumor was he was good with explosives."

"A blind man?" Hansi asked.

"They said he rigged them just by the feel of his hands, if you can believe it."

"It sounds dangerous enough with two good eyes," Hansi said.

"Indeed. In fact, several years back something went wrong with one of his jobs, a bad accident. They pulled him above ground, and he started working for the uniform company."

"Why are you telling us all of this?" Karin asked.

"Selfish reasons, I guess," Kurt said. "When I overheard you saying you had a letter for Herr Bittendorf, I thought maybe I could learn something more about his death. The accident and circumstances seem too mysterious to me. Nobody will talk about it. I miss him. Ever since then, I can't escape the feeling there was something he wanted to tell me but couldn't. And she doesn't even shed a tear."

"The manager?" Karin asked.

Kurt nodded. "She's his sister."

They were at the Hauptbahnhof now. Kurt accompanied them to the platform where a small group had gathered to wait for the train from Koblenz.

"Now tell me," he said. "How did you know Herr Bittendorf?

"We didn't, really," Hansi answered, looking at Karin. "We met him without knowing who he was," he continued, measuring his words, "but it wasn't in the best circumstance I'm afraid. Karin discovered his name almost by chance, really. And we came here hoping he could help me find my father."

Kurt looked confused.

"It's complicated, but my father was arrested and now virtually disappeared."

"And this had something to do with Bittendorf?"

"We wanted to ask him."

The train arrived and passengers began to board.

"I'm really sorry about your friend," Karin said, giving Kurt a quick kiss on each cheek.

Hansi shook Kurt's hand and thanked him.

Kurt took them both by the arms and pulled them close.

"When the war is over, come back to Trier and look for me at the warehouse, if it's still standing. We can be friends and talk about more pleasant things."

He turned and broke into a run, in an instant disappearing among the afternoon travelers and soldiers that swarmed around the station.

Hansi and Karin found the last two seats in a second class compartment filled with men whose noses were buried in their newspapers.

"I'm sorry, Hansi," Karin said quietly.

He let his shoulders fall. They were no closer to finding his father than the moment they left Luxembourg.

The bell rang signaling departure. Hansi looked out the window, grateful for the barrier between himself and the chaos outside. He simply wanted to go home.

Karin put her hand in his. He tensed. What was she doing?

"I'm sorry for yesterday," she said, just above a whisper. "It's really not what you think—it's just that the way we parted last Sunday—I just thought that yesterday you might have come for a different reason."

"Like Peter?"

"No, that's not it. I just meant that I was surprised, of course, to see you again, and was expecting, I guess, that you'd—well—that you'd apologize before asking me to help again."

Hansi closed his eyes. She was right. He had shut her out after finding the key and expected her to jump back in without explanation. And was jealous for it!

"Oh," was all he could manage while the train sat motionless—the world itself frozen in his dread.

The seconds grew into minutes and the newspapers fluttered. Murmurs rippled through the compartment.

Then loud thumps and the sound of the doors sliding somewhere along the train. The car fell silent. Quick footsteps, figures in the next car.

A shock wave reverberated through Hansi's legs at the sight of the two men. The first one, a lean-faced man wearing the black trench coat of the Gestapo, locked eyes immediately on Karin and Hansi. With a quick nod, a puffed-faced police officer threw the door open. The Gestapo man stepped inside and pointed.

"You! Come with us!"

CHAPTER FORTY

Hansi's impulse to repeat a window escape was dashed by the sight of police officers outside, mirroring the movements of the men inside. And in the next instant, a second officer entered from the rear of the car. They were blocked in every direction.

The Gestapo man led them past wide-eyed passengers onto the platform where silent gawkers parted without instruction. Eventually, they came to a door along the back of the station and passed into a room full of musty suitcases. The door closed behind them.

The agent turned to Karin. "Please tell me, Fraulein, what brings you two to Trier this afternoon?" His tone was surprisingly calm.

Karin rubbed her palms on her skirt and took a deep breath.

"We came to visit the Porta Nigra," she stammered. "For a school project."

The agent paused, seeming to manipulate even the silence to his purpose, and then continued. "Is that all?"

"Yes, that's all."

"Excuse me, sir, but we really shouldn't miss our train," Hansi said.

"There are other trains," the agent said without even looking at him.

"You didn't visit Trier Uniformem at 27 Metzelstraße?"

Hansi's face tightened.

"We got lost," Karin answered. "We stopped there to ask for directions."

The agent tilted his head slightly and narrowed his eyes. "So, you got lost looking for the Porta Nigra, the most prominent landmark in town?" The puffy-faced officer grinned.

"We got caught up in the excitement of the parade and got turned around, I guess," she answered. Hansi was amazed.

"Let me ask you, Fraulein, do the trains run on time here in the Reich?"

Karin seemed confused by the direction, but answered, "Of course."

The agent looked at his watch and smiled that fake smile all too familiar now to Hansi. "The train to Luxembourg is now five minutes late. This is unthinkable. But it is waiting for you, on my orders, under one condition."

Karin's eyes widened.

"Just tell me the truth."

Karin took another deep breath and glanced at Hansi. "I am, sir. I swear it," she said.

Hansi's heart slammed against the inside of his chest.

"You swear? You've told me everything?"

"Yes, sir."

Karin's performance, brilliant as it was, left Hansi gripped with fear. He was convinced the agent not only knew exactly where they had been, but who they talked to and why. This was how they worked, he was sure, never asking a question without knowing the answer in advance.

The officer sucked in his breath through clenched teeth. "I give you one last chance, Fraulein. Is there nothing you want to tell me about a letter, for a certain Herr Bittendorf?"

The trap snapped shut. Send the train on its way, Hansi thought.

"No," Karin said. "I don't know what you're talking about."

"Do you take me for a fool, Fraulein?" the agent said, leaning close to Karin and drawing out each word. "Let's have a look in your bag."

Hansi's couldn't breathe.

Karin, eyes locked on the agent, held out her bag. The agent snatched it away, flipped it open, and dumped the contents with a shocking crash. A glance sent the accompanying officer to the floor where he began to sift through the books, pencils, and papers scattered at Karin's feet. His movements became frantic. He looked up, as though it was his fault that there was no letter.

Color drained from the agent's face. His body began to quiver, and then a thin line of blood emerged from his lip where he had been biting down. He wiped it away with a sweep of his thumb and then spit. Finally, without looking up he waved vaguely at the door.

"Don't let me ever find you in Trier again!"

Karin gathered a few of her spit- and blood-spattered belongings before Hansi dragged her out the door. They flew across the platform and into the car, collapsing on the floor panting. A shrill whistle bellowed its protest at having to wait so long, and then the train lurched forward.

CHAPTER FORTY-ONE

Unwilling to face the stares of the crowded compartment, they sat in the noisy space by the doors where the rails flickered underneath through cracks in the floor. But at least they were alone.

"I can't keep putting you in danger like this," Hansi said.

"You didn't," she said. "I left the note on your door, remember? We needed to find Bittendorf. Without me, what would you have said to his sister?"

"I don't know," Hansi replied. "Or what I would have said to that agent. What happened to the letter?"

Karin managed a faint smile. "There never was one."

"Then what would you have done if Bittendorf had really been at the warehouse?"

"I hadn't thought that far ahead. I guess I would have just talked to him."

"It doesn't make sense," Hansi said.

"Yes, poor Bittendorf, I feel terrible for him."

"No, the Gestapo. They were looking for us."

Karin pressed her lips together. "Why?"

"Rather, who?"

"Do you think the border officers called the Gestapo? Why would they care about a couple of students visiting the Roman ruins?"

Hansi let the question hang. Outside, they had passed from hills and vineyards to farms and villages near the city. Someone had certainly warned the Gestapo. Frau Gerta? She would have had to act quickly. Then it hit him.

"Karin, how did you get to the Gare so fast this afternoon? You were waiting for me when I arrived, and if I'm not mistaken, you had further to go from your school than I did."

"I rode the tram. There's a stop just down the corner from school."

"Did anyone see you get on? Did anyone know where you were going?"

Karin looked down.

"What?" Hansi said. "Were you followed?"

"I'm sorry Hansi," Karin said. "I'm really sorry."

"It's all right, Karin, you didn't know. Who was it?"

Karin looked up at him with soft blue eyes that penetrated to Hansi's heart in a way that spoke of betrayal, but not the kind of betrayal he had expected.

"Peter rode with me."

Hansi closed his eyes.

"But it's not what you think. I can explain."

The train braked with a jolt. Hansi pulled himself up and opened the door adjoining the cars, filling the space with a rush of sound. He stepped across the joint on the sliding floor and pushed into the next car.

"Hansi, don't!" Karin followed, but the gap between them grew.

Hansi pressed on, driven by a storm of rage and shame. But at himself. For hoping. For trusting.

The train slowed, the platforms slid into view, and the train shuddered to a stop. He jumped out, the brakes hissing as if laughing at him. His head throbbed, the same throb as the night of the bombing. He bolted for the passageway at the end of the platform, ignoring Karin behind him, and then bounded down the steps two at a time. At the bottom, he stopped dead.

Standing in his path were two gendarmes, and behind them, a face that he couldn't escape—Herr Blik.

Behind him, the tracks and yard offered hope of escape. He would just have to beat them up the stairs.

When he turned, it was too late. Karin stood at the top, tears streaming down her face. Two more gendarmes stood as bookends beside her.

The officers grabbed Hansi, and Blik waited for Karin.

"It's not what you think!" Karin called, but Hansi ignored her.

They dragged him across the plaza and shoved him into the second of two black Mercedes waiting at the curb. The cars sped off up the Grand Rue toward the central city. Hansi wondered if jumping out would kill him. But he would have to climb over the officers on either side of him first.

Minutes later, Hansi's rage turned to surprise when they passed through the center of the city, where he expected to stop at police headquarters. Surprise became fear when they entered the familiar neighborhood and turned onto the unforgettable street. The red Nazi flag over the Blik house welcomed him with crisp salutes in the afternoon breeze.

The cars zoomed past the house and doubled back on the alley behind. The heavy sedans whooshed down the narrow lane, leaving a wake of swirling leaves before screeching to a halt at the rear entrance.

Karin was rushed inside first and then Hansi. He was made to sit in Blik's office, in the padded armchair across from his great desk. The door closed and locked behind him. A silhouette filled the translucent glass. He was alone, utterly alone.

In the silence, Hansi pondered the afternoon. Karin had sent him the note, and he was all too eager to accept it. Had she tricked him? Had she set the trap herself or simply complied with Blik's own plan? Why let me go all the way to Trier?

The more he considered these questions, the less he could blame Karin. She was probably in another room right now facing her father's questions. Perhaps she had told Fritz where she was headed. Or told her father in passing, and his suspicions took over. He put the border guards on alert, and they called the Gestapo. It was a long chain but the only conclusion that made sense.

At the bottom of it all, Hansi couldn't escape his constant companion, shame. He had been a child at the mention of Peter. Karin's offer to help find Bittendorf had been sincere, and he had let petty jealousy get in the way.

His back turned to the door, Hansi heard the noise in the hall but didn't see the silhouette disappear. He also failed to see the new one fill the frame. He was so absorbed in his own despair that he ignored the faint click when the door handle turned. The door swung open on well-oiled hinges. But the thump of a heavy footstep made Hansi jump in the seat. A scrape and another thump, and Hansi spun around. The terror that seized him was that of seeing an evil ghost alive from the dead. The coat, the eyes, the marred face were unmistakable: Schlinge!

CHAPTER FORTY-TWO

Schlinge was a living corpse. His face looked like he had fought a bear and lost. He moved with great exertion, dragging a leg behind him. His unworldly presence alone pressed Hansi to the chair.

"You have been an elusive prey," he said, his voice raspier than Hansi remembered. "But the chase is over now. And you have something of mine. Would you care to return it now?" Schlinge's voice oozed with sarcasm.

"I don't understand," Hansi lied.

"That knife was a personal gift from the Führer himself. I will send someone to your flat to find it. What is your mother's name again? Marie, wasn't it?"

Hansi shuddered. Schlinge shuffled behind Blik's desk and sat down, landing heavily on the thick padding. "But for now, the time of games has ended. It is now time to tell me everything, Hansi."

"I told you; I know nothing."

"That kind of attitude will not help you in your present trouble, I'm afraid."

"What have you done with my father?" Hansi said.

"Tell me, what has your father done that would attract my attention? Why should I have anything to do with him?"

"The Gestapo have everything to do with everything, especially when it comes to the disappearance of innocent people."

"Innocent? How amusing! No one is innocent these days, and certainly not terrorists!"

Rage conquered Hansi's fear. He wondered if Schlinge could do anything if he leaped over the desk and clamped his hands around the man's neck.

"Then you admit you have him?"

"Very clever. I have much greater concerns than a small-town terrorist. The fates of nations are at stake. My present concern is removing a certain nuisance from my work." He bore his gaze right at Hansi.

"I want to see Herr Blik," Hansi said.

"Herr Blik is comforting his daughter. She has had quite a shock, learning the truth that you are one of the terrorists."

"She'll never believe him! She knows you're behind all of this!"

"Don't be so sure. Despite everything, Karin remains a good German daughter. When we explain to her what this so-called 'Resistance' is all about—smuggling, kidnapping, sabotage—and what you and your father have been up to, she'll come around."

"That's ridiculous."

"You underestimate our power of persuasion. Perceptions are reality, especially when the doctor administers something to help Karin rest. In the meantime, Herr Blik has instructed me to clean up everything else."

"So he's the one in charge."

Schlinge sat up. "For now. Every play needs an actor for the sake of the audience. But when the play is over, the director also steps forward to receive the applause. In a few days, the play will be over, and Herr Blik's part will be finished. He will return to Berlin and begin rehearsals for the next show."

A few days? Was Schlinge saying the German invasion was coming in a few days?

"Why are you telling me this?" Hansi asked, without thinking.

"You disappoint me, Hansi Broussard. I thought you were more clever than this. You listen in on my conversation, elude my grasp at the station, and again in Strassen." Schlinge hacked an evil chuckle. "Don't you realize, es macht nichts? It doesn't matter because you've no one to tell what you know. You fail to understand that I do not permit nuisances to interrupt my work. Not now, not ever."

Schlinge stood up, revealing a Luger that he pointed right at Hansi's heart. "It's time to go. Get up."

Hansi rose carefully, unable to take his eyes off the black hole at the end of the barrel.

"Put away any thoughts you might have of trying another of your silly escape attempts," Schlinge said. "For the moment, that is. You will walk carefully to the door, we will go to my car in the back, take a short ride, and only then will you escape. Of course, I will stop that attempt once and for all. But for now, should you make any sudden moves or loud sounds, I'll be forced to ruin Herr Blik's carpet with your blood. He would be very upset, but Fraulein Karin—the poor dear—she would never recover from the trauma of it. You don't want that on your conscience."

"What do you know about conscience?" Hansi snorted.

Schlinge moved in close behind Hansi and jabbed the gun into Hansi's side. They crossed the room to the door where the guard stood outside.

"Now turn on the handle and say nothing," Schlinge instructed.

The officer outside turned. "Is everything all right?"

"I'm taking this one down to headquarters for questioning. Tell Herr Blik I will speak with him later."

Schlinge twisted Hansi toward the rear of the house. Hansi looked for a way of escape, but gendarmes were stationed at both ends of the hallway.

Footsteps thumped down the stairs behind them. Hansi slowed. Schlinge jabbed the barrel to his ribs and whispered sharply, "Keep going!"

"Schlinge, is that you?" It was Blik. And while Hansi didn't trust him, it was clear that Schlinge had not shared the nuisance-removal plan with him. Hansi stopped.

"I was just taking the boy down to headquarters for further questioning, Herr Blik. I'm sure your daughter has had quite a shock learning the truth about him, and I don't wish to trouble you further. We were just on our way out."

Herr Blik reached the landing. "Just a minute, Schlinge. A word—in my office—now."

Hansi detected a flash of worry in Schlinge's good eye.

"This one is quite elusive, sir. I'm sure you don't want him slipping away again. Do you have somewhere in the house that these men might secure him?"

Blik looked at the gendarmes. "The wine cellar is off the kitchen in back. Leave him to them and come with me."

"But sir, I'd prefer to secure him myself."

"Then be quick about it!" Blik said and slammed his office door.

Schlinge let out a breath. Then, with another hard jab, prodded Hansi on. A gendarme led the way, finding the kitchen and then the door to the wine cellar. He swung it open. Stairs descended into the dark.

Hansi hesitated but Schlinge didn't. Schlinge's hand struck him squarely between the shoulder blades, propelling him out into the empty space. And then everything went black.

CHAPTER FORTY-THREE

Hansi awoke to the gritty taste of dirt in his mouth. His cheek rested on a cool stone floor. Rolling on his back, pain erupted in the corner of his forehead. His arm was numb and heavy, but he lifted it to touch the source of pain. A chain rattled and stopped his wrist with a jolt. In the faint light, he saw the other end, bolted onto a brick post between racks of bottles.

A wine cellar and a prison?

He twisted to a sitting position to let his head clear. In the pool of light at the base of the stairs, a figure stood guard.

"Are you hurt?" The voice was familiar.

"I don't know," Hansi replied, his mind still a fog.

The man approached Hansi, saw the handcuffs, and swore, Hansi assumed because he didn't understand the German. He reached into his pocket.

"Fritz? Is that you?"

"Indeed."

Hansi felt the touch of Fritz's bony hand around his wrist, gentle but confident. A click and rattle and Hansi was free.

"Can you stand?" Fritz asked, lifting him. "You've got to get out of here before they come back."

Hansi struggled to his feet, pain exploding in every joint, but his mind sputtered back to life.

Fritz led him deep into the cellar to a wall covered with columns of dusty bottles. Fritz reached between sections, and something clicked as the rack mysteriously slid forward and away, revealing a narrow passageway.

"Go as far as you can and find the metal rungs. Climb and twist the latch anti-clockwise. Run as fast and long as you can. Now hurry."

Hansi turned and saw Fritz's face in the light. His eyes were bright and sharp. Hansi grasped Fritz's arm. "Why did you do this?"

"I saw firsthand what the Germans did in the last war—too many friends lost because of fools like them. But these Nazis are worse than fools—they're more like wild dogs. Fighting children, no less! I'll not have it, I tell you. I'll not have it."

"I didn't get the chance to thank you before, Fritz."

"Go!"

Fritz's plan worked, but running from Karin's house to the city had left Hansi in agony from head to toe. Heaving, he staggered forward, driven by a single desire. Schlinge would discover he'd been fooled and explode. Hansi could never hope to outrun Schlinge's Mercedes. But Maman had to get out. Not Saturday when Uncle Pit came with the truck, but today, now. Hansi had to warn her.

Near the city center Hansi remembered a bicycle shop he knew. On lazy Sunday afternoons, he would dream about the shiny new models displayed in the window. The bell on the door shook violently when he entered. Hansi stumbled to the rear of the store and slammed into the counter, where the shopkeeper, a short, wide-faced, middle-aged man looked up over his spectacles with sudden fear.

"Your phone—may I use it please?" Hansi could hardly get the words out.

"Is everything all right, son?" the man asked.

"I've got to call my mother—it's an emergency," Hansi said, trying to gain control.

"What kind of emergency? Shall I call the gendarmes? The doctor?" The man was reaching for the phone and near to dialing.

"No gendarmes!" Hansi barked, startling the man. "I must speak to her myself—and quickly!" Hansi swept behind the counter and snatched the phone. The man jumped back, losing his spectacles.

The phone buzzed in Hansi's ear, but no answer. He waited, his hand shaking.

Answer!

Nothing. Hansi slammed the phone back on its cradle.

"Young man!" the shopkeeper said, indignant. "I have but one telephone and I insist you treat it more carefully! If this is such an emergency, I must call the gendarmes. I'm sure they can help—"

"No!" Hansi shouted. "Do you have a car? Can you drive me home? My Maman is in great danger, and I must warn her!"

The shopkeeper blinked repeatedly, suddenly aware of his lost spectacles. "I have a car, but I cannot leave the shop. We don't close until six. You're upset, I can see. Let me call my brother. He has a car and might be able to come by and drive you home."

Hansi had no time for a maybe. "Can I borrow a bicycle?" he said. "I promise I'll return it as soon as I can."

The man pressed his spectacles higher on the bridge of his nose. "Borrow one? We rent them on occasion, but…"

The man replaced his spectacles.

"Look, I don't know what you're up to, but I don't like the sound of this. I'm going to call the gendarmes." He picked up the phone and began to dial.

Hansi, heart in his throat, lunged across the counter and grabbed the cord. He pulled with all his might and ripped it from the wall.

The man's mouth fell open. He staggered backward into a shelf, which sent a box of metal parts crashing to the floor.

"I'm sorry, Monsieur," Hansi said, running to the front of the shop. He was speaking about the phone—and something more. He was sorry for what he was about to do next.

CHAPTER FORTY-FOUR

Barreling down the Avenue Monterey, Hansi never saw the shopkeeper shaking his fist at him from the sidewalk. The man left him no choice, having resisted his every demand, or nearly. The only option left was the one thing Hansi didn't want to do—steal a bike.

The bike was a beauty—a three-speed leisure model of French design with sparkling chrome and glossy red paint. Hansi accelerated easily down the street and sped past the Gendarmerie Centrale, weaving through the early evening traffic, past the Place Guillaume toward the central bus station and Cathédrale beyond.

The freedom and fresh air cleared Hansi's mind. It was time to honor the promise made to Papa—he would take Maman straight to Manolo's.

Schlinge's words echoed too: *a few days*. Schlinge had as much as told Hansi the invasion was imminent, so did anyone else know? Had the government prepared? Were they going to warn the citizens?

And Karin. He might never see her again. She hadn't sprung the trap, at least not knowingly. He was sorry for the way he had mistrusted her and blocked her out. And now, with war coming, there was so much he wanted to tell her but probably never would. What must she think of him now? Would she believe the lies Blik fed her about him? Did Karin know what was coming and her own father's part in it?

The questions had to wait. Everything came back to Papa. Hansi was no closer to finding his father than the day he and Karin went to Differdange. They had found the key, the box, the clues; but what did they mean? What did Papa want him to know? Want him to do?

It did no good to despair. The world was in chaos, but he had one thing to do: warn Maman.

The chill wind cut through Hansi's lightweight jacket as he passed the Cathédrale at top speed and banked left in front of a truck on the Avenue de la Gare. The horn blared as he sped past and began to accelerate again, pumping his legs like the pistons of a locomotive. Hansi was sprinting along the cliff now, passing the Parc du Casemates and nearing the plunge down the hill to the Rue du Grunde. Just as he braked at the top of the hill, there came the seesaw of sirens, somewhere on the far side of the cliffs.

Bounding over a manhole, Hansi's foot slipped, and the bicycle wobbled beneath him as it started down the hill. Speed built rapidly on the steep decline—too rapidly—and he was suddenly alarmed. The bike was a common model with a hand brake in the front, which he dare not use lest he go sailing over the handlebars, and a coaster brake in the rear that he could engage with his foot. He tried the coaster brake, and the rear wheel locked and skidded for an instant until Hansi let off. He was going so fast that the smallest touch on the brake locked the wheel and sent the back end of his bike fishtailing side to side.

Accelerating ever more, Hansi glanced down to the bottom of the hill and shuddered. A dump truck full of stone chugging up the Rue du Grund was entering the intersection directly in his path. It moved so slowly that a line of cars had stacked up behind it. Hansi was going too fast to turn and was unsure of the brakes.

The sirens drew nearer. Two red lights pulsed on the far end of the valley, approaching the Grund from the opposite side. Schlinge had taken the longer but faster route that avoided the central city.

Fear tightened Hansi's grip on the handlebars. The bike rattled with speed. Disaster would explode in an instant. He would lie mangled, broken, or dead at the bottom of the hill, unable to warn Maman.

Thinking was overwhelmed by instinct, and Hansi did the least sensible thing of all: he jumped off. While the bike continued riderless down the hill, Hansi hit the pavement shoulder-first. His head smacked the pavement with a buzzing clang, and he began to roll. The flurry lasted only seconds before he met the curb with a crack and came to rest in a sewer grate near the bottom of the hill.

Dazed, he looked up just to see what would have happened had he not jumped. The bike hit the bottom of the hill and leapt into the intersection. The dump truck driver slammed on the brakes, but too late. The bike slammed into the left-front fender and was crushed. The mangled mass of metal would never carry another rider.

The sirens, very close now, focused Hansi's mind. He staggered to his feet, every fiber ablaze with pain. Adrenaline fueled his stride, and he broke into a run. The driver of the dump truck and several others had gotten out and were exchanging shocked stares at the twisted bike when Hansi rushed past. He had to beat the sirens to his flat. Nothing else mattered.

Rounding the bend past St. John's brought his building in sight. The sirens stopped and so did Hansi. He was too late. The black sedans were parked directly in front of his flat. The doors were opening.

Hansi dashed into a doorway at the last instant and peered into the street. Schlinge, dragging his leg behind him, was heading inside.

Hansi pressed himself against the cold concrete to catch his breath. What would they do to Maman? He played a scenario out in his mind: Schlinge would begin with a pleasant inquiry—is Hansi home? When Maman answered in the negative, Schlinge would continue probing to find out what she knew. Gratefully, that was not much. He would push hard, and Hansi wasn't at all confident he would believe her.

Terror rose from within. Schlinge might ask about the knife and demand she return it. Would she know about it? Hansi was certain Maman would be suspicious of the Gestapo and tell Schlinge as little as possible. Schlinge would be furious, but would he really hurt her in front of the gendarmes?

Hansi was torn. If he moved in to help, he would fall right into Schlinge's lap. If he held back, Schlinge could wait for hours. Hansi feared what an impatient Schlinge might do in the meantime. There had to be another way.

CHAPTER FORTY-FIVE

Crouched down in the doorway, Hansi inched his head out enough to study the windows of his flat. The curtains didn't move. He crept carefully out and ducked behind a parked car on his side of the street. Carefully he backtracked up the street out of sight before running once more. Within moments he was at St. John's.

The main doors to the school were locked, but after running across the courtyard, Hansi found the doors to the church still open. Inside the empty sanctuary, he kept to the wall, passing the flickering candle-lit niche up the side until he came to an archway in the corner covered by a velvety maroon curtain. Hansi had seen Father Jean disappear through this archway countless times and knew the passageway led to his private residence, but he had never been there.

Hansi paused. The boundary between public and private space was clear. The curtain represented another kind of boundary too: the one in his relationship with Father Jean, the one between doubting and daring to trust him. Because of Maman, he would cross it.

Beyond the curtain, the passageway was arched stone leading to a dark wooden door marked "Pastoral Residence." Hansi knocked and waited. A few seconds passed with no response, and

Hansi knocked again. Again, there was no response and so Hansi tried once more—harder and with more urgency.

Imagining Schlinge with his mother brewed panic inside.

He pounded furiously.

"Please!" he called. "Father Jean!"

The lock turned from inside.

Expecting Father Jean, Hansi couldn't hide his surprise to see Sister Elaine. Short and stout, her brown eyes lit the plump face bursting out of her veil. She snatched Hansi by the shirt and pulled him inside to a small sitting room.

"Oh, good heavens!" she cried, squeezing him like a grandmother. "Thank the Lord you are safe! Wait right here! I'll get Father Jean—he'll be so grateful to see you." She disappeared through an adjoining doorway while Hansi waited. The room was plain but comfortable, with soft chairs and a short table on which rested a vase of fresh flowers. He stood waiting while a commotion could be heard somewhere deeper in the residence, followed by heavy footfalls.

The expression of relief on Father Jean's face compounded Hansi's surprise. *Were they expecting me?*

"Thank the Lord you're here!" the Father said. "But you're hurt! What's happened to you? Sister Elaine, gather something to dress those scrapes, please. And some tea. Hansi, please sit down."

"There's no time, Father," Hansi replied. "It's Maman. She's in trouble, and I need your help. The Gestapo, they're with her, right now at our flat. They're waiting for me, I know, and something terrible is going to happen!"

"Alright, son. Let's sort this out. Please, sit down," Father Jean ushered Hansi to one of the nearby chairs. He reluctantly took a seat but with great difficulty because the knee that had borne the brunt of his fall had already swollen stiff.

"Your mother is fine," Father Jean continued. "I just spoke with her on the telephone. In fact, I was on the phone with her when you arrived."

Hansi tried to swallow but his mouth was dry. "But you don't understand; the Gestapo arrived not five minutes ago."

"I'm sorry, son, I didn't make myself clear. Your mother is safe because she's not at home."

Hansi bolted up, wincing. "Then where is she?"

"She's at a safe house. I'll take you there presently, as soon as we've had time to clean you up a bit."

"A safe house?"

"Yes, that's what they call it—a safe place where people in danger can hide. When the Germans come for good, we will need many of them, to protect those who will try to fight back."

"The Resistance?"

"Then you know already. Yes, the Resistance has provided this place for you and your mother for a few days until we can make other arrangements."

"Then you're a member too?"

"Hmmm, yes, but of course I need not tell you that you must never repeat a word of this, to anyone. I cannot even tell Sister Elaine what I'm doing. For her own protection. It's better for her, should anyone ask her, that she truly does not know. It's easier than to try to lie."

"The Gestapo would interrogate her?"

"I don't like telling you these things, Hansi, but in the days to come, you'll learn soon enough. There are stories coming out of Poland that since the German invasion both nuns and priests have not only been interrogated but also put in prison. And worse may be yet to come, I'm afraid."

"How did Maman find out about this safe house? How did she know about the Gestapo coming?"

"Your mother got a call not even an hour ago from a stranger—a certain young girl—warning her to leave the house immediately."

"Karin!" Hansi said.

"Your German friend?"

"Yes, but I thought…" Hansi's voice trailed off.

"Your mother called me immediately and I instructed her to come at once. One more call and it was all arranged. They came for her and took her straight there. I was on the phone with her when I thought my door was going to jump off its hinges." He smiled.

Sister Elaine returned with a bowl of water, cloth bandages, and a medical kit. Father Jean exchanged a knowing glance at Hansi and pressed his lips together reminding Hansi to keep his secret. She quickly surveyed his injuries and began with the worst, his leg. Hansi's pant leg was shredded along its length, an oozing mass of flesh and blood mixed with debris that had plowed tiny furrows in his flesh. Sister Elaine tugged gingerly at the cloth but stopped.

"A doctor should see this, Father. If it gets infected…"

"I'll take Hansi directly to the hospital," Father Jean said. "He'll be safe there and they can dress his wounds properly. For now, let's try to clean this up as best we can. And about that tea, Sister. Is the kettle on?"

Just then a buzzer rang, not once, but several times in rapid succession. Father Jean locked eyes with Sister Elaine in an anxious glance, but he said calmly, "Would you mind seeing who it is?"

Sister Elaine left, and Father Jean retrieved a white tube from the medical kit.

"Put some on your leg, all around, and quickly. We may not make it to the hospital just yet."

Hansi complied while Father Jean retrieved his beret and a set of keys from a nearby cabinet.

Sister Elaine returned. "It's the gendarmes," she said, out of breath. "Two of them. And a third man, without uniform. His face…"

"Schlinge—he's Gestapo!" Hansi's mind raced, wondering how they knew to come here.

"I told them you were indisposed at the moment," the sister said, "but they demand to see you, at once." She eyed the beret. "Are you leaving?"

"Tell them to go around to the church where I'm receiving confessions," Father Jean said, his voice completely calm. "That may give us enough time."

The buzzer sounded again, accompanied by incessant pounding on the door.

"Go, Sister, but whatever you do, don't let them in."

Sister Elaine's face paled, but she complied.

Father Jean led Hansi further into the residence to the back door. After a quick glance into the lengthening shadows, the Father stepped outside and led Hansi down a covered walk to a small garage. Inside was a small vehicle covered by a gray tarpaulin.

Father Jean pulled the cover off a yellow Renault coupe, a surprisingly sporty two-seater. "A gift to the parish when an old friend passed away a few years ago," he said. "I save it for special occasions, and I guess this qualifies." He exhaled deeply, mouthed a silent prayer, and then crossed himself before turning the key. The motor cranked, sputtered, and then thundered to life. When he looked up at Hansi standing there, a smile had broken across his face. "Ready?" he asked. Hansi nodded. "Then God go with you," Father Jean said with a tug on his beret. He revved the engine and popped the clutch. The coupe leapt forward.

Windows along the Rue du Grund rattled in their frames as the coupe tore down the street. It roared past Hansi's flat heading east along the river through the winding streets of the Grund.

Surprised but by no means fooled, the black sedans joined in pursuit. Their powerful engines and Father Jean's lack of experience allowed them to close so quickly that by the time the coupe was heading up the valley at the edge of the village they were right behind.

Hansi saw none of it. He didn't see the coupe swerve from side to side, torturing the tires, and climbing higher as the river fell farther and farther below. Hansi didn't see the sedans behind it, edging forward, bumping the coupe from behind. And Hansi didn't see the expression on Father Jean's face—exhilaration at first, changing to worry as the sedans closed, and lastly terror when the coupe took a blow from a sedan and lost control. Instead, Hansi was moving in the opposite direction up the Rue du Grund. He was halfway up the hill when Father Jean's coupe left the road and plunged down the bank toward the river. Hansi never saw the crash, the explosion, or Father Jean thrown clear, lying crumpled on the riverbank.

By the time Hansi looked back into the valley from the top of the cliffs, he had no idea what caused the plume of smoke now rising on the horizon. Climbing onto the tram on the Avenue de la Gare, the only thing Hansi knew was that he was free from Schlinge and on his way to see Maman. And grateful that Father Jean's diversion had worked.

CHAPTER FORTY-SIX

The scrapes up Hansi's arm and leg burned like fire. Despite the pain, he collapsed with relief into the half-empty tram, slumping against the window with a sudden sleepiness. If Schlinge had known where Hansi was, he could have taken him without a fight.

As the tram sparked and rattled down the street, Hansi struggled to make sense of the remnants of his wrecked world. How did Schlinge know to visit Father Jean? Did Schlinge know about the Resistance? And once he caught up to Father Jean, wouldn't he learn where to look next?

The tram squealed to a stop in the plaza and let the handful of passengers out. Hansi grasped a brass handle to pull himself up but fell back when his vision suddenly blurred. He rubbed his eyes and blinked to try to clear his view.

"Are you alright?" came a voice from up front. The conductor had been clearing the car of trash and belongings left behind.

"Just dizzy, I guess," Hansi replied, grasping the handle again.

The conductor took him by the arm. "Steady now, son. What happened to you? Have you been in some kind of fight?"

The tram seemed to be spinning around its center, but with the conductor's help, Hansi managed to move down the aisle. "I… I fell off my bike."

Hansi didn't realize how much of his weight the conductor was bearing. They reached the steps of the tram and stopped.

"I can't let you go like this," the conductor said, helping Hansi to the last bench by the door. "You need to see a doctor." He turned toward the bustling crowd outside.

"No," Hansi groaned, fumbling for something to grab on to. "I just need to get across the street." His hand found a pole and he pulled himself forward. The other hand swatted air. The conductor caught it.

"You're in no shape to go out there yourself," the conductor said. "You're liable to fall and crack your head worse than you have already. There's bound to be a gendarme nearby. I'm going to get you some help, just hold on."

Hansi grabbed the conductor with both hands. With the little strength he had left, he drew the man's face close to his own. White spots began to flood his view. "Please, sir, no gendarmes!"

The conductor hesitated. "Are you in some kind of trouble, son?"

Hansi's hands shook involuntarily. "I beg you, please don't call the gendarmes."

The words dribbled out in a whisper, the last of his energy. He let go, fading into a sea of black, just beyond reach of the conductor's outstretched arms. He glanced off a bench before hitting the floor with a dull thud. The world spun wildly. Hansi closed his eyes to shut it out and focused every effort on trying to speak.

"Manolo" echoed through his mind, and, he hoped, across his lips.

Hansi awoke in a strange bed in a strange room. The window looking up to a dark alley told him he was below ground level. A faint light fell upon the thin curtain, providing the room's only illumination.

Maman was sitting at the end of the bed.

"Where am I?" Hansi asked, his voice soft and raspy.

"A safe place," she answered, sliding forward to take his hand.

"How did I get here?"

"Manolo said a man brought you to the restaurant."

"The conductor?"

"Yes, you had fainted on the tram. The doctor thinks you suffered a concussion. But he said if you feel better in the morning, we can travel."

"To Aunt Milly's?"

"Just rest, Hansi. We can talk later."

"Please, Maman, I want to know. Are we not going to Aunt Milly's?"

"I'm afraid it's no longer safe there for us, Hansi."

"No longer safe? Says who?"

"I've spoken to Manolo; I told him our plans. He thinks it would be better if we leave the country, at least for a while. He is working on finding a place for us in France."

Papa's words seared him with shame. If anything happens to me, promise me you'll go to Manolo. He'll know what to do."

Hansi hadn't kept the promise until it was too late and only after Maman was in danger.

"And what about Papa?" he said, the intensity gone from his voice. "How can we just leave him?"

The question hung in the air for a moment. His mother was trembling.

Hansi sat up. "Did something happen, Maman?"

"I spoke with Monsieur Pfaffenschneider today, while you were sleeping. The negotiations broke down. There will be no release. No one will speak to him any longer. He apologized profoundly, Hansi, but there's nothing more he can do. And with what's happened to you, he also urges us to leave the country."

They're all giving up, Hansi thought. But why?

"I learned something today," he said. "The Germans are planning something. Something in the next few days. Something big."

"The invasion? Oh, dear heavens!" she said, covering her mouth.

"We can't leave now, don't you see? Not without Papa!" Hansi took ahold of his mother by the shoulders. "Maman, please listen to me. We have friends here to help us—Monsieur Pfaffenschneider, Manolo, Father Jean, others in the Resistance—they'll help us. We can't leave!"

Maman looked down, her shoulders quaking.

"What is it, Maman? What happened?"

She looked up, her face sparkling with tears in the faint light.

"What? What is it?"

"There's nothing we can do now, Hansi,"

"Do about what? What are you talking about? Is Papa all right?"

"It's Father Jean."

"Did they catch him?" As soon as he asked, Hansi wished he hadn't.

Maman seemed not to hear his question. "I don't understand it. He is always so careful with his car."

"What happened?"

"There's been an accident. Something wrong with the brakes."

"Is he...?"

"I'm sorry, dear, it's true. He's dead."

CHAPTER FORTY-SEVEN

Maman explained that Father Jean lost control and his car plunged down the steep bank along the Pétrusse and was killed instantly.

"I don't believe it," Hansi protested.

"I can hardly believe it myself. He was such a good man," Maman said.

"No, Maman. I don't believe it was an accident."

She shook her head. "What on earth do you mean?"

Maman had enough to worry about, so Hansi didn't reply. He was convinced Schlinge chased Father Jean off the road. His fear of the man was matched only by his hatred.

Manolo was now in charge of their safety. The plan was to hide out in the city for a few days, perhaps a week, until the Resistance secured their passage to France.

In the meantime, he gave them strict instructions not only to stay in the flat, but to keep the curtains closed, the lights off, and voices to a whisper.

"Gestapo men—they walk the street, this street!" he said, pointing through the wall. He tapped his watch. "We move you soon. No worry. Very soon."

Being hidden away in the two-room flat became tiresome at once. Manolo needn't have worried about them making noise, for the flat had neither phonograph nor radio. The few books were not helpful either—Italian volumes without pictures except for a dusty three-volume encyclopedia. Hansi had to look at them in the bathroom where he could close the door and turn on the light. Another time he watched raindrops bounce off the asphalt in the back alley, peeking through gaps in the curtains while Maman dozed or did needlework in a rocking chair. Very few words passed between them. By the end of the first day the boredom was unbearable.

On the morning of the second day, while Maman was still asleep, Manolo delivered some food and supplies. He brought bread and cheese, mineral water, hard salami, plums, a small suitcase full of odd-fitting clothes, some toiletries, and, for Hansi, a blank sketchbook and pencil.

"It's not much, my boy, but not long now and I find you and Mama better place. More room, fresh air."

"We can never repay you," Hansi replied. "Thank you, Manolo."

Manolo smiled. "Your father helps many people. Not just now, with war coming, but before. When I come to Luxembourg, he helped me and my family. Nobody help me but your father." Tears filled his eyes. "Hansi, let me tell you. No Papa, no ristorante."

"I want to ask you something, Manolo," Hansi said. "You have no idea where my father is, do you?"

Manolo looked away, hesitating. "No, Hansi. Everyone works hard to find him. A friend in the gendarmes, he tries very hard. We need more time. Good news soon, yes?" Manolo put on his cap and pulled his coat tight. "Rain never stops. I must go back to the ristorante."

Hansi walked him to the door. Manolo drew back the curtain over the window just enough to see a figure across the street and then flipped the porch light on and then quickly off. The figure moved off.

"I come later, Hansi. Say hello to Mama. Don't worry, my boy. Soon! Very soon!"

Hansi touched Manolo's arm. "We're not waiting for Papa, are we?"

Manolo hesitated again.

"I can see it in your eyes," Hansi said. "You know something you're not telling me. Please, Manolo, I want to know the truth. Please tell me."

Manolo's face was tight with pain. "But your poor Mama. I don't want her to worry. She is weak. She needs rest. Somewhere far away, somewhere safe."

"Tell me," Hansi repeated, tugging at Manolo's coat. "Is Papa… dead?"

Manolo removed his cap and turned back to Hansi. "I don't know," he said in a low voice. "My Luxembourgish is not so good. But I speak to you man to man. From now on, you are the man of the house. I'm sorry, Hansi, but we make plans for the worst. In Poland, they have Resistance men before the Germans come. Gestapo in Poland makes trouble, frightens people, beating people. Some people," he paused, "disappear." He patted Hansi on the arm. "No court, no trial."

Hansi couldn't believe what he was hearing.

Manolo closed his eyes before speaking slowly. "No body for the family. No priest, no church. Only nothing."

Hansi understood his Luxembourgish completely.

"I'm sorry. That's why you and Mama must go. If your Papa never comes back and the Germans come, you'll never be safe. They hunt like wolves—wives, children, the whole family. Go to France, be safe."

Manolo opened the door to leave. A blast of wind caught it and blew it wide open, showering Hansi with sheets of frigid rain. He stood there, watching Manolo's bulky silhouette ascend to the street and disappear into the chilling grayness.

Maman appeared beside Hansi. She closed the door with a shudder. "Is everything all right?"

Hansi could not look at her. He could hardly speak. "Yes, Maman," he muttered. "Everything is fine."

Manolo's revelation was the gust against Hansi's house of cards. After all he had been through, from his first encounter with Schlinge at the Casemates to his narrow escape at St. John's, facing a real bomb seemed preferable to facing the bomb of this final truth—that all hope of seeing his father again was lost.

Hansi went directly to the bedroom, locked the door behind him, and fell into bed. Cramming his face deep into the pillow, he wept.

He lay there all day.

When he finally emerged, it was dark outside but still raining. Manolo had returned, sitting at the table, still in his raincoat. Maman was pouring tea into his cup.

"Everything is ready," Manolo said, warming his hands over the steam. "Tomorrow morning a truck comes, furniture inside.

Two large—" He couldn't find the word, so he drew the shape of a box with his fingers. "For clothes."

"Wardrobes," Hansi said.

"Yes! Men will bring wardrobes here. Later, other men will come back. They will knock on the door three times." He demonstrated the precise rhythm on the table—tap, tap-tap. "They wait five minutes and come inside. You and Mama hide inside."

"The wardrobes?" Maman asked, incredulous.

He nodded.

"One hour only, Mama. I promise." He smiled. "You and Hansi go to France. You and Hansi are safe."

"That's it?" Hansi asked. "We'll live in France, pretending to be French?"

Manolo frowned. "Yes." He got up, thanked Maman for the tea, and put his coat back on. He signaled the watch and waited for the return signal.

"Thank you, Manolo," Maman said.

Manolo tipped his hat and disappeared down the street.

Maman plopped down at the table and started to cry. "It's terribly selfish of me, I know, but I wish I had had a chance to gather a few things from our flat," she said. "There just wasn't time. I know I can always get other clothes, but some things you can't replace. To leave our photo album behind is too hard to bear."

Hansi understood. Was this how they'd go? Simply close the wardrobes and leave? Forever? Without Papa?

The brown leather album was a wedding gift. It was the family archive—pictures, birth certificates, even a lock of Hansi's baby hair.

He got an idea.

CHAPTER FORTY-EIGHT

Rain drummed against the windows all evening, sending Maman to bed early.

Hansi took advantage of the opportunity. Once he was sure she was sleeping soundly, he retrieved the envelope from under his mattress, stowed it into his bag, and slipped out the front door. With no umbrella, the cold drops quickly penetrated his thin cotton jacket.

Hansi climbed a few steps to bring his eyes level with the sidewalk. He scanned the street—it looked empty as far as he could tell, so he continued. At the top of the stairs, he paused again to peer intently into the dark doorway across the street. It was impossible to tell if the lookout was still there. He would take the chance.

Hansi waited for a surge in the shower and stood up. A final glance and the doorway had not changed. He walked briskly away until he came to the corner and looked back. The street was empty.

The first task was getting his bearings. The street names were unfamiliar to him, and with the blackout it was impossible to distinguish landmarks or even walk toward the glow of the city. For what seemed like forever, Hansi wandered the streets, pelted by the rain, until he stumbled across tram tracks. He waited at a nearby stop, shivering under the never-ending sheets, until the tram finally arrived. He was lucky in two respects—the tram was heading toward the City Center and it was warm.

The Grund seemed alien that night. The streets were hidden and deserted. St. John's was just a dark memory of Father Jean. Hansi would have passed his own building except for the habit of memory, which reminded him he had walked far enough.

Hansi kept on, to the second building down. The windows were difficult to make out but there was just enough light to count three up and two to the right. He knelt and found a stone. The first missed and so did the second before the third one found its mark and rattled off the pane. The window came open.

"Peter, it's me! Hansi!"

They met inside on the first-floor landing.

"You're the last person I'd expect to see again," Peter said. "I figured you ran off like Paul."

Hansi ignored the insult. "Do you still see Karin after school?"

Peter hesitated. "Maybe I do, maybe I don't. Are you still sore over that?"

"No. I never was upset about that."

"You sure fooled me. If jealousy was a sickness, you'd be in the hospital." Peter seemed to enjoy provoking Hansi.

"Look, Peter, that's not why I'm here," Hansi said. "I need your help. I need you to give her something after school."

"Didn't you hear? They've closed school until further notice."

Hansi looked down. "Because of Father Jean. Yes, I heard," he said.

Peter shook his head disparagingly. "My father said he was drunk yesterday and crashed his car."

"Who told him that?"

"I don't know, but that's what everyone seems to think."

"It's a lie, Peter. I don't care what you've heard, it's a lie. Father Jean was a good man."

"How would you know?"

"I can't explain now. There's no time. But believe me, Peter, Father Jean wasn't drunk, and his crash was no accident. Everything terrible in Luxembourg happens for one reason: the Germans."

"That's rich, Hansi, blaming Germany for all that's wrong in the world. I think you're just mad that your little Fraulein likes me more than you. If you came all this way on a night like tonight to try to convince me that Karin is part of the evil conspiracy, you've let yourself get soaked for nothing!"

Hansi wanted to punch Peter right in the mouth.

"That's not what I meant! Forget I said anything about Germany. I need your help, Peter. I need you to take this note to Karin tomorrow. Please, will you do it for me?" He shoved the envelope into Peter's hands and squeezed them shut.

Peter jerked his hands away. "And why should I?"

Hansi drew close to Peter and looked him right in the eye. "Because if you don't, Karin could get hurt."

Peter stepped back. "Oh, I see now. Your little love letter is going to protect her. And win her back in the process. How touching! Do you think I'm that stupid? Come on, Hansi, what kind of fool do you take me for?" Peter threw the envelope down at Hansi's feet.

"Peter, please listen to me." Hansi picked the letter up. "If I was trying to—well—win her back as you say, why would I come to you?"

The question penetrated.

"I came to you because I can't go to her. I can't go near her house."

"Are you in trouble?"

Hansi nodded.

"And I can't trust the post. So, will you please just take this to her?"

Peter paused, suddenly serious.

"Not unless you tell me what's going on. Why are you in trouble, and why do you have to warn Karin?"

Hansi hesitated, unsure whether he should take the risk of telling Peter anything more. But after a moment, he realized he had little choice.

"I can't explain everything, Peter, but the Germans are planning something, and it's coming any day now."

"The invasion? Any day? How do you know?"

"I don't know. But I need to warn Karin. Look, if I'm wrong, all the better. No one gets hurt, and I'll be gone from Luxembourg anyway. But I need you to deliver this note. Please, Peter, I'm begging you!"

Hansi thrust the envelope forward. Peter stared at it, glanced at Hansi, and then back at the envelope. Then slowly he reached up and took it.

Hansi gripped Peter's arm. "Thank you," he said. "Tomorrow, don't forget."

Hansi was shivering when he flew out the door and took off up the alley. He ignored the splashes he was making, anxious to regenerate some body heat. In front of his own building, he slowed and jumped the steps before slipping into the back entrance. A pool quickly formed around his feet when he paused inside to listen.

The stairwell was empty when Hansi got to the second floor and retrieved his key. He slid it into the lock with extreme care and turned it slowly before passing inside. The air was heavy and stale in the dark hallway. In the living room, he checked the curtains before turning on the lamp. His throat seized—everything in the room, from picture frames to pillows, books to chairs, was upturned in a random heap on the floor.

He was fortunate to find Maman's album in the pile of books and papers in the center of the floor. He stowed it in his bag and went to his room. It had been similarly violated, and Dieter's box was gone.

With a chair from the kitchen, Hansi returned to the hallway. He opened the small utility closet at the end of the hall and placed the chair inside so he could step up and reach its ceiling. He slid his hand along the edge of a wooden panel that provided access to the attic. With a firm push the panel gave way and Hansi stepped up onto the shelf in the closet. The attic was completely dark, but Hansi knew exactly where to find the tin box his father used to store important papers.

In a moment Hansi was down and had the box open. He pushed aside a bundle of old letters, some receipts, and other official-looking papers for what he was most interested in—an envelope full of money. He never told Maman and Papa he had discovered the box and the family's emergency fund. It would be helpful in France.

He put the envelope in his shirt pocket, grateful the Gestapo had not found it. But when he set the box down and got up to leave, Hansi saw something sparkle at the bottom of the box. His heart leapt when he realized what it was—the slender shaft of a folding knife emblazoned with the Nazi eagle and swastika: Schlinge's knife! Without another thought, Hansi put the knife in his pocket.

Errand completed, he was anxious to leave. He stepped down off the chair and started to drag it back to the kitchen. The thought struck him—*how silly if I'm never returning*.

He let go and stepped backward, striking something that wasn't in the hall before. A shock wave reverberated through his body when he realized that the something was a *someone*. And before he could react, that someone had his arm around Hansi's chest and the other over his mouth. He was trapped.

CHAPTER FORTY-NINE

"Don't say a word," the man whispered sharply, close to Hansi's ear. The man spoke with an accent, but it wasn't German. And he was restraining Hansi using only his hands.

The man waited and then whispered again. "Do not shout and I will release you, understood?"

Hansi nodded but still, the man held on. Hansi nodded again, more vigorously before the man finally released him.

"You should not be here," the man said. "We must return at once."

Immediately Hansi realized two things: the man was not a Gestapo agent and his accent was Italian. He must have been watching the safe house when Hansi left, perhaps even from the darkened doorway across the street.

"Did anyone see you enter the building? Anyone in the stairway when you came in?"

Hansi shook his head.

"Are you sure?"

"Our building is quiet this time of night. No one knows I'm here, I'm sure of it."

The man stepped into the front room and peered down at the street. Then he crossed to the back and scanned the alley before returning to the hallway. He approached the door, listened, and then motioned to Hansi to follow. They crept carefully out of the building, but then the man picked up speed, walking quickly and silently through the dark behind the row of flats. Finally, when they had reached the cliffs and the Pont Adolphe, he spoke again.

"You put your mother and all of us in great danger," he said. In the light of the streetlamp, Hansi got his first good look at the man. In a gray sweater and woolen cap, his tall and square frame reminded Hansi of a younger version of Manolo, with the same dark eyes that darted at every sound.

"So you are a part of the Resistance too?" Hansi asked.

"Listen, don't speak! If anyone stops us along the way, I am Raul, and you are coming to visit my son Antonio. That is all you need to know."

"Look, I'm sorry—I didn't think I would be putting anyone at risk."

"Leave the thinking to others. What were you doing there?"

"I wanted to get a photo album for my mother, that's all," Hansi said.

The man called Raul said nothing. He pressed on, striding more briskly than before, forcing Hansi to alternate between walking fast and occasionally jogging to keep up. Winding through the dark streets they eventually came back to the safe house and slipped quietly back inside. After a quick peek at his mother, who was still sleeping soundly, Hansi went straight to bed.

The next morning, Hansi awoke to the sound of rain drumming on the window. Maman sat with a cup of coffee in the kitchen. Raul had stood guard all night and before he left gave Maman plenty of reason to be upset with Hansi. But after she had sorted through the belongings Hansi had retrieved and thumbed through the black and white photographs in the album, a smile broke across her face.

When the truck arrived around ten o'clock to unload the wardrobes, Manolo lectured both of them. Maman nodded with feigned contrition.

Before he left, Manolo made them climb inside the wardrobes to test their fit. The larger of the two, reaching nearly to the ceiling, provided plenty of room for Maman to sit on a small suitcase. But after only a few seconds with the door closed she had to get out.

Hansi was worried.

"I'll be fine when the time comes," she said, not entirely convincing. "But not before."

Hansi's wardrobe was little more than a plain wooden box painted dull yellow, chipping at the corners and edges. Climbing inside, Hansi found it to be too short to stand in and not wide enough to sit. He could either crouch with his head bent or sit with his shoulders twisted—neither option comfortable.

The minutes of the afternoon ticked by as slowly as the raindrops dripping off the gutter in a plop-plop-plop. At three, according to Manolo's instructions, Hansi helped Maman climb in and take her seat on the suitcase in her wardrobe. He handed her an extra blanket from the bed and asked, "Are you going to be all right, Maman?"

She nodded nervously.

"Then I'll see you soon," he said, gently kissing her on each cheek before closing the door.

Manolo's strict instructions to say nothing once they were inside would help Hansi, but he would barely have enough time.

He moved quietly into the bedroom and grabbed two corners of the blanket he had positioned under his bed earlier in the day. He pulled it across the floor, out of the bedroom, and into the front room, every book from Manolo's shelves riding on it. Quickly he transferred the volumes from the blanket to the wardrobe, stuffed the blanket on top, and closed the door. With any luck, the movers wouldn't know the difference. Then, after a last look at the larger wardrobe, Hansi returned to the bedroom, slid open the window, and climbed out into the narrow back alley.

The rain had eased when Hansi slid along the buildings. In the cool mist every sound was amplified—every crunch beneath his shoe seemed to echo through the street. Under low, gray clouds, he pulled his jacket close and made a wide circuit around the block. In a dark doorway, he waited.

Before long, the low rumble of an engine rose in the distance. The sound grew and Hansi watched a black truck pass by. When he peered out, the truck slowed and stopped in front of the safe house. From deep in the shadow Hansi watched as two men got out, entered the flat, and then returned with first the large, and then the smaller wardrobe. Hansi mouthed a silent prayer for his mother being jostled inside. The men worked quickly, covering the wardrobes with a gray tarpaulin before securing everything with ropes. Doors slammed, gears groaned, and the truck rolled off. A moment later, Raul appeared on the sidewalk and walked casually away.

Hansi waited about five minutes longer, just to be sure. Only then, certain the street was clear, did he edge into the light. Like the night before, he had an errand in mind, but this time not in the Grund.

CHAPTER FIFTY

Hansi plunged into the stream of pedestrians on the Avenue de la Gare and strode quickly toward the city. A cold breeze channeled by the deep valley met him at the Pont Adolphe, wringing itself of the last of the rain. At the Parc du Casemates, he headed to the familiar spot where many a daydream had been captured in his sketchbook. A lifetime ago.

Karin was sitting on his bench—the one from which he had first seen her so many weeks before. He was relieved—Peter had come through. The collar of her navy woolen coat was turned up and secured by a red scarf. The ponytail was gone, replaced by blond waves spilling out beneath a knit cap and cascading down her shoulders. Hansi's heart quickened when he saw her.

When their eyes met, Hansi saw the color drain from her reddened cheeks. He drew closer and she sprung up from the bench, clutching the straps of her shoulder bag so tightly that Hansi could see the raised tendons of her wrists. She said nothing.

"Thanks for coming," Hansi said. "I wasn't sure you would."

Karin, her entire body quivering, bit her lip. "I was convinced you wouldn't."

"Huh?" Hansi asked, confused. "What do you mean?"

"Father told me you were dead," she blurted. "That crash involving the priest."

"Tell your father I'm sorry to disappoint him," Hansi replied. "Father Jean died alone."

Karin turned away.

"I'm sorry," Hansi said. "I'm sorry for a lot of things."

She didn't move.

"I should have trusted you. Not just with helping me look for my father, but other things too."

"What other things?"

Hansi scraped his lower lip with his teeth, struggling for the words. "Peter," he said. "I'm a fool to think…"

"To think that there was really something between him and me? A boy like Peter? Really, Hansi, I tried to tell you, there is nothing and there never has been. He liked to follow me around, that's all."

"It didn't look that way. Peter said it himself. You felt sorry for me and that's why you helped me." Hansi shook himself. "Look, it doesn't matter—about Peter that is. That's not why I'm here."

"Peter said those things, I didn't."

"You didn't disagree as I recall."

"I was upset at you. You left me behind when you went to the Dumont's house. After that day we had spent together, working side by side, you didn't trust me. I told you I wouldn't speak to my father and I haven't, even to this day. Even after he tried to convince me you were part of the terrorist network, I refused to believe him. I still refuse. With Peter, I only wanted to make you jealous. And I didn't tell my father we were going to Trier, I swear!"

Hansi took a deep breath. "Why would your father say such things about me?"

"I don't know," she answered.

"Did he tell you what Schlinge said to me?"

Karin shook her head.

"Schlinge promised to take me away and kill me. Your father wanted to speak to him right away, and so Schlinge threw me down the stairs of your cellar instead. Did he tell you that? Did he tell you if Fritz hadn't helped me escape, Schlinge would have come down and finished the job?"

"Is that why you came here, to make me hate my father?"

"No, Karin, but you must open your eyes. Your father knows everything—not just what Schlinge has been up to with me, but more. Much more."

"What do you mean?"

"Schlinge told me something is about to happen. Something big—so big that everything will change."

"I don't understand."

"It can only be one thing, Karin—an invasion."

"No, Hansi!"

"I'm afraid so. I wish it were anything else, but that's why I had to meet you here."

"What do you expect me to do, Hansi? Call the gendarmes, have them arrest my father?"

"I want you to come with me."

Her eyes lifted. "Did you find another clue?"

He shook his head.

"To France. With Maman and me."

CHAPTER FIFTY-ONE

Karin's expression changed. "You're serious."

"My mother is on her way now."

Karin shook her head. "I couldn't even begin to talk to my parents about this—"

"You wouldn't."

She touched his arm. "How could I? Just… disappear?"

"Karin, listen to me very carefully. Your father hasn't told you about what's really happening in Poland. The German army is ruthless. They've bombed cities, burned villages, arrested and killed hundreds, maybe thousands of innocent people. No one is safe—"

"What does this have to do with me leaving?"

"Once France and Britain move, they will punish Germany. Just like after the last war. If you go home to Berlin, war will come. You won't be safe. Please, Karin, come with me."

Karin buried her face in her hands. "I can't, Hansi," she said. "I just can't."

Hansi pulled her hands away and took them in his. He had never wanted anything as much as he did in that moment. What words were powerless to do, perhaps his eyes could accomplish.

"Please, Karin," he said, barely above a whisper. "I'm begging you."

Her gaze betrayed the battle inside. He waited. His appeal at its end. A cold gust from deep in the valley swept over them, chilling her expression. She pushed away.

"No. No one knows the future. And even if what you say is true, my place is still at home. Even such as it is. I'm sorry, Hansi."

Hansi exhaled slowly and closed his eyes.

What did you expect? Let's escape to France! Sure, let's go!

Raindrops dampened his upturned face. In the silence, he forced back tears, more at himself for asking than her for answering.

He reached into his bag.

"I have something for you," he said, his voice quaking.

Karin unfolded a piece of paper, a drawing. The scene was of the city skyline, at night, glowing beneath sparkling stars. There was the Cathedral, the Palace, the casemate walls, and the Grund. And at the center, the round silhouette of the Ferris wheel. The night of the fair he had poured every bit of skill into capturing the serenity and magic of the moment they enjoyed together at the top of the world.

"It's beautiful, Hansi," Karin said, tears at the rims of her eyes.

Though he could not speak, in that moment he could see every raindrop, each one a sparkling diamond falling from the sky. They fell in slow motion, each one a soft caress on her golden head and luminous face. She was never more beautiful.

His body quaked at the torture of a disintegrating heart and punishing head—this is the end.

"Addi, " he said.

"Auf wiedersehen, Hansi," she whispered back, turning away.

He sucked in a breath and turned. Each step up, a thousand tons.

Where the walk turned behind the rocks, Hansi stopped. He turned for one last look. Unsettled clouds churned overhead, but then, as if in the eye of the storm, the gusts calmed for an instant.

Karin, still beside the bench, looked up and their eyes met.

She broke into a run, and they embraced on the edge of the cliff as the gusts swept over them. Hansi held her tight, breathing deeply through her golden hair. She shuddered in his arms. For the first time in his life, he felt free and unafraid. And sad as he never knew sadness before.

The spell was broken by the sound of a revving engine coming from the edge of the park. Hansi and Karin looked up and through the mist saw a brown truck coming to a stop on the far side of the park. The markings were unmistakable: Trier Uniformem.

Hansi swept Karin behind an outcropping of rock. First one and then a second dark figure emerged from the truck. The first one removed a hat-sized cardboard box from the back of the truck, and together they disappeared into the museum building nearby. Then the street fell quiet.

Convinced they were gone, Hansi stepped out from behind the rocks, taking Karin by the hand, and ran up the sidewalk. They ran across the spongy grass and arrived at the truck, where he knelt near the rear tire. He ran his hand through a thin coating of red mud.

"This is from the Thillenberg mines," he said, rubbing his fingers together. "This is the truck that nearly killed us at the mill."

"But how could it be?" Karin said. "Kurt said Bittendorf's truck crashed."

"That's what he was told."

Hansi stepped to the back of the truck. Karin followed. He opened one side and Karin the other. He climbed inside and began pushing away the blue and brown uniforms that hung in their racks. Karin joined him and searched the other side.

"What are we looking for?" she asked.

Hansi knelt and ran his hands along the smooth metal floor.

"Explosives."

"Didn't you see the box?"

"Explosives come in crates. I expected wooden crates. The Gestapo wouldn't let something like Bittendorf's death stop them. Whoever's driving this truck now is probably still smuggling explosives." He stood up. "Keep looking. I'm going to check out the cab."

He climbed through the doorway at the front of the cargo section as a new shower began to drum on the roof. He bent down to feel under the dash and seats. If not explosives, perhaps he could find written evidence he could take to the Army.

Crawling below the level of the windshield, he failed to see the car that turned into the park up ahead. He also failed to see it switch its headlights off. Karin, digging through the uniforms in the back, missed it, too. Neither one noticed the car cut its engine and roll forward, stopping silently only meters away.

Hansi's hand hit upon a piece of paper.

"This truck was definitely in Differdange," Hansi called out, trying his luck now beneath the other seat.

"How do you know?" Karin asked.

Hansi stood up and Karin came forward. They were facing forward letting the faint light illuminate a crumpled map, upon which a dark pencil line had marked a route from Differdange to Luxembourg City and scribbled the word "Kasematten," the Casemates.

"At least you found something," she said. "There's nothing back here,"

"What are you looking for, my dear?" The voice came from behind the truck, deep and familiar.

Karin spun around. Hansi looked up.

Herr Blik, like a phantom, stepped out of the mist, pistol raised.

CHAPTER FIFTY-TWO

In the growing shower, Blik's chin was tucked under the shelter of his wide-brimmed hat. His teeth were bared in a sneer, and his eyes, black and cold, bored right into Karin.

"To say I'm disappointed would be an understatement, my dear. A severe understatement."

"Why are you here, Father?"

"You have deliberately disobeyed me, Karin. You have forfeited the right to ask questions. Step to the side, please."

Hansi saw it in his eyes. Blik would pull the trigger as soon as Karin moved away.

"Not until you answer me. What is this truck doing here? What were the men unloading?"

Blik forced a cunning grin. "What does it look like, Karin? I'd say they are delivering uniforms, don't you? Now stand aside."

Hansi's mind revved beyond its limit. Fleeing through the front doors of the cab would take precious seconds. Blik would get a clear shot.

"Put that away and I will," Karin said.

"I will do no such thing. This mongrel has hypnotized you against me. He is a dangerous criminal, who has evaded us for the last time."

"Hansi? That's ridiculous!"

"Come now, Karin, let's examine that. He was at the Gare the afternoon of the bombing. He knows the prime suspect, and his father is the secondary one. If he is so innocent, then why does he refuse to speak to the police and insist on fleeing every time an official tries to speak with him? And why does he continue to associate with the underground terrorist movement in this country? Open your eyes, Karin, before it's too late. Now for the last time, stand aside!"

Karin trembled but didn't budge.

While they had been arguing, Hansi took advantage of the only option. Slowly, he moved his arm backward, careful to keep it hidden behind Karin's body. Without taking his eyes off Blik, he found what he was looking for rising from the center of the floor. Grasping it, his body twisted.

"What are you doing?" Blik snarled, but it was too late.

Hansi jerked on the handbrake and the truck let go.

Blik's eyes ballooned in the instant before he jumped.

Karin screamed and fell back into Hansi.

The momentum pressed them against the dashboard. The truck hurtled down the slope toward a turnaround at the edge of the cliff.

Hansi had traded Blik's bullet for a horrible crash that would kill them both. He'd been a fool. Again.

The truck wobbled and hit the curb, lurching Hansi and Karin from the center of the cab. Hansi's arm slipped around Karin's waist, and he managed a quick twist to shield her from the crash against the far door, which came with a jolt.

The curb slowed the truck, but only for a moment, serving instead to correct the course down the slope. The turnaround loomed ahead. The barrier at the edge of the cliff was built for humans, not a truck.

As the truck accelerated, its center of gravity shifted back to the middle. Hansi got an idea, but Karin's body pinned him against the door. He found her hips and pushed.

"The wheel!"

He flung her forward.

She slid across the dashboard, arms outstretched. Her hands were only centimeters from the steering wheel when she tripped over the handbrake, glanced off the gear shift, and went down.

Hansi braced for the crash against the barrier and the open air beyond the cliff.

But Karin saved them, grasping the steering wheel as she fell.

The force of the turn jerked the truck sideways. The tires squealed, then one lifted, and then the truck teetered for a moment until the far curb finished it off.

The truck smacked on its side, tossing the insides like it was a toy in the hands of a giant. Its flank ground against the stone curb in a shower of sparks, bleeding it of its speed. The truck scraped to a halt at the bottom of the slope, only meters from the barrier.

For a moment all was silent except for the dying rhythm of a spinning tire.

Hansi clawed away a mass of uniforms. Somehow, he had ended up in the cargo compartment amidst the mass of blue and brown shirts, trousers, and coveralls. Something was jabbing him in his side—a hanger—but by some miracle, he was unhurt.

"Karin?" he called.

Her head appeared in the passage between the cargo compartment and the cab, now horizontal in front of him.

Her eyes were mere slits, and she was rubbing her head.

"Are you alright?"

"I think so," she replied, blinking slowly.

Hansi crawled to her. She was never so beautiful. He wanted to take her in his arms.

"You saved us," he said.

"We've got to get out of here," she said. "It may be too late already. Come on."

Karin climbed over him and the jumbled uniforms to exit first. Hansi followed. Outside, the rain was steady. Karin stopped in thought. Back up the slope in the growing fog, Blik was hunched over but upright and moving toward them.

"This way," Hansi said, pointing at the exit of the park, the same place they had escaped Schlinge the first day they met.

"No," Karin said. "I can't go. But you can, Hansi, and you must."

"I can't just leave you here—"

"Don't worry, I'll deal with Father. He'll be furious and lock me in my room for a while, but once he realizes you're gone, he'll calm down."

Hansi hesitated.

"Go!" she said. "Before something terrible happens!"

Time stopped as the words echoed in Hansi's mind. Blik, a shadow in the distance, moved clumsily down the slope, dragging one leg behind him. Karin, clutching Hansi's hands, was pleading with her eyes. Hansi imagined her locked away in her room. Then the realization exploded in his mind.

"Do you remember the day we first met, Karin?"

"Yes, Hansi, but there's no time—"

"Do you remember the tunnel when the lights went out? Remember the voices?

"Yes—no! What do you mean?"

"One of them said he needed someone 'comfortable with the dark.'"

"So?"

"Don't you see? Bittendorf. He's comfortable with the dark."

"Yes, he's blind. I don't follow."

"Bittendorf was in the tunnel that day. With Schlinge. They were preparing something bigger than the bombing of the Gare. Something right here!"

"Are you sure?"

"As sure as anything I've known since the day I met you," he said, turning toward the cliffs.

A look of fear swept over her.

"Where are you going?"

Hansi took her by the shoulders and drew his face close. He tried to cover the knot in his throat with a brave smile. He looked deep into her eyes and embraced her one last time. "Tell your father I've jumped a tram for the Gare."

She pushed him away, tears streaming down her face.

"You're going to the tunnels," she said.

Nodding, he stepped away.

Karin broke into a run up the slope, fading into the mist toward her father. Hansi didn't see them meet. He was flying down the sidewalk, the same sidewalk he and Karin had used to flee from Schlinge, but this time in the opposite direction toward the tunnel and the dangers inside. His heart throbbed and the rain stung his face. He doubted he would ever see Karin again. Deep down, he wondered if he'd ever see anyone again.

CHAPTER FIFTY-THREE

A chain hung across the entrance to the tunnel with a wooden sign: Closed for Repairs. He stepped over it and entered with caution—the lights in the tunnel were off. The air-raid shelter chamber where he and Karin exchanged their first words was completely dark. Hands along the damp wall guided him to the back of the chamber and the door.

It was locked, not a surprise. He felt the keyhole below the handle. Schlinge's knife might fit. He ran his fingers along the shaft to locate the tab that released the blade. In the darkness, the knife slipped out of his hand and clattered to the floor.

On his knees he slid his hands along the tunnel floor, cold and sandy and wet. His heart quickened. This mission might end before it begins. Frantically he made a wider sweep, touching a bench in one direction and the bottom of the door in the other. Flakes of metal along the bottom of the door frame stuck to his fingers. His quick movements almost missed it. A fingertip grazed something heavy. The knife was lengthwise in the corner of the floor.

More careful now, Hansi found the tab and pressed it. The narrow blade sprung out. He found the keyhole and inserted the tip of the knife. It slid in about halfway before wedging tight. He twisted, gently at first and then with force—the mechanism moved a little, and so he twisted in the other direction. The knife slid in further. The ancient mechanism seemed to be crumbling inside.

Hope rose. He worked harder, rattling the lock and thumping the door against the bolt. His hands burned from the effort, and still the door held. Then, about to give up, he experienced three things happening at once: a loud click, the door letting go, and his body falling backward. The door swung open and clanged against the wall with a noise loud enough to wake the city above him.

He froze. There was nothing to be done. *Here I am.*

A tense minute ticked by while the tunnel remained silent, so he stood up and felt for the door.

His stomach dropped. At the keyhole, only a short stump of metal was left. The hilt was lost in the darkness, his only weapon gone.

At least the door was open. He stepped through only to be met by an unwelcome air, cold and stale. He continued one hand against the rough stone wall and the other out in front. The corridor sloped down. He moved along for a few minutes, straining both his ears and eyes for something other than silent darkness.

He was moving well, feeling his way, drawing the path in his mind. He decided to count steps—both for proportions and to focus his mind on something other than the darkness.

The one-hundred-and-fourteenth step seemed to miss the floor. Then it hit something not far below, but by then his balance was lost. Momentum carried him forward, the next step lower than the one before, and he realized he had missed a flight of steps.

By instinct, he flung his arms forward. He hit the floor, hands first, elbows next, chin third, then the rest of his body across the sharp stones. He plowed across the floor until THUNK—he struck something hard.

The white burst was only in his mind. He sat up against the cool stone and let his head clear. It could have been worse. It could have been deadly.

On his hands and knees, he felt his surroundings to sketch the scene in his mind. He had come to an intersection of two tunnels, the second lower than the first—hence the steps. The lower tunnel sloped decidedly to his left. Deeper. Something urged him to go that way. But from now on, he would slide his feet.

A few steps on, his shoe scuffed something that moved under his sole. He jumped at the thought of a snake but in the next instant argued against the idea—snakes were both uncommon and unlikely to inhabit the cold of a casemate tunnel. A few steps later he brushed up against the thing again—it only moved when he pushed against it.

He dropped down and found it. A cord or rope of some kind, but the texture was wrong. Rough and, in some places, sticky. As far as he could reach in both directions the length of the tunnel. Then he found a second one. The covering was a kind of cloth wrapping. He found a gap and dug through the stickiness to a hard core.

A new chill swept through him. These were not ropes, but wires. Wires for explosives.

CHAPTER FIFTY-FOUR

Hansi crouched and used the wire to guide him on. Soon his legs began to burn, and so he raised up and shuffled on as before, keeping contact with a foot or an occasional hand. He continued this way for several minutes and progressed more quickly as he gained confidence. Ahead, he could make out the wire's path shift from the right of the tunnel to the left and then disappear beyond a corner.

Hansi stopped—could he really see or was his mind playing tricks?

He blinked. The distinct shape of the tunnel was visible, he was sure—smooth floor, jagged top and sides. Ahead, it intersected with another passageway, the source of the light.

He came to the corner and paused. The wire turned left. He listened and discerned the slightest of sounds—a mix of voices and movements. His pulse quickened.

Hansi edged his face around the corner. The wire disappeared into darkness. In the opposite direction, about twenty meters up the corridor, a thin strip of light leaked from under a door. The source of the sounds.

He followed the wire into the darkness. The tunnel curved right and sloped down. Beyond the last of the light, he shuffled forward as before.

His hand came to an opening on the right. His foot tapped a metal threshold. He stooped and, taking the wires in both hands, followed them through the doorway. The wall fell away on both sides and the sound of his shuffling changed—he had come to a room or chamber. He inched forward into the space, the wires his only guide. A short meter later, he stopped. The sheathing was gone, the bare wires exposed. A half a meter more the wires came to two metal posts anchored into a wooden block. Metal nuts secured the main wires, and beyond them a web of other bare wires. Everything was covered by sticky goo.

Hansi's heart thundered in his chest. He followed one of the wires. It continued up and then over the side of a wooden crate. Carefully he reached inside. His fingers came upon a slender tube and then another, and another.

Panic filled the chamber. He followed a second and then a third of the spidery wires, each to a new crate. He counted at least three crates to the right, left, high, and deep. Alone in the dark, his mind sketched a terrifying image—an entire room full of explosives.

His body began to shake. Not only was he in danger, but the staggering dimensions of the chamber made it clear the entire city was in grave peril. Rumor and legend told of secret tunnels leading to the Grand Ducal Palace. Schlinge's hints made terrible sense now—these explosives were the big something, the event that would change everything. These crates were more terrible than the bombing of the Gare and, he was forced to admit, even Papa's arrest. Alone in the dark, his body racked with pain, Hansi could not escape the conclusion—everything the Gestapo had done in Luxembourg led to this room. The destructive power contained in these crates was aimed not just at the Casemates or the Grand Ducal palace, but the nation itself.

A second revelation followed the first—and with greater power. He had held the truth from people he could have trusted. He might have gone to Manolo sooner; he could have trusted Father Jean, the superintendent, or even Monsieur Pfaffenschneider. But now it was too late. What he knew about Schlinge, Bittendorf, and Dieter was useless. The nation would pay for his failure.

The accusations growled like a demon in the dark. He should have left Karin out of this. He didn't really love her—he was indulging a selfish, boyish, romantic fantasy.

Powerless and paralyzed, Hansi quivered, fell against the doorframe, and sank down. Perhaps at this very moment, Bittendorf stooped over the plunger, snickering over another job well done, counting down the final seconds until everything would end in a singular, spectacular flash.

Water from deep in the rocks, cold trickles in a pool at the base of the wall, soaked quickly through Hansi's pants, startling him out of his despair.

Another voice—from a deeper, truer place—rose in a whisper.

Get up.

Hansi obeyed. Perhaps he could do something—

The knife! No—that was gone. *But the wires—*

Hansi dropped to the wires and began to rub away the globs from the terminals. He pinched a nut with his fingers and twisted. The nuts were torqued tight, and his fingers were soon raw from the effort. He moved on to crates. The wires came out of the dynamite sticks easily, but there were countless wires and countless sticks. Without light he could work for hours and never be sure he got them all. And though he really knew nothing about explosives, he was confident they worked in a chain reaction—blowing one stick was as good as blowing them all.

He came to the last option. If by some miracle he could escape, he could warn someone, anyone. Maybe now the gendarmes would finally believe him.

Hansi turned, grabbed the metal doorframe, and pulled himself through. He felt for where the wall turned, shuffled his feet across the wires, and positioned himself in the center of the passageway. He would run, back to the light, back to the corridor, and out.

He never took a step, blinded by the sudden, intense, and overwhelming light.

CHAPTER FIFTY-FIVE

Hansi shielded his eyes, lost his balance, and fell. But then came the realization, with great relief, that he had not been blown to bits. The lights in the tunnel had simply come on. His eyes adjusted and beheld what before only his mind could imagine—the chamber, as big as his living room, a web of shimmering wire covering crates stacked three and four high.

He got up and started running up the passageway, guided by the caged bulbs above him. He had rounded the curve, which brought the first intersection into view, when he heard the scrape of a metal door. And then voices. He stopped dead.

"Check everything one more time and be quick about it. I'll be waiting for you by the plunger." Schlinge!

"Come with me. It will go faster with your eyes," Bittendorf answered.

"I don't want to get any closer to that stuff than I have to," Schlinge said, irritated. "Besides, you're the expert. Now get on with it."

Bittendorf laughed. "Yes, that might be far enough."

"What?"

"Nothing. I'll be there in a minute. We'll roll the dice together."

There was a scuffing sound.

"Take your hands off me!" Bittendorf bellowed.

"What are you talking about?" Schlinge asked.

"Nothing. Like my old trench mate said, 'You never wish you had less wire.'"

"We gave you everything you requested."

Bittendorf laughed again. "No one could get the plans for this place. They don't exist. How was I to know the chamber was twice as far as it looks from up top? But no matter. We're like the rest of these rats down here. The only difference being that if I've got it wrong, I'll know what hits me."

"You fool! Stop talking and do what you're told."

"Whatever you say. As I figure it, I'm a dead man either way. A boom or a bang. The crates or a Gestapo pistol. Me—I'd rather go on my own, in a manner of speaking. I've been on borrowed time since '15 when that mustard gas blew back on me at Verdun. Ever since, I've seen more than enough misery for a blind man." He laughed again. "Hey, that's a joke, isn't it?"

Schlinge didn't reply. Hansi heard heavy, shuffling steps approaching. He froze for a minute, thinking, and got an idea.

When Bittendorf appeared in the corridor, Hansi had retreated past the chamber and pressed himself tightly against the wall.

Bittendorf kept a hand on the wall as he moved and would now and again stop, stoop, and touch the wires. His pale, wandering eyes reflected his concentration.

At the doorway of the chamber he paused, tossed his head back, and sniffed the air like an opossum. Hansi held his breath. Bittendorf turned and entered. Once inside, Hansi let out a slow, silent breath.

Bittendorf made soft rustling sounds as he worked. After a few minutes he reappeared outside the chamber, and Hansi held his breath again. Bittendorf turned back up the corridor, repeating his method of crouching, touching, and shuffling. And then, after a few steps, he stopped.

He rotated his head slowly back. Hansi's lungs screamed for air. If not for Bittendorf's blindness, he would have been staring right at Hansi. Hansi's lungs hurt. Then Bittendorf turned to leave.

A few seconds more, and Hansi could breathe.

Bittendorf took one step, then another, and then stopped.

"You, along the wall, what do you want?" he asked.

Hansi clenched every muscle in his frame trying to squeeze another few seconds out.

"It's no use pretending—I know you're there. I knew it when I first came around the bend."

Hansi let go. His breath made guttural, animal sounds.

Bittendorf let out a twisted smile and started up again. "Hansi, is it? You should have left when you had the chance. You're a sausage in the pot now," he chuckled.

Hansi followed.

"Are you really going to go through with this? Don't you realize what you're doing? Don't you know where you are?"

"Thillenberg mine or the Eiffel Tower—it makes no difference to me, boy. I'm boiling right beside you. We're somewhere in Luxembourg City, right?"

"In the casemate tunnels. Below the city. Perhaps below the Palace," Hansi replied.

"You did a good job holding your breath," Bittendorf said, "but you were too close. The air is cool back around the curve. You've been busy—it's warmer down this way, I can feel it."

"Don't you care that you'll kill hundreds, maybe thousands of people?"

"Hundreds, that's nothing. And I've seen thousands dead already. When I had good eyes. Back in '15, we filled the trenches until there was no room left. And now it's starting again. This time it won't be thousands, though. It'll be millions. I'm just glad I won't have to see it again."

"But why help the Germans?"

"That's my business, boy. And you should've kept your nose out of it. If Schlinge finds out you're down here…" Bittendorf stopped and then chuckled. "I guess it's not likely to matter whether Schlinge knows you're here or not."

"Why are you helping him?" Hansi pressed, grabbing Bittendorf's shirt. "You don't have to do this!"

Bittendorf reacted like he had been touched by a live wire. "Get away from me!" He tried to move on, but Hansi squeezed around him and stood in front of him. Bittendorf's movements grew agitated, jerky.

"The Gestapo told your sister you were dead," Hansi said. "Did you know that? They told her you died in a crash."

Bittendorf flailed his arms out in front, narrowly missing him.

"Leave her out of this. And leave me alone!" He took another step forward and swung, missing again.

"You don't have to do this—you really don't!" Hansi pleaded.

Bittendorf swung, striking his hand on the wall, and swore. "You don't know them like I do—I've got no choice. Now get out of my way!"

Hansi backed further up and glanced up the corridor. He could see the intersection up ahead.

"I know that the Gestapo lies and Schlinge is their chief liar," Hansi said. "They'll do and say anything to get what they want. What have they told you?" Bittendorf gyrated like a man possessed. "Tell me," Hansi said, lowering his voice. "Please, Herr Bittendorf, tell me."

Bittendorf closed his eyes, pressed his lips tightly together, and the movements settled. "They've got her," he finally said.

"Your sister? Where? How?"

"Schlinge said if I didn't help him, they'd take her. He said they'd put her in a camp and make her work until she's paid for all I've done." His voice wavered.

"All you've done?" Hansi asked.

"The accident. At Thillenberg in Differdange. After the war. I mis-wired a junction block and twelve men died in the explosion. Men with wives and children. The Gestapo said if I didn't do this job for them, they'd make my sister a slave until she paid the debts I still owe. It'll kill her!"

"But they can't do that!" Hansi protested.

"They can't? Says who, Der Führer?" Bittendorf wiped his eyes and shook himself like a dog does when he gets wet. "Look, boy, I don't know what you think you're doing down here and how you think you're going to stop me from blowing that room. It's too late for fighting the Gestapo. They're like rats—get rid of one and two show up to take their place. You might have time to get out of here before I set her off, if you hurry and if Schlinge doesn't find you first. But if you don't get out of my way, I'll tie you up with my own hands and throw you in there with the others, I swear it. You're not going to stop me!"

"Others? Where?" Hansi had Bittendorf by the shirt collar, pleading with him.

"The cells are that way," he said, pointing over his shoulder. "Just beyond the explosives—that's where they keep them."

CHAPTER FIFTY-SIX

Hansi felt new life rise in his limbs.

"How much longer?"

"Until I blow her? Ten minutes, no more. The Gestapo rats are anxious to get on with this."

"That's not enough time. Stall them. I've got to get my father out."

"You're better off saying your prayers and goodbyes if you ask me," Bittendorf said, turning away. "Those cells are locked tight."

"Help me," Hansi said. "Please."

Bittendorf snorted.

"Tell you what. I'll take you to Schlinge and you can ask for the keys."

He trudged off.

Hansi erupted with rage. He flung himself at Bittendorf and pounded his fists on his back. It was like pounding the stone tunnel.

"You monster! How can you be so heartless?"

Bittendorf turned and brought his thick arm around in a giant swat that knocked Hansi to the floor. His tailbone smacked the tunnel floor with an electric burst of pain.

"You're right, boy. I am a monster," Bittendorf said. "My heart died a long time ago. The rest of me is about to follow, and I'll be glad. But you'd better hurry—those ten minutes I'm giving you are ticking away. You give me any more trouble, and I'll end it right here."

He turned back up the corridor and left.

Hansi considered another attack. Anything that would keep Bittendorf away from that plunger. But then a picture emerged in his mind, a picture of his father only meters away. In his cell reaching out to him. Ten minutes was not much time at all, but it was better than no time. Bittendorf was right. It was over.

The moment was as near to Bittendorf pushing the plunger as Hansi could imagine, if not for seeing his father. Something let go inside. Tears blinded him as he ran back down the corridor.

Past the chamber the line of ceiling lights ended, and the passage widened. By the faint light that remained, Hansi saw a row of iron-barred cells on his right.

"Papa! Papa!" Hansi called in panic. But no answer came from the cells.

One by one Hansi peered into them. The first was empty except for a chain anchored into the rock wall. In the second, he saw the shadow of a rat scurry by. The third, fourth, and fifth cells were completely invisible in the dark.

"Papa! Papa! Are you there?" Hansi called again as he moved back and forth. He rattled the doors and waited. Nothing but silence replied. Would Bittendorf have been so cruel?

Hansi kept running, rattling, calling, and listening. Panic choked him. How long had it been? Was Bittendorf keeping time? Would there be any warning before the end, a brief dimming of the lights, an electric-buzzing sound, a clap of thunder?

His chest heaved from the effort. With a groan from the pit of his soul, he called out once more.

He felt a sensation in his head—of something lifting it from his neck. Then his legs gave out. Hansi reached for the bars in front of him and then realized it didn't really matter anymore. He let go, staggered a step, and simply sat down. The final drops of energy seeped out of him like moisture through the cracks in the walls.

Hansi listed and sank slowly down until he came to rest on the stone floor. Tears drained off his face into the cool pool below. He waited for the end.

Whether Hansi waited ten seconds, ten minutes, or an hour—he had no idea. However long, he became aware of a faint tapping sound somewhere in the darkness.

It might have been a rat, but the longer it persisted, with a regular beat and metallic sound—he could not disregard the signal. Or the rising hope.

Hansi lifted his head. "Papa, is that you?"

Tap-tap-tap. Faster. Tap-tap-tap.

On the surge of adrenaline, he scrambled to the last cell and pressed his face between the bars, without care for the rust shards cutting into his face. There, in the back of the cell, was that a shadow within a shadow?

Tap-tap-tap. Something definitely moved!

"It's me, Papa! I'm here!"

The taps drummed repeatedly. The signal brought Hansi new life. He climbed to his feet and gripped the bars. With strength from another world, he shook the bars. The sound echoed over the shower of rust sprinkling down. Yet there was more than enough good iron to hold the door fast. He shook it with the violence and desperation of being trapped inside himself. Still, the ancient door would not yield. His strength evaporated as quickly as it had risen.

"Hansi!" The voice was raspy and faint but recognizable.

Hansi jumped at the sound and then threw himself against the gate, once again hoping against hope that years of moisture and inattention would have their effect. Up and down, the corridor the bars rattled like a machine gun. Hansi coughed rust, spit, and shook with all his might—a wild animal. The pain in his head, hands, and arms was unbearable. And still by the time his last ounce of energy was gone, the gate had yielded only a few years of rust. His hands, frozen in their pained grip, opened just enough. He let go and fell—a heap of despair at the foot of the gate. He couldn't even cry.

A hand touched his shoulder. "I'm here, son."

An unsteady hand stroked his hair. Hansi reached up. The fingers were thin, rough, and cold.

"You're bleeding," Papa said.

"I'm sorry," Hansi said, crushed beneath a sudden wave of shame. The tears came. "I don't have the key."

"No time for that, son. You must go quickly."

"I'm not leaving you."

"But the wires—you must cut the wires."

This statement was like ammonia in Hansi's nostrils. "You know about the explosives?"

"Everything. But there's no time."

"I have no tools," Hansi said.

"You must try. If that room goes…" His voice faltered.

Hansi didn't need him to finish. Countless lives—indeed the entire nation—would be lost.

"Go!"

The strength in Papa's voice—even when all hope was lost, thinking of others rather than himself—revived Hansi enough to get up.

He staggered back up the corridor toward the light. In the chamber, he fell to his knees at the terminal block. With swollen, raw hands he took hold of the insulated wires and began to pull, bend, twist, and wiggle as fast and frantically as he could. The thought repeated for the thousandth time since the door—if only Schlinge's knife had survived. And for the thousandth time, the thought was wasted.

As the seconds ticked by without even the slightest progress, Hansi's rational mind began to lose control. He no longer cared to save himself. Or the Grand Duchy. What drove him now, strange as it was to his own thoughts, was a simple desire not to disappoint Papa. And so, like an animal, Hansi bent low, bit down on the wire, and began to chew. The canvas jacket and rubber gave way and the insulation tasted awful. The wire sliced his lips and gums. He slid the wire back to his molars, smashed his eyes closed, and bit with wild force. He saw white spots, heard a crack, and then the bolt of pure pain snapped his head back. He twisted in agony, hands clasped on his jaw, which had exploded with pain. He tripped over the wires and crashed into the wall of crates.

His mouth filled with blood. A chunk of tooth passed over his tongue.

The pain sharpened his thoughts. Papa was counting on him.

Papa would figure this out. But how?

He wouldn't waste effort lamenting the lack of tools, that was certain. He would focus on the problem. He would use what was at hand.

At hand.

Hansi's hands were on the crates. The force of his fall against them cracked several slats.

He pushed off and spit a mouthful of gooey blood. His jaw pulsed with every heartbeat. Then he found a broken slat and pulled it free. Then a second.

He knelt at the block where the bare wires fanned out from the terminal. He pressed the broken slats on opposite sides of the thumbscrews that held the wires in place on the post. He squeezed hard and turned.

SNAP! A slat broke and drove a splinter deep into the center of Hansi's hand. The stab hardly registered among his inventory of pain. This was the solution—he knew it in his heart—if only Bittendorf would grant him the time. And Hansi's body— swollen, numb, throbbing—would obey.

He threw himself against the crates again and tore off new slats. This time he doubled the wood on each side of the nut.

He clamped once more and twisted, this time building up the pressure gently and steadily. He could no longer feel his hands, his forearms quivered. His temples thundered as though his own head was between the slats.

With the last of his effort, he closed his eyes and whispered, "Please, God."

Hansi didn't know whether it was the prayer, the double slats, the steady pressure, or some combination of the three. The slats held long enough for the thumbscrew to turn—just a little.

Hope met terror in a head-on collision. He shook uncontrollably, fumbled, and dropped the slats. His body was betraying him in the moment of victory.

Hansi screamed. The cry rose from the pit of his stomach, arched his back, and echoed up and down the corridor. He didn't care who heard it. It broke the shakes. He returned to his work—clamped his fingers, raw and throbbing, around the nut and twisted. This time the effort paid off—the nut turned, then an entire rotation, and more. He dropped the slats and finished it off by hand. The nut had hardly hit the floor before he ripped away the lead and wires feeding the crates.

He stepped back, panting, and leaned against the doorframe. Cool water dripped onto his neck and trickled down his back. His body begged for mercy, but his mind pressed on. He knew almost nothing about explosives but had learned in science class that electricity depended on two wires—one positive, the other negative. He hoped that was the case here. He couldn't rest until he was sure.

Minutes later, he was sure. The second nut yielded to the same process.

Still, he could not rest. Not while Papa was trapped.

Hansi picked up the terminal block and two lead wires. Using the block of wood as a spool, he began to wind the wires. As he wrapped, he moved backward toward the door and the tunnel beyond.

At the doorframe, something reached from the dark and jabbed him square in the back. He dropped the bundle.

CHAPTER FIFTY-SEVEN

Hansi pivoted. The muzzle of a German Luger was pointed directly at his heart.

His first thought was Schlinge, but as his eye followed the black metal barrel up past the hammer, across the top of the slender hand, and up the sleeve of the blue cotton shirt, Hansi saw a twenty-something man not at all like Schlinge. The fair face; soft, sandy hair; and dark eyes were those he remembered from the Gare. The pistol quivered in his hand.

"Bittendorf said I'd find a rat down here," he said. "I just didn't expect one so small." He looked at the wires. "Or so resourceful. You'll wish you hadn't done this."

"You're Dieter Dumont!" Hansi blurted.

"And you're a nuisance." Dieter gestured Hansi out into the corridor and then up the tunnel, away from the cells.

"Where are you taking me?" Hansi asked.

"Somewhere you can't cause any more trouble."

"But what about my father?" Dieter waved Hansi forward. "You can't just leave him down there!"

Dieter let out a devilish grin. "I won't," he said. "You will. You're the one leaving him here, wondering for the rest of your life how close you came to being a hero. Who knows, maybe you won't have that long to wonder. Now move along!"

If not for the gun in his face, Hansi would have torn into Dieter. His rage burned hotter than the broken molar, swollen hands, and aching joints.

"Just like your poor mother," he said, not quite under his breath.

"What did you say?"

"I said, 'Just like your poor mother.' Just like you left her to die at the Gare." Hansi barely finished the sentence when he felt the sting of Dieter's free hand across his face. The tears rose but Hansi held them back.

"Then we understand each other," Dieter said calmly. He raised the pistol to Hansi's eyes. "Now move."

They retreated up the tunnel all the way to the room from which Hansi had heard the voices. The door was open. Inside, seated at a table with his back to the door, was Bittendorf.

Along with the table, the room contained a couple of chairs, two bunk beds, and a gray plywood cabinet. Just above the table, a solitary bulb seemed to float in a cloud of cigarette smoke. Wisps swirled and a figure moved out of the darkness from the corner, sending a tremor down Hansi's hamstring muscles. His hair was messed and his shirt collar open, but Herr Blik's gaze showed no sign of injury from the runaway truck.

"Here's your rat," Dieter said to Bittendorf as he shoved Hansi into the other chair. "He's been gnawing on your cables."

Herr Blik stepped around the table and flicked his cigarette to the floor. "You've made your choice, young man," he said. "But not a wise one, that much is clear."

Then he spoke to Bittendorf. "Only a fool would leave such a threat running loose down here. Herr Schlinge will be most disappointed when he hears about it. Most disappointed."

"He's just a boy," Bittendorf growled. "And no ordinary boy can undo what I've done."

"Well, then," Blik said, with a wicked smile back to Hansi. "He's given you a compliment. Indeed, you are no ordinary boy. How did you manage to disconnect the wires? Are you a demolitions expert—or is there someone else with you?" He was yelling the second question at Bittendorf.

"There's no one else down there. I would have seen them." He laughed. "My papa taught me to use the glue. It keeps everything together and everybody away—rats and little boys. It must be your blasting caps. My work is good."

"You better go see for yourself," Dieter said.

"I can't see. Did you forget?" Bittendorf enjoyed the joke.

"Be quick about it!" Blik added. "You've already wasted more than your share of the rotten air down here."

Bittendorf stood up clumsily and left the room.

Hansi considered making his own break for the door. Perhaps he could outrun Dieter and Blik up the tunnel and warn someone, anyone. But Dieter's pistol hand had grown steadier in the presence of Blik.

"Shall I lock him up with his father?" Dieter asked.

"No time for that," Blik answered. "Besides, I'm not the sentimental type. I don't go much for tearful reunions. Or tearful goodbyes. Have Bittendorf tie him to the bed here when he comes back."

"No wonder Karin despises you!" Hansi sputtered.

Blik's backhand was sharp across Hansi's face. He didn't care.

"She was temporarily distracted by your attention," Blik said, "but she's a good girl, and an even better German, and will always trust her father over a street urchin like you."

"I should have known it. You've been behind this all along. The first time I met you I should have smelled it."

Another slap, but Hansi was numb.

"Yes," Blik answered, "but in your foolishness, you never had a chance of finding out. So blinded you were, by looking for your father and your selfish infatuation with Karin. You missed the whole point. And made it as easy to catch you as catching a puppy with a sausage."

"You think you'll blow up the Casemates and the Palace without everyone knowing it's the Germans behind it?" Hansi asked.

"We've already convinced the gendarmes. The Grand Duchess will be dead, and the army—if you can call it one— is powerless. We'll happily cooperate with the Luxembourg authorities and show the Prime Minister the evidence which proves your father's guilt. That is if the Prime Minister survives. And he will have no choice but to beg Germany for protection. We'll not fire a single shot, and the nation will be ours. That much closer to Paris." He smiled with satisfaction.

Hansi stared into his cold eyes. "I think you've forgotten something."

Blik seemed hardly to notice.

"Or someone, I should say."

Blik's smile faded. Dieter moved the pistol closer.

"Where's Schlinge?" Hansi asked.

"You should be glad he's not here," Blik replied. "I think he'd kill you right here."

"I don't doubt it," Hansi said. "Which makes his absence all the more curious. Where did he go, I wonder?"

Blik stepped forward. "Speak up, boy."

"I think your man Schlinge has something else on his mind besides killing me." He paused, looked at the door, and then back at Blik. "Or taking orders from you."

Blik grabbed him by the collar and pulled him close. "What are you talking about?"

"If he were here, you could ask him," Hansi replied. "You could ask him if there's enough wire between the crates and the plunger. I heard Bittendorf tell him the wires are too short. The surprise you get when you push the plunger will be your last."

"That's ridiculous," Blik fumed. "Our own engineers calculated the requirements. Schlinge supervised it himself—" The words caught in his throat. His face turned white.

"Schlinge is probably halfway to Germany already, conveniently beyond the reach of the authorities. But when the dust settles and Germany takes over, guess who takes over for you?"

Hansi enraging Blik brought only temporary relief from the overwhelming sadness of the faces in his mind: Madame Dumont, unaware of her son's duplicity; Father Jean, hopeful and courageous; Manolo, constantly looking over his shoulder for the next source of terror. Maman, waiting patiently and praying; Papa, clinging to life alone in his cold dark hell. Finally, Karin— Hansi was sure she was unaware of her father's wicked betrayal.

The grief was interrupted by the sting of Blik's hand once again. This time it woke Hansi up and pushed him to a place he never knew existed—the place where he realized his own life was lost. And a place of freedom to act in a way a person clinging to life never would.

He ignored the grief. He ignored the slap. He ignored Dieter's Luger. He leapt from the chair and launched himself at Blik. Driven by the cumulative pain, despair, and defeat, Hansi hit Karin's father with a fury more animal than human.

The blow to Blik's midsection made a sound like air being let out of a bag. The force of Hansi's rage drove them both backward until they crashed into the wall with a dull thud.

Dieter waved the gun nervously. "Stop! I'll shoot!" he stammered.

"No, you fool!" Blik gasped, "Get the boy off me!"

Hansi's arms were wrapped around Blik, and his head wedged between the man's torso and the wall. Blik squirmed. Hansi churned his legs to regain the upper position until he felt a sharp crack on the top of his head. His arms relaxed for long enough for Blik to twist free. Hansi expected the next sensation to be a bullet.

Instead, in the next instant, two things happened at once: Dieter's gun went off and everything went dark.

CHAPTER FIFTY-EIGHT

The darkness was so sudden and overwhelming that Hansi wondered if he was dead and passing into the next life. The sharp throb sprouting from his forehead convinced him he was very much alive. Something had knocked the power out.

Hansi put his hand down to find the floor and instead came upon the heel of a shoe. Karin's father? It didn't matter.

He drew a sketch of the room in his mind, and he gathered himself on all fours to face the direction he hoped was the doorway. He started out, reminded of the table when he plowed into it with his shoulder.

Over the high-frequency echo in his ears, left over from the gunshot, he heard a scraping sound from across the room and then the shuffle of feet. He froze. Dieter was looking for him.

More steps, a thump, and then a loud crash. Dieter swore, his voice farther away now and lower to the floor. It was Hansi's chance. He crawled under the table and found the doorframe.

He was in the tunnel. Dieter was thrashing about in the room, yelling. Hansi stood up and put his hands on the wall as he moved. There was not much time.

At the intersection to the main tunnel, Hansi paused, wondering if he heard voices. The sounds weren't coming from where he expected, where Bittendorf was making his repairs, but from far up the corridor. And then, straining his eyes, he thought he saw a faint flicker of light. Was Schlinge coming back? Who was with him?

Just then Dieter let out a rage-filled howl. He must have realized Hansi had escaped. They would find their way outside and be upon him in no time. Ahead, Bittendorf was unaffected by the power failure. He was certainly at the end of his repairs. For Hansi, there was only one choice.

Relying on his memory of the corridor, He began to run. He ran with his right arm feeling the edge of the tunnel and his left arm extended forward like a battering ram. Building up speed he rounded the curve, scraping his hand over the rough stones of the tunnel wall. Soon, he knew, the tunnel would make a sharp right turn into the room of explosives, and if Hansi had any speed left perhaps he could surprise Bittendorf and knock him over. If by some miracle he could accomplish even this, Hansi had no idea what would come after that.

The wall fell away, Hansi planted his left foot and wheeled hard to the right. Two strides more and he would be through the threshold and on top of Bittendorf.

Too late Hansi realized he had forgotten an important detail in his mental sketch of the tunnel. His foot caught the threshold, thrusting his body forward. A sharp crack sent a bolt of pain through his shoulder like someone had hit him with a club. It was the doorframe, and when Hansi hit it, his body spun around so that he entered the room almost backward, completely out of control.

Hansi merely glanced off the hulk of Bittendorf. His heels caught the junction box and he fell back into the mesh of wires, which broke his fall against the wooden crates of dynamite. He was unhurt but in far greater danger, for now he was trapped at the giant man's feet.

The surprise had failed utterly, and now Hansi felt the strong arms of his captor moving steadily to find him. Hansi twisted and flailed like a wild animal caught in a snare, but Bittendorf was patient. He found Hansi's shoulder and clamped the vise of his grip on it. Hansi swung at him, but the blows bounced off Bittendorf's thick body. Then Hansi's left sleeve caught fast in the wire mesh, leaving him stuck like a fly in a spiderweb. Bittendorf moved closer and sat down on Hansi to stop him from kicking. His free hand moved past Hansi's shoulder and found his neck. The other hand would follow and soon it would be over.

Suddenly Hansi's sleeve ripped free from the mesh and he realized he was holding a piece of wire. Driven by the panic that overwhelmed him, he reached for Bittendorf's neck.

"You've been a nuisance long enough," Bittendorf said calmly. He relaxed the grip of one hand, snatched the wire, and wrapped it around Hansi's own neck. Hansi's entire body spasmed, but Bittendorf was too heavy and there was nothing he could do.

As Bittendorf tightened the wire, Hansi began to experience light-headedness that he knew signaled the end. But there were no images that flashed before his eyes like he expected. Instead, his mind slipped into a darkness that matched that of the room. This was it. A rush of sadness filled his soul.

But then, at the last instant when Hansi thought he would slip away forever, he saw a strange light glowing behind Bittendorf's head. Forming a bizarre halo, it was not at all what Hansi envisioned for the end. Perhaps it was a sign. He should forgive the man.

The vision changed. The light grew and Bittendorf's face became clear. His head was raised upward, and the narrow eyes rolled back into their sockets.

And then everything vanished.

CHAPTER FIFTY-NINE

Hansi's eyes hurt from a bright light overhead. Then slowly his focus changed to reveal details of a clear bulb hanging from the ceiling, swaying gently. Blinking brought other objects into view the rough-hewn ceiling, wooden slats just overhead, and a loose thread hanging down. He was on his back, and when he tried to raise up every inch of him awoke with pain, the strongest being a burning around his neck. His throat felt thick, like the time he got a plum stuck in it and, until it finally passed, brought pain so sharp Hansi thought he might choke to death. This was not what Hansi expected it would be like waking up on the other side of death.

Something moved in front of the light—the figure leaned in over Hansi's head. Hansi flinched, bringing a fresh spasm of pain from his right shoulder, but the man only smiled. Hansi studied his bright eyes and remembered. It was Captain Bertrand.

"Easy son," he said, his voice calm and confident. He put his hand on Hansi's shoulder. "You're safe now."

"Where am I?" Hansi croaked, all moisture missing from his mouth.

"You're in the guard room," the captain answered, lifting a glass to Hansi's lips.

Hansi swallowed painfully and then tried to sit up. He felt like he had been run over by a freight train.

"Papa?" he said, his voice stronger.

"He's going to be all right, Hansi. The doctor is coming. Don't strain yourself, son," he said.

"I must go to him," Hansi said, trying again to rise up. Now he could see his surroundings. Dieter was in a chair, head hung down, arms bound, and under close watch by two of Captain Bertrand's men. The Luger was at the center of the table. Bittendorf was tied up in the other chair. Karin's father lay slumped at the base of the wall, unmoving.

"Listen carefully, Hansi. That's not a good idea at the moment. The keys to the cells are gone——" the captain's eyes were fixed on Dieter, "so we must cut him out. They're doing it now, and fortunately, the bars are old and rusty. I'm sure they'll have him out in no time, but the best thing for us is to wait here. You know for yourself the tunnels are narrow down there. We'd only be in the way."

The pain served to clear Hansi's mind. He bolted upright, swung his legs over the side, and touched his feet to the floor. "The wires!" he gasped. "Have you cut the wires?"

The captain sprung forward just in time to catch Hansi, whose legs were too weak to hold him. He eased Hansi back down. "It's all been taken care of," the captain assured him. "Thanks to you."

But Hansi was determined to sit up, despite the pain. He rubbed his neck and exhaled deeply. Captain Bertrand relented and helped him find a comfortable position.

"What happened?" Hansi asked.

Captain Bertrand's eyebrows shot up. "We were hoping you could tell us. All we know is that you were very brave, Hansi. When we arrived, there was very little for us to do but to secure these two and start to work freeing your father. It seems you did the bulk of the work for us."

"I don't understand," Hansi said. "How did you find me?"

Just then a man stepped through the doorway into the room, as if on cue. Hansi recognized him immediately as the man called Raul, Manolo's lookout.

"You are a persistent one," he said with a smile. "But I was lucky. After your last—shall I say, 'adventure'—Manolo had me put a second man on watch. He was watching the alleyway from the apartment above you when you slipped out."

"Is Maman all right? Did she make it to France?"

"Yes, and because of what you've done here, she's on her way back," Raul replied. "But not in a wardrobe," he added with a wink.

Hansi could hardly believe the good news he was hearing.

Raul continued. "We followed you to the park and that's when things got interesting."

"You were there?" Hansi asked.

"After we warned you about sneaking out of your house the first time, we were surprised that you would do it again. So, when we saw you with the girl, we were going to move in on you right away."

"Karin! Is she all right?"

Captain Bertrand stepped forward. "I don't know, Hansi. Did she have something to do with all this?"

"No," Hansi said, and then explained. "She helped me search for my father, that's all. But her own father, is he—?" Hansi stopped and looked at Blik, lying on the floor.

Captain Bertrand nodded. "Who was he?"

"His name is… was Blik. Maximillian Blik."

"The diplomat?" Captain Bertrand his eyes widened. "You're saying the one behind this conspiracy is a German diplomat?"

Hansi frowned. "Some say Blik was just the actor, not the director. If you know what I mean." He watched Dieter and Bittendorf for a reaction. Dieter looked away.

"And who is the director?" the captain asked.

"His name is Schlinge. Did you arrest him?"

"We've rounded up a few others," the captain replied. "What does he look like?"

"If you've met him, he's not someone you forget. His face was mangled in the bombing of the Gare, and he walks with a limp. He was here, just now."

Captain Bertrand raised an eyebrow and flicked his head to order the pair of soldiers at the door to head out at once. Then he pressed his lips together and exhaled deeply. "I hate to say it, Hansi, but he may have slipped away."

"He tried to kill me," Hansi said. "More than once."

"Try not to worry, son. The Gestapo is finished here in Luxembourg. The army has been watching things for some time now, and we've had our suspicions about Dieter, Bittendorf, and others. We believed there was a conspiracy brewing against the Grand Duchy—that was their pattern in Czechoslovakia and Poland. We also believed the Gestapo was behind it all but couldn't prove it. Not until now." He smiled and nodded to Hansi.

"The Foreign Minister is meeting with the German Ambassador at this very moment. He's ending the arrangement between the gendarmerie and the Gestapo immediately. I've been assured that by morning the only Germans left in Luxembourg will be the ambassador and his dog. And given what almost happened this evening, I wouldn't be surprised if Schlinge was across the border already."

"But how did you know to come down here? Now?"

Raul stepped forward. "When we saw you two climb in the truck, it all started to make sense. We knew about Bittendorf's past and unfortunately his present. When we realized it was his truck, we knew something was going on here in the tunnels. That's when I called Captain Bertrand. Once he and his men arrived, we moved in."

"We've been begging the gendarmes for months to secure the Casemates," Captain Bertrand added. "There are tunnels down here nobody knows about, and they need to be sealed off. What you did today makes our point painfully clear."

Just then a soldier appeared in the doorway. "We've cut the door open. We're bringing him out now."

The words still echoed in the chamber when Hansi leapt from the bed and was out the door, racing past the team of engineers working in the explosives room toward the bright glow that was now the prison chamber. An array of arc lights mounted on metal stands had been brought in for the work of opening the cell. Hansi clawed his way through the mass of soldiers crammed in the corridor and pulled himself along the face of the cells by the bars. The bright light revealed how dismal the conditions his father endured. Dark water stood in every wrinkle of the stone floor and rust had nearly consumed every manmade feature— the metal bunks, the chains holding them, the waste buckets, and wash basins. By the time Hansi reached the last cell, his hands were covered in a gritty red paste.

A broad-shouldered man in goggles, holding a large hacksaw, stepped back from the entrance when Hansi appeared. "That's his son!" someone called, followed by "He defused the dynamite!"

Hansi stepped between the freshly cut bars, sparkling under the bright lights. A white coat stood out among the soldiers huddled around the figure on the floor, who was hidden in shadow. Hansi rushed forward until the arms of a soldier stopped him short.

"Just a second, son."

The doctor directed the soldiers to lift his father onto a stretcher. His father's frame seemed so slight in the strong arms of the team. The instant he touched down on the stretcher, Hansi broke free.

"Papa!"

Hansi, ignoring his father's condition, flung himself upon him.

"Careful, son," the doctor said. "He's very weak."

Papa was swaddled in thick woolen blankets like a newborn baby. All that showed was his colorless face, with sunken eyes, blistered lips, and matted beard. When Hansi tried to wipe the hair from his father's face, he left a streak of rust in an angle across his forehead.

Papa opened his mouth in an attempt to speak, but his voice was but a faint rasp.

Hansi leaned down and put his ear above Papa's mouth.

"My son," he whispered, "...already a man."

The soldiers lifted the stretcher. Hansi pushed in and took hold of the rail with them, ignoring the pain in his swollen hands. He didn't let go until they were safe in the ambulance together.

Three beds awaited them at the hospital that night. With Papa and Maman at his side, Hansi never slept so peacefully.

CHAPTER SIXTY

Not a single cloud disturbed the deep blue sky above the Casemates. From his desk at St. John's school, Hansi stared out the window, waiting for the afternoon bell to release him. The golden maples along the tops of the wall trembled in the warm breeze, the gentle cascades of leaves swirling over the wall and into the valley. Gone were the summertime days of carefree walks along the wall. Gone was the desire to join his friends in make-believe battles and adventures. Gone were Hansi's dreams of Count Sigefroi and his sword fights defending the city to the last man. The reality of the past days had smashed all that, leaving Hansi alone in his thoughts.

From the moment he stepped out of the hospital two weeks ago, Hansi was an instant national hero. News of his exploits broke immediately. The *Lëtzebuerger Zeitung* ran a special section explaining how Hansi, by looking for his father, not only discovered the explosives but spoiled what they called "The Casemate Conspiracy." It described his "uncommon bravery" and "inspiring patriotism," phrases strange to him. Further investigation revealed that the plan to blow up the Casemates was really an attempt to destroy the Grand Duchal Palace, assassinate the Grand Duchess, and throw the nation into chaos. "As a result of Hansi's tireless effort, putting himself in the gravest mortal danger," the *Zeitung* continued, "the Palace, the Royal Family, indeed the entire nation, is saved."

Immediately after the explosives were disarmed, the Luxembourg National Guard led by Captain Bertrand seized control of the Gendarmerie and quickly purged it of all Gestapo agents and German influences. For a while, at least, Luxembourg remained independent.

Yet everyone knew the victory was a temporary one. The war in Poland was almost over—the speed of Germany's blitzkrieg, the lightning war, struck terror in the heart of every European, both east and west. In response to the invasion of Poland, Britain and France declared war but so far seemed only capable of issuing statements rather than firing weapons. Everyone believed that as soon as the guns fell silent in the east, Germany would look west. Soon enough, all Luxembourgers expected, war would come. And while many put their hopes in France to protect the tiny nation, still more expected a defensive line west of their common border. And so preparations for a German invasion resumed.

A few days after being released from the hospital, Hansi, Papa, and Maman were summoned to the Grand Ducal Palace. Hansi wore his best pair of wool trousers and a freshly pressed white shirt that was normally reserved for church. A long, black sedan picked them up at their flat in the Grund and delivered them to the entrance of the Great Hall, where they were met by Her Royal Highness's Chief of Staff. He led them across thick carpet beneath high ceilings to a set of doors.

Hansi's breath was short and his legs weak. He tugged at the collar of his shirt and nervously wiped the perspiration away from his forehead.

The Chief of Staff, a fit, silver-haired man with refined features, caught Hansi's gaze and smiled.

"Nothing to worry about, my dear boy. The Grand Duchess is more nervous to meet you, a real hero." He snapped a quick wink, which put Hansi at slight ease, and then nodded to another attendant.

A pair of servants at the entrance opened two doors. The Great Hall, an ornate room sparkling in the light of a dozen chandeliers, was packed to its limit with people Hansi later learned were dignitaries from every corner of the Grand Duchy including the Prime Minister, members of Parliament, the armed forces, the Mayor of Luxembourg City, and even the president of Father's steel mill.

A band started the Luxembourg National Anthem just as Hansi and his parents stepped into the room. The floor was a river of golden glass, so polished Hansi could see his own reflection in it. They strode forward, Hansi between his mother and father, three hundred pairs of eyes riveted on them as they passed by. One man caught Hansi's glance—a white-haired man in a black silk coat whose lapel proudly displayed some kind of medal. When their eyes met, the man nodded gracefully. Hansi looked to see who the man was acknowledging and found that everyone was looking only at him.

At the front of the hall, they arrived at a short platform where the Grand Duchess waited. She stood tall in a somber-looking woolen suit, her silver hair sweeping back to accentuate her firm jaw and bright eyes. She held Hansi in the same gaze of affection. Then the anthem ended, and the room fell silent.

Hansi felt a nudge from behind. It was Papa gently urging him to keep going. Suddenly he felt self-conscious stepping away from his parents, but the Grand Duchess smiled warmly and extended her hand in a motion ushering him to come forward. He took a breath, ascended two thickly carpeted steps, and then stopped, alone above the audience, every eye on him, face to face with the Grand Duchess.

One of the assistants was holding a brown leather case. The Duchess turned, reached inside, and retrieved a red silk ribbon to which a gold medal was attached. She held it high and spread the ribbon open with her fingers to slip it over his head.

"Throughout the centuries," she declared in a strong voice, "our beloved homeland has entertained unwanted foreign guests, sometimes forcing us to submit to them against our will. Yet brave and fearless citizens, driven by their love of freedom, devotion to our homeland, and the desire to preserve our unique place among the nations, have always come to the aid of our people, even at the gravest threat to their very lives. Our nation bestows a small token of our eternal gratitude upon such heroes who exhibit such rare courage that compels them to risk everything for the sake of our homeland. We call it the Order of the Red Lion, so named because it represents the ferocity of its brave recipients. Today, Hansi Broussard of the Grund of Luxembourg, on behalf of a grateful nation it is my great honor and distinct pleasure to award you your rightful place among those who have come before you in this most sacred Order."

The Grand Duchess stepped forward, and Hansi bowed his head. Suddenly another assistant whispered something quickly to her and the Grand Duchess stopped. There was an awkward moment during which Hansi realized she was staring at the red streak around his neck, still sore from the wire Bittendorf used to choke him. He looked up and smiled. "It feels fine," he said, and the Grand Duchess seemed relieved. She lowered the medal gently over his head and let it come to rest around his neck. She touched his shoulder, the signal to look up. She ushered him to face the audience. As he turned, the dam finally burst—the room let forth a tidal wave of applause and thunderous approval, now and then accentuated with splashes of "Well done!" and "Bravo!" Hansi found himself short of breath. Maman, beaming, looked like time had reversed itself upon her. Papa fought to keep control of his quaking chin.

Only two weeks later, the scene had faded into a distant dream. Life for Hansi settled back to an uncomfortable normal. Papa was back at work and Hansi back at school, although without Father Jean it was nothing like before. Concentration was impossible. Nothing seemed interesting or enjoyable, not even his sketchbook.

One autumn afternoon in Father Jean's old classroom, Hansi slumped at his desk, staring out the window to study the spidery cracks and mossy brick of the Casemates. They were the one constant in his life—the fortress, silent and strong but calling out the deepest whispers of his heart. He couldn't stop thinking about Karin.

His last moment with her had been outside the tunnel. He had known then that he might not see her again, and it turned out to be true. Two days after Dieter Dumont killed her father, she and her mother returned to Germany. Hansi would have done anything to try to see her before she left, but the doctors insisted he not leave the hospital, and Papa and Maman wouldn't override them. Hansi couldn't imagine the shock Karin endured learning of Blik's death, much less his treachery.

Yet more than anything, Hansi wished he could have seen her one last time, out from under the shadow of the conspiracy and betrayal, to tell her how he felt, how much she meant to him. He had never felt such affection for anyone, and yet it was mixed with so much pain that the two feelings seemed unable to exist separately. He longed to hold her in his arms again, like the moment before they parted, without fear and without embarrassment. And without the threat of danger nearby. They had not even said a proper goodbye.

The bell rang, pulling Hansi back into the room. He stayed seated as if unplugged from the energy that made the other students jump up and scurry out. He looked at Sister Margarite, out of place behind Father Jean's desk, wishing for the scolding stare of the man who never tolerated Hansi's daydreaming. Instead, her expression was gentle.

The students gone, Hansi finally stood up and started across the room.

"Hansi," the sister called.

"I'm sorry, Sister," Hansi began. "I was daydreaming. I know."

"It's all right, son." She retrieved something from the desk drawer, an envelope marked simply: HANSI.

"Father Jean's brother brought this to me. He said to tell you they found it in your friend's house. He thought you might like to see it."

CHAPTER SIXTY-ONE

The stiff breeze on the top of the Casemates wall sent a chill through Hansi as he looked down on the spire of St. John's and the Grund beyond. Standing along the railing where he saw Karin for the first time, he retrieved an envelope from his pocket, broke the seal, and pulled out the letter.

My dearest Hansi,

When last I saw you at the entrance of the tunnel, you had a strange sadness in your eyes. I know now that you were saying goodbye. I understand why you couldn't say the words, or perhaps refused to. I wouldn't have wanted to either.

I am sorry for so many things. I'm sorry that I pressed you to let me speak with Father. What a fool I was to think he could help you. He was never the man I thought him to be, and as bitter as that is to face, I see that now. You saw him so clearly and yet you weren't harsh toward me.

Most of all I am sorry to leave you. Berlin was never my home and never will be. The only time I've been at home is with you. From the moment we met, you didn't care that I was German and spoke with a funny accent.

I will always remember our days together. Even when I was afraid, I never wanted to be anywhere else but with you.

Whatever the war brings, no matter where we are, one truth will endure: You will be Prince Hansi forever in my heart.

Love,

Karin

Hansi let his stare linger on the words: You will be Prince Hansi forever in my heart.

A train moved up the far side of the valley, heading east toward the Moselle River, Trier, and the Rhine Valley beyond. He imagined Karin staring out the window and tried to see her face again, to look once more into her deep blue eyes. Even now he could not summon the clear picture of her he wanted. Strong gusts lashed his tear-filled eyes. Nothing had ever hurt so much.

Returning the letter to the envelope, Hansi noticed a lock of golden hair tucked inside. He brought it to his nose and took in a long breath, but the only scent was of a cold autumn wind.

A few strands were snatched by the breeze. The swirls lifted them up and out over the wall, and into the abyss.

Hansi clenched his fist to protect those that remained, crushing the letter in the process. The wisps danced but for a moment above the valley, then swept east, where they were hopelessly gone, lost forever in the gusts above the Grund.